TOMORROW'S CHIP PAPER

A NOVEL BY

RYAN BRACHA

Ryan Bracha   Tomorrow's Chip Paper

Copyright 2013 © Ryan Bracha

Abrachadabra Books

In association with

Paddy's Daddy Publishing

All rights reserved. No part of this publication may be reproduced or transmitted in any form or by any means without permission of the author.

All the characters in this book are fictitious and any resemblance to actual persons, living or dead, is purely coincidental.

By the same author:

Strangers Are Just Friends You Haven't Killed Yet

The Banjo String Snapped but the Band Played on

Bogies, and other equally messed up tales of love, lust, drugs and grandad porn

Paul Carter is a Dead Man

For Rebecca

And everybody else who showed me support,
I'm more humbled than any of you will ever know.

Like me, on Facebook…

Follow me, on Twitter…

Kill me, on Television…

Prologue

Day three. I think. I've been in and out of consciousness too many times to follow the concept of time. I would kill for a drink of water right now. My eyes feel sticky as hell. I'm struggling to remove my tongue from the roof of my mouth. I stopped shouting for help ages ago. It's funny, but throughout my own worries, the fact that I'm feeling a few hours from death, all I can think of is her. Did she get out? I pray to a God I don't believe in that she did. God, Jesus, Allah, Ganesha, Adi Purush, Nirankar, Jah, Jehovah, The Light, all of those bastards. Maybe one of them will forget that I don't exist in their rolodex of believers and throw me a bone. For sure, if they help me out and leave a card I'll even join their crew. For now though, I'm here and helpless. If anybody's looking for me then they need to look sharp, because I can feel myself slipping away here. I'd take the bobbies right now, take what I've got coming to me, and face the music. And dance. I just need to know she's okay, I need her to know that I'm okay, alive. Barely. For sure if she didn't make it I'm gonna make sure each and every one of them pays. I'll track them down, each and every one of them, I don't give a single fuck if they're harder, faster, more tooled up than me, and- This is all sounding very fucking familiar. I sound like him. But the thing is, I don't care, she's everything to me. We've been through far too much for me to let them do this. If they've done anything to her I'll hit them where it hurts, no doubt about that. I can feel myself fading again. I fall into a dream, and in it I'm still here, trapped, only this time I can hear somebody through the rubble, a girl's voice, shouting my name, crying out for me. The crying gets closer and closer as she digs through for me. Dust falls onto my face as she disturbs the shit around me, fills my watering eyes with dust and creates this sludgy grey film over my vision, and fills my lungs with the billions of particles she's shaking loose. I'm trying to call out for her to stop but she's not hearing me, and if she is she's ignoring me, and I'm choking, throwing up liquid cement into the tiny hole I'm stuck in. Now everything's just noise as I'm just chucking up this cement shit over myself and into my tomb. The vibrations are shaking more and more of the dusty shit loose, and this girl's still shouting for me, and I'm trying to tell her to calm it, to let me get my breath, but I can't for all this stuff I'm throwing up. The vibrations begin to feel closer and closer to me, like she's getting near and thin strips of light begin to pierce my tomb, and what comes to mind is Kerplunk from when I was a kid. Back in my old life. The straws being pulled from the holes, only this time instead of marbles dropping onto me it's shards of lights, and the dust particles are dancing in and out of these shards, doing some sort of tango before my eyes. The cement vomit is slowing, but still oozing out of my face as I'm suddenly feeling all serene, watching these particles circle each other, their dance floor ever increasing as the shards become more and more. Behind the grey sludge in my eyes I see a figure standing over me, pulling me from the wreckage. I'm slowly aware that this is no longer a dream, my eyes flicker open to see this figure. I can feel myself being hauled from my tomb, the hands that lift me feel massive, nothing like what I'm expecting from the girl's voice of my dream. My head rocks heavily as this hero of mine stomps over the debris that surrounds us. As he, or she, carries me out into the light of day I let out a howl as my skull is rocked by this new sensation, even with my eyes closed tightly

the pain is unbearable. My hero drops me roughly to the floor and I'm vaguely aware of the wet grass beneath my back, the moisture seeping through my clothes and cooling my skin. My brain becomes accustomed to it eventually, and I feel moved to finally open my streaming eyes. I blink the salty tears away and focus on the figure which stands over me, its massive frame leaning down and staring at me intently. My throat feels raw as I dry retch over the grass beneath me. As I figure out what's happened I roll over, licking and sucking at the blades of grass to take whatever moisture I can, I don't give a single fuck that there could have been dogs shitting and pissing all over it, I just need water. My hero pulls me onto my back and lowers something to my lips, pouring liquid into my mouth as I hungrily devour what they're giving to me, I splutter as my eagerness forces the water down the wrong hole, a heavy hand thumps against my back and a familiar voice talks to me under the soundtrack of my coughing. I rub my eyes with the back of my filthy hands, and try to regain my breath. My hero stands over me, shading me from the searing continental sun. My eyes travel from his feet, past his huge legs and torso, and the silhouette of his massive frame returns my gaze. The hulking monster squats before me and the features of his face become ever more familiar. Cristiano. He smiles at me.
"Tommy man, you look like shit."
I have to acknowledge this with a nod and a weary smile, because he's probably right.

Chapter 1 - October

Delicious Treats

Another crumb fell silently onto his lap like a suicidal beige speck, joining the millions that had perished before it, sitting broken and forlorn like limbless biscuity soldiers across a polyester battlefield. His left hand slowly edged to the packet to bring more future crumbs to his face, his right hand cradled the wireless mouse from above and guided it across the generic mouse-mat he purchased from Walmart a few months prior to now. His eyes darted across the images upon his seventeen inch flat screen monitor, taking in the information before him. The silence was punctuated by his slow contented crunches of sweet short-crust pastry surrounded by chocolate, halted only by him taking the time to absorb fresh information on his screen, milking the imagery for all he could before the crunching would recommence, his tiny blue marbles drinking in the flesh, wiring it to his appreciative brain, which would assist in diverting the blood from the rest of his body to the rising erection between his legs. The crumbs around his lap, disrupted from the increasing bulge beneath them, trembling and rolling away in a vaguely edible landslide to fall further, creating an artistic spread around the base of his blue padded office chair, thinning out the further away from him they lay. His left hand was by now no longer bothered by the delicious treats he had previously been feasting on, as it was now assisting with the delight he was experiencing in line with the delicious treats his eyes were now feasting upon. The ball of his palm massaged the bulb of his cock through the rough material that encased it, his thumb wandering down the shaft to his balls. His stroke was halted briefly, by the small pop up in the corner of his screen. Lucy. The little vixen.

Lucy: Hi Davey :) xx

He smiled. Lucy. Older than her thirteen years would have you believe. She knew him as Davey. Melissa knew him as Aaron. Jenny knew him as Cody. He responded.

Davey: Hi sexy pants :) missed you, where you been at? xx

Lucy: Been to the mall with mom, got some new sneakers :D xx

Davey: awesome!!! :D I bet they look neat!!! you could send me a pic of you in nothin but them! :P xx

Lucy: maybe I will ;) xx

Davey: ur hot xx

A flutter shot through his balls, he'd exchanged pictures with Lucy, but nothing spectacular, a few shots of her in her pyjamas making attempts to look sultry in her bedroom mirror, she was beginning to warm to his advances though. He knew how to play the long game, he'd done it many times before. To Gary this was a hobby, not an obsession, there were guys in the club that went way too far and Gary wasn't like that, he knew how people would see him if they knew about his hobby, but he wasn't hurting anybody. Here in his room he could be whoever he wanted to be. Davey was a teenage punk, kicking against the system, a real whizz with his poetry, he could make his female peers melt with his words, he was tough, but tender. His room was covered in posters from films that belied his tender age, he was a flawed rebel. And Lucy just lapped it up. He'd see her sweet little pussy before long. Aaron was the sports star at his school, bold, brash, and incredibly dense, but he was perfect for Melissa, she was ditzy, confident, a girl who was beginning to become aware of her own blossoming sexuality.

Lucy: so watcha upta? xx

Davey: thinkin of u xx

Lucy: lolz, what u thinkin? xx

Davey: how much i wanna kiss u xx

Lucy: lmao xx

Davey: not kidding, i wish we lived in the same town, i wish we could make it together, think i might love u xx

This was a bold move as far as his experience went, it could go one of two ways, either she'd disappear forever, or she'd try to play it cool. He sat, quietly, watching the screen, his hand firmly massaging his cock. His heartbeat steadily increased, panic taking him over. His hands rose to the keyboard to hammer out a retraction, anything to get her back on board, his heart turning as she responded.

Lucy: for real? Xx

Davey: for real :) will u go on cam so i can see u?

Ryan Bracha   Tomorrow's Chip Paper

mines broken still so i can't xx

Lucy: sure :) xx

Gary's hand massaged his crotch harder and harder, anticipation rising within him as the pop-up arrived, black screen to denote that Lucy's camera was loading. He massaged harder still. Her camera activated, but to his utter dismay there was no Lucy. As he typed a message to ask her to appear on screen a flash of confusion hit him. Her bedroom looked familiar. He knew that room. He knew the woman in the framed photographs across chest of drawers that filled the majority of the screen. That room. Why did he know it? Then it hit him like a hammer to the chest. That room was downstairs. That woman in the photographs. It was his late mother. A wave of sickness washed over him as he rose unsteadily and ambled to his bedroom door. No longer was he preoccupied with seeing a naked pubescent girl, a sense of impending doom now the prominent feeling. His hand shook as he fumbled at the bedroom door and opened it tentatively. What he didn't expect to see was the petite smiling face of a young looking woman of about five feet looking back at him, much less did he expect the hand cannon that she had pointed at him.

Dyson of Innocence

This creep sickened her. The blood around his head wound congealed as he wept pathetically into his carpet. His trousers utterly filthy from where he had shit and pissed himself through fear when she dragged him at gunpoint down the stairs and into the lounge. They all did it, without fail. These men who were strong enough to take advantage of children, but would find themselves reduced to shit covered cowards when faced with their maker.

Maybe the doubts in her own mind were right, perhaps this was entrapment, but it was justifiable entrapment. If they weren't attempting, and failing, to see her, naked, as a thirteen year old girl, or indeed boy, then they would be doing the same with an actual child, and succeeding. Like a Dyson of innocence, sweeping mercilessly across the internet devouring all that stood before them, to satisfy their own demands, to fulfil their own deviant needs. Not one of the creeps before this one ever said sorry. Between them all they couldn't summon enough remorse to fill a thimble. They all felt sorry for themselves as they shivered in fear, caked in their own faeces. They felt nothing for their countless victims though, who they presumably saw as collateral damage in their missions for sexual gratification. She was here to prevent that damage. What had gone before she could nothing about, the proverbial horse had bolted on that front, but she could do everything in her admittedly great power to limit future pain, the domino effect of abuse victims becoming abusers. Her prey would have no idea of the future pain they would cause, and if they did then they certainly didn't care. They deserved what she put them through. Like this one here, weeping and spluttering, only five minutes earlier was masturbating himself into a frenzy at the thought of witnessing young flesh presented before him. Nobody would blame her for what she did, she was providing a service to the world, and she was paying from her own pocket to provide this service. The world could thank her later, for now she had work to do. She placed herself on the arm of a green chair in the corner of the lounge.

"*Davey*, good to finally meet you face to face, although I suspect that it has come as quite the shock to you that my breasts are larger than you would usually prefer."

He whimpered into the floor, his face streaming with snot, spit, and tears. His blood-red eyes daring not to look up and face his tormentor as she gazed at him without pity. She stood from where she had been seated, an anger rising within her as she took confident strides toward him, and lay a heavy boot into his submissive face, drawing from him a howl of pain, as he rolled over and lay, his broken teeth falling from his mouth, appearing as small yellow islands in a sea of red on the carpet beneath his rapidly swelling face. The girl moved back to the chair, disgustedly wiping her bloody boot against the fabric of the armchair, and shifted her gaze back to her prey, the sight of him denying her anger the chance to subside, and she whipped round, delivering another boot to his face, a howl emanating from the filthy beast after the clearly audible noise of his jaw snapping. He rolled onto his back, his hands drawn to his blackened face, his glistening, swollen eyes looking at her now in sadness, the limp jaw bone hanging open from where it was once held to his skull. They had all looked at her in this same way. If it had been anybody else she might have felt something for their plight, some sort of sympathy, but this, this beast had to pay, for his past crimes, and what would have been his future crimes. He needed to feel pain for what he had caused, and would cause, if he hadn't found himself in his current predicament. She had done this so many times by now, there was no point in dragging this out. They were all the same, no amount of talking would make a difference, he was to be punished, they all needed to be punished, and Liezel was the girl to do it.

Since she'd been involved in the organisation, Liezel had made this her own personal mission, to remove every piece of scum like the one that lay before her from existence, rapists and paedophiles, men and women who had no rightful place on this Earth. People who had been given the blessing of life, and had chosen to spend it seeking sexual gratification in places that it did not belong, and if that desire for gratification was not reciprocated, then it was simply taken. These people had spent the lives that they had been granted ruining those of others for an obscene compulsion. No matter how many times the organisation presented them to her, to research them, to watch them do what they did, she could not allow it to go on before her eyes. Sure, there were the thieves and the crooks, they would take advantage of the stupidity of others, and were targeted for their greed. She could live with that. But those that took advantage of innocent children, and vulnerable women, she could not stand by and watch happen, no matter what they told her, or how much they took exception, she would act, and to hell with the consequences. Whenever a dossier was pushed her way, she just *knew* when it would be something like this. Dietmann would act sheepishly, would be vague with the details surrounding the target, and send her on her way. And it was happening more and more. This wouldn't bother her in the grand scheme of things, but something about *why* they still gave her assignments that they knew would end like this, it sat uneasily with her. Did they want to keep her busy and out of the way? Since her game she had learned to trust nobody but herself. Of course, she respected

what the others had to offer, and what they could do for her, but she was in this to get everything she could, with a view to getting out unscathed at the other side. This whole charade of disappearing from the face of the Earth, and undertaking tasks for the organisation didn't sit well with her either, she was now at their mercy. The whole world believed she was dead, so she could die at any point and there would be a distinct lack of action by the authorities. This was her issue to come to terms with though, so she turned her attention to the pervert before her.
"Do you have anything to say Gary?"
The delirious beast's eyes gazed at her sadly, through the padding of the swollen flesh around them, like glistening red piss holes in purple snow, whatever emotion he was attempting to convey was struggling to get through the paralysis she had beaten into his face, his muscles doing their best to simply keep his smashed jaw attached to his head, let alone summon up the power to display anything other than beaten indifference. She'd been here enough times to know it was actually fear, and desperation, a struggle to come up with anything that might help him out of this situation that his predatory instincts had got him into. Plain and simple, he knew that he was fucked. He let out a high whine, punctuated by gurgling, unsure of whether this meant he had anything to say or if his pain simply needed an outlet, Liezel approached his body and stood over him, a cold glaze coating her stare, and she pumped a silenced bullet into his crotch, the wounded beast screamed into the air, his hands reaching at the red stain pouring onto the carpet beneath him, clawing at the nothing that his cock had become. Conscious of the noise he was making Liezel silenced him with two bullets to the face, pocketed her gun, and began her ritual.

Into the Precipice

He awoke to a crackling noise that encompassed every aspect of his hearing, steadily revealing itself to be a familiar sound of fire, from every angle. His vision corrected itself as he gradually regained consciousness, and rose from his waking bed, a hard, hot metal frame, creaking springs that roared in anguish for every movement that he made. An overwhelming heat was upon him, and beneath the crackling an echo of laughter rocked through his surroundings, it was the laughter of children. He took in his surroundings. Rusted orange bars that stretched up beyond the limit of his vision into a pitch black distance, vines of barbed wire weaving between the bars seemed to grow from the stone floor. In every direction there were others in positions just like him, each hunched over in their prison cells, each on wired metal bedframes, each of them appearing to wake here in unison. To his right a hunched figure, ten or fifteen feet away, faced away from him, head in hands, a low groan emanating from it. The frame of it gave it away as another man. His head rising slowly from its cradle. Gary tried to call out to him, to try to discover what this place was, but nothing but the same low groan came from his face. He lifted his hands to explore where his mouth should have been, but instead of the usual lips, teeth and tongue, his fingers were met by a dry, crusted hole. Shreds of his skin fell like pale, translucent cornflakes of DNA from the surface he was fingering. Panic stricken, Gary rose from his bed, his screams for help only coming out as the monotonous groan he was already accustomed to. From all around him the same wails began. A chorus of anguish, all in the same key. The people in the other cells began standing too, all turning to face each other, to take in their environment. Gary was horrified to discover that each one of them appeared to have suffered the same injury as he. The man in the next cell was pallid, his sickly complexion contrasted against the deep red hole from which the whine gushed, he had no mouth, no nose, no cheeks. Just coal black eyeballs staring back at him in horror, beyond him another, and another. Men, and women, all grey as far as he could see, imprisoned by rusted bars and barbed wire ivy that clawed the cavern above them. Between the cells small figures danced through, their laughter mocking the terrified prisoners. Each of the figures approached a cell of their choice, and faced its occupant. A girl, no more than eight or nine, wearing a white dress with floral embroidery, her light brown hair tied up in bunches, a small spattering of freckles across her nose and cheeks stood before him. She laughed derisively at his naked form. He wanted to ask her what this place was, who she was, why he was here but in his heart of hearts he knew. This was hell. And anyhow, he no longer had the facility to ask anything anymore. The girl pointed at his shrivelled cock and howled with laughter, and the floor around his bed fell away, the rocks collapsing to reveal flames, licking the air about them. The little girl fell to her knees and stared intently into the fire, reaching her hands into the precipice. Gary tried to tell her "No! You'll hurt yourself!" But the low groan told her nothing, her eyes rose from the fire she was watching, and met his. Her face creased into a smile dripping with intent, and from the fire she pulled a scorching orange poker, the skin from her hand melting away from the bone like rose candle wax, but her grip held ever tighter to the metal, and if he had a nose then he would have been sickened by the smell of burnt skin. In his head he whimpered pathetically as the girl held the iron close to him, jabbing it forward into the air before him. He leapt in fear onto the bedframe as more of the floor fell away beneath him, which amused the girl further still. In the corner of his eye the man in the next cell, for all the agony he must have been in, simply let out the hollow groan, quickly drowned out in the sea of noise, as a young boy in an immaculately pressed sailor outfit whipped his dry grey torso with burning orange wire, fireworks of sparks exploding with each strike, the child displaying a great amount of strength that belied his tiny frame. His focus arrived back at his own personal tormentor, as she thrust the poker into his waist, deeper and deeper into his skin. The agony ripped through his every inch, his low hum joining in with the chorus once more, and overcame every ounce of his being. For whatever reason he found himself aroused beyond his own belief, his flaccid grey whistle filling with something, against his own will his erection began to grow bigger than anything it had ever been in life, the flames below his bed grew larger, threatening to engulf him. His body shrank, his whole becoming the erection that grew from the pain that the little girl subjected him to. As the cock became bigger than he was, the little girl grinned with malice, waved at him with the ends of the four fingers of her hand, and sliced the burning hot poker through the ashen flesh of his member, which peeled and flaked away, dropping into the furnace below. Overwhelmed by the pain, calmness filtered into him, the cavernous arena of punishment blackening, the rusted bars dropping away, the fire extinguished, the little girl becoming nothing. Then blackness. A blackness that flushed out the agony and allowed him a moment's respite, and from the silence a faint click echoed in his mind. And another click. And another. It became a crackle. That crackle again. The fire. His eyes opened to view those bars, this same rusted prison cell with the barbed wire ivy entwined to beyond the limit of his vision. And the whole process began again.

Chapter 2 - January

My Goon

I wander aimlessly through the aisles, my eyes shut tight, my fingertips dragging through the different materials, disturbing the sleeves, they'll be leaving behind them a rippled rainbow of greens, and yellows, and reds. The sensation of the velvet, and silk feel wonderful against my skin. I love how certain things feel. Some people hate the texture of cotton wool, I find it comforting, it reminds me of my dad before he died. The feel of dry dusty sand pouring through my hands makes the inside of my forearms tickle, and I love it. Here in the shop I'm alone except for the girl at the counter. She's beautiful, tall and unfeasibly slim, dark skinned with jet black hair, lustrous and full atop her uncovered forehead. I loved the way that her brown eyes beamed at me the second I approached her. Her pure white teeth are entirely contrasted against the darkness, and it feels to me that they are on show a lot, her smile seems so natural. I wish I looked like her. Her beauty is so unassuming. Effortless. She probably doesn't even realise how lovely she is. There's a light jazz soundtrack coming from some hidden speaker somewhere, and aside from the sound of the coat hangers rattling gently behind me as my fingers explore the array of fabrics available to them the shop is silent, serene. I feel it pass me by, silk, lace, velvet, cotton, and I stop at one which feels nice. My eyes still closed I pinch the material and rub it between my thumb and forefinger; I don't know what colour it is, what style it is, or anything. I just want to know how it feels, consider how my skin will feel beneath it. It feels, right. Now I know, I open my eyes.

Ryan Bracha — Tomorrow's Chip Paper

It is gorgeous. It's purple, my favourite colour, the long billowy sleeves hang lower than the waist line and I want to wear it now. I want Tom to see me wearing it and tell me I look fit, in that way he does. He's such a goon, but he's the reason I'm here in this boutique, with the place to myself and taking my own sweet time to find what I want. Half of having the place to myself is luxury, the other half is necessity. *But he's my goon*. I turn to the counter girl, who smiles and heads my way.

"I'd like to try this please."

"Of course, come with me please, I will show you to our change rooms."

I follow her as she glides ahead. If Tom were here I know he'd be watching her arse. He'd try not to, but even I have to admit that she's out of this world. I would kill to look like her. Tom tells me I'm the most beautiful girl he's ever met, but I don't think I am. He's met better. I know I'm not ugly, but I'm nowhere near this girl's league. Tom would tell me otherwise but sometimes I feel that's just out of duty. I mean, he does say that it's his job to make me feel like the fittest girl on Earth, but he does it with that look in his eyes, like he truly believes it, and that he wants me to believe it. When I'm with him I do, but when we're apart, well, I kind of just go to shit a little bit.

    We approach the changing room and she spins on her feet as she drags the curtain open and beams at me, allowing me access to the bright and airy cubicle. Before she pulls the curtain closed again she tells me to give her a shout if I need anything. The full length mirror on the wall gives me a top to bottom view of myself as I peel my dress over my head. The Mediterranean sun has done wonders for my skin. It feels healthy, and rich. I turn to watch my body in the bright artificial light. I have to admit, I am looking the best I ever have, and my exercise regime is starting to pay off. As I drop the blouse down over me it feels divine. The cool material glides down over me and I thumb it against my tummy as I close my eyes and smile. I'm buying it. I'm going to wear it tonight when I give Tom the news, I want him to share how nice it feels, the knowing, the anticipation. I can't wait to see his face. He'll be over the moon.

    I open the curtain to the counter girl, her face fixed with that questioning look, melting into pleasure as I nod and confirm that I'm going to take it, passing it to her and letting her know I'm still looking, there's no point having the place to myself and only buying one thing, no, I'm taking full advantage. She's wrapping my blouse at the counter and I'm at the shoe section. I want to look my best for him. I want to see that look in his eyes. I love that look. At the shoes I'm scrutinising them, devouring every inch of them with my eyes, I want to be able to look down and feel brilliant when I'm wearing them. I want to feel brilliant without even looking down, to know that my feet look and feel like they are wrapped in a blanket of deliciousness. Shoes are the foundation of any person, if the foundation looks good, then the rest can only follow suit. On the other side of the coin, it doesn't matter how good you look, how well you present yourself, if the foundations look like shit. The foolish girl builds her house upon the shit. The shoes in front of me sparkle in the bright lights of the boutique. I move slowly from left to right, taking in their beauty, which takes my breath away further for every pair I pass. The smell of brand new top quality leather fills my nostrils, and I inhale it with delight, so deeply that I can taste it, the aroma coats my throat, and I love it. I stop at a pair of Westwood shoes, they're black with a heavy looking buckle at the top, and another at the ankle strap. They're called Temptation. How apt. My fingers stroke the leather, I want them on my feet, I need them in my life. I pull them eagerly from the shelf, slipping my feet out of the sandals I'm wearing, and delight in the sensation of increasing at least 4 inches in height when I slide them under the soles of my feet. I love it. Without buckling them up I walk a few feet, then swing round and head back. The glee in my face is clearly evident as the counter girl's eyes light up, and she asks me which ones I'm looking at. I tell her and she purrs in agreement that they are beautiful. I'm having them.

The Art of Bending Reality

Jess has been out and about for a while, doing her Pretty Woman thing, getting the whole shop to herself, loves it dunt she? She'd probably say as much herself. For sure, that's her thing, she loves everything bless her. In the meantime I'm having a mooch around Barcelona, sightseeing and that, Las Ramblas man, absolutely crazy, places like this are mint. In the day it's a tourist's dream, it's all going on, some of the characters that hang out round here crack me up. I've been watching a fella that does caricatures go to town on this one woman, in reality she's pretty non-descript, her wavy brown hair looks slightly from the nineties, this curled under fringe and loose rings that drop down by her ears. Her gurning self-conscious smile holds like she's frozen in time, scared that she might spoil the image that the fella is currently scrawling onto his easel. Only her eyes moving as she follows her companion round behind the caricature fella. The companion, her boyfriend, lover, husband, whoever, is dancing around in stitches at the drawing, like it's the funniest thing he's ever seen. For sure, it might be, but I'll be honest, to me it's not that funny. I suppose it takes all sorts though, I've become slightly less judgmental in recent years, since Jess has been around, since, well, since then. She's always been a lot more easy-going, and open minded than me, but it's started to filter into my personality too. The picture that the fella is scribbling down is pretty good, if a little generic. He's got all the usual suspects as far as features go. The big eyes and massive lashes, the dots for freckles, even though she doesn't have any, at least from where I'm sitting. Her self-conscious gurning smile has been turned into a huge mouth with protruding front teeth. Below that she's got the tiniest neck ever, and this drops to a small body, with huge tits, driving a convertible car away from *La Sagrada Familia*. She doesn't have huge tits. The art of bending reality is truly a skill in my book, even if this fella will perform the same trick on every single person that sits before him until he decides to retire, he's got the skills for it. Probably gets bored with it sometimes. For sure, I'd probably draw not-so-subtle cocks and balls all over them if it were me. He finishes up his work and spins the easel round to show the woman what he's done, she claps with delight and falls over laughing at the hilarity of it all. That picture will now go on a great journey, rolled up and bound with an elastic band, back to whichever hotel she's based at. It'll sit rolled up in the corner of her hotel room until they're ready for heading home and when the whole family's round to hear about their holiday it'll get unleashed at the same time as the photos. The kids will be in stitches, granny Mavis will be having a chuckle in the corner, and it'll be the best thing they've ever seen, that ten Euros will be the best money they've ever spent. For about an hour. Then they'll move on with their lives, the picture getting ever browner, curled in the corners, dying slowly but still no less important in its minor feature in their lives. Amazing how the smallest thing can provide so much joy to some people. Again, I'm trying to be less judgmental, but it's not for me. Give me a couple of grams in my pocket, the millions of Euros I'm sitting on, and my woman. Don't get me wrong, we'll have those same kinds of giggles together, that innocent laughter caused by the daftest of stuff, but I've got this aversion to being seen to enjoy such trivial shit. I suppose that says more about me than it does these fools here, but the fact of it is that I don't give a fuck. The couple wander off, arm in arm, and they're replaced by a pair of French kids, yammering at each other incessantly, which gives me my reason to vacate the area and wander further up the main strip. A guy with a long brown Jesus beard strums at his guitar and belts a Beatles tune out, and he's pretty good. A small group of appreciative teenagers sit cross legged in front of him, making up the entirety of his stoned hipster audience. The stink of weed emanates from them, and that's another reason I love this place, that whole lawlessness of it all, but low key. These guys aren't causing any trouble, they're just chilling out, playing their part in the grand show that is Las Ramblas. I stand and watch the musician, my foot tapping away to his rendition of Helter Skelter, and pleasantly surprised when one of the teens holds a spliff up to me, which I'm happy to take, and pull a strong toke into my lungs, holding it in and nodding in appreciation as he gazes up at me in stoned wonder. I pass it back to him after another huge toke, and nod back, throwing a friendly "Alright?" his way, which he reciprocates in the form of a "Yeah man," in an Australian accent. The weed mildly hits me and a mellow buzz washes over me, and it dawns on me that I've not had a spliff in ages. It's good weed too. Beardy starts up with Hey Hey My My by Neil Young, or My My Hey Hey, I get them mixed up, and I'm in my element here, the guy's got some right tunes in his repertoire. The spliff comes back around and I take a couple off and send it round again, before nodding a thanks again to the young Aussie and wandering off with that old familiar fuzzy feeling, and a smile on my face, Neil Young, the old Crazy Horse rattling around my stoned brain. Ambling through the tourists my newly paranoid mind turns to Jess, she's had her couple of hours being a classy version of Julia Roberts, and I think that should be enough. It's almost as if she's feeling my paranoia right there, because my phone buzzes, and it's her gorgeous face looking back at me from the display. The picture I took in Florence outside *Piazza di Santa Croce*, the first stop off on our perpetual road trip, her gorgeous smiling face, looking like a sexy pig in shit. I call her that sometimes, sexy pig, pisses her off.

"Heyyyyy baby, all done?" I ask, my mind swimming in thoughts of what she might have bought, what delights that might wait when she gets me alone tonight. I cannot wait for that!

"Hiya, yeah I'm done, where are you?"

"Las Ramblas, been having fun with the stoners, might have had a little toot."

"Tommmmmm!" She drags it out, I know she'll be feasting off that little revelation for the next few hours but she knows I'm not killing anybody with it, and the fact is that I told her, so she can't bust my balls too much, that's the secret you see, she wouldn't have known if I didn't tell her, so I get points for

honesty, how cool is that?
"I know, I know, I'm sorry, just getting into the spirit of the city, stay where you are anyway baby, I'll come find you."

<u>Definitely Not Only Together Through Circumstance</u>

The waiter stands over them. Watching them intently as Tom's eyes scan the menu. Jess knows he hasn't got a clue what he's about to order, but he does enjoy looking authoritative on stuff like this. Typical man, she thinks affectionately. His eyes flick up to her.
"What you having?"
She smiles at him and looks up to the waiter.
"Tortilla de patatas, por favor, cambrer." The pronunciation rolls from her tongue effortlessly, the ability to sound native to whichever country she was in was something of a skill of hers. The waiter nods as he scribbles down her order, and tilts his head slightly to address Tom, who is still poring over the foreign language before him, but the confusion leaks slowly into his features.
"Senor?"
Tom looks to Jess. He hates situations like this, where he looks stupid in front of his girlfriend, and an uneasy feeling rises within him, almost of frustration, but her bright beaming eyes disarm the feeling, and she is moved to ask.
"What do you want to eat baby?"
He shrugs, then considers.
"Owt meaty."
She laughs, and looks at the menu.
"Sausages?"
His face lights up and he nods eagerly like a child being asked if they'd like to take a spontaneous trip to Disneyworld. Jess places her gaze upon the waiter

and rolls off the order on behalf of her beau.
"Botifarra amb mongetes, por favor."
"Dunt sound meaty."
"Catalan pork sausages baby, don't worry." She puts him at ease and rests her hand on his, and the waiter wanders off to place their order.

It is at this moment that they both feel extremely happy with their lives, but are both well aware of the dangers that face them, and their good fortune to have made it unscathed so far. Between them they have pissed some very bad people off, and killed some even badder people, and stolen ten million Euros in cash. For the last two years, since the most eventful twelve months of their short lives they have moved from country to country, keeping the lowest profile they possibly can. They have seen some of Europe's most beautiful sights, melted into the throngs of other sightseeing couples.

Recently they have felt more at ease, as if they are finally getting away with their crimes against criminals. They feel less inclined to look over their shoulder at every turn, and although they are still very aware that they need to sleep with one eye open, they have begun to talk of finding somewhere to settle, like their old colleague, Cristiano, their cohort in the grand murdering, and theft from, Terence Wilcox, AKA Philip Hoxton, AKA a lot of other names, the head of a multinational organisation that specialised in twisted games to test the morality of the human race. With the fall of Wilcox, they are not sure that they'll ever have an idea what to ever expect. They can assume that the organisation fell apart, that the team that they had once worked with were not searching for them, and Cristiano. Or they could imagine that Ada, their one time heroine, the cold blooded killer and expert manipulator, has maybe taken over the huge network that was at the disposal of her employer. That the same network was moving Heaven and Earth to track them down, and that the games they forced upon criminals, lowlifes, and egomaniacs were no longer being held. At one time, every other face in the crowd was Ada, or Dietmann, or worse still Yannick, but that fear had gradually dissipated over time as they became comfortable with the lifestyle they were now forced to live. The millions of Euros eased the hassle somewhat. Now here, in Barcelona, they feel happy. Tom felt comfortable with allowing Jess out of his sight, if only briefly, to go about her business, shopping for the clothes she was wearing tonight, to help her feel even slightly normal for once. His hand slides from under hers and reaches into his pocket, his fingers rolling nervously over the ring that nestles there. He has been waiting to do this since Amsterdam, but there was always something that stopped him, something inside him that feared the rejection. A small, insecure part of him felt that she was still a thousand leagues above him, better than him, and this was still some ridiculously evil game against him. He sometimes feels that they are perhaps together through circumstance, rather than out and out choice. Jess takes a sip of her water, a nervousness of her own threw her stomach up and down, waves of nausea lap at her insides.

The silence between them grows unusually uncomfortable, as both work through their inner turmoil, edging ever closer to speaking up. Jess eventually breaks it.
"I love you, you know?" She says, with genuine warmth.
Tom smiles sheepishly, and looks her deep in the eyes.

"I know, I love you too, I dunno what I'd do wi'out you." His fingers sweating up as they make the leap, curling around the diamond ring, balling into a fist and dragging it from its long term slumber in his pocket, she watches his arm bringing the fist up like a heavy crane hauling its load over a building yard, onto the table and coming to rest by her hand. Her fingers move slightly to touch him, but his hand remains balled. The silence falls between them again as he stares at her, his mouth seeming to want to say something, but his mind stopping it.

"Are you okay?" She asks, conscious that this is in danger of turning into something awkward, and they have never had an awkward moment between them in all of their time together. He doesn't answer her straight away, and seems to be taking some sort of mental plunge, as his fist turns over, the fingers peeling away like a flower bud unfurling in Spring, to reveal a stigma made of a circle of sparkling white gold, and a huge immaculate diamond. Their eyes both rise from the ring in his palm, to meet each other's. He smiles at her, an expectant look in his eyes.

"Wanna marry us?" He asks.

She feels the anxiety flush away in an instant as her heart explodes in her chest, her stomach looping the loop and her innards dance with joy.

"Tom, of course I do!" She leaps up from her chair, flinging her arms around his neck as he rises to meet her, relishing her previous decision to purchase such high shoes. He squeezes her as tight as she did him, admitting to nobody that there are tears in his own eyes.

"And anyway," She whispers into his ear, "I'm gonna have to marry you now, pregnant aren't I?"

Self-Imposed Exile

Whoosh! The axe dropped effortlessly through the log that somewhat optimistically believed it might provide any kind of resistance to the weapon, or the beast that wielded it. Chop! Chop! Chop! Chop! None of the brave wooden soldiers providing much more of a challenge than any of their predecessors. As the axe wedged deep into the shredded chopping surface and as the low winter sun shone on his back he wiped the warm sweat from his brow with the back of his forearm, then hoisted the chopped logs up across his muscular chest, and carried them to the store at the back of the cabin, dropping them to where a recently diminished pile once stood.

Leaning against the wooden structure of the cabin that had been his home for the last two years he emitted a long sigh, and took in the view across the valley, a lammergeyer soared across the clear blue sky, dropping the bones of some unfortunate carcass down onto the rocks below and swooping down to feast on the marrow. Cristiano was fascinated by the birds that nested around this area, especially the Egyptian vultures, *The Pharaoh's Chicken,* although most of them had made the trip over Gibraltar into Africa for the winter. This self-imposed exile from society had given him an opportunity to read, and learn more, to educate himself on a great many things. He enjoyed reading, absorbing new information, proving to himself that he was not the lumbering imbecile that he had forever been taken to be, by childhood friends, his parents, the organisation, that had him pegged as the brainless muscle. He proved to them that he was not brainless, no the brainless one was Hoxton, Wilcox, whatever his name was, given that he had had them beaten out of his old wrinkled skull and been left to be discovered by the Ada, or any one of the rest of his sycophantic employees. Like the pathetic old fool that he turned out to be. The way he'd feigned indifference when Cristiano held his withered frame in his fists, like he'd accepted his fate. He did not beg, or pray, he simply let his body fall heavy, and waited for Cristiano to do his work. To the old man's credit he held on, a man who had seen enough fights to never give up, so it was left to Cristiano to put him out of his misery, and empty his gun into him. The old man's murder never felt special in any way after the deed, it was just a case of another life ended by Cristiano and his power, that it freed him from the shackles of the organisation was merely a fantastic by product of his desire to end Hoxton.

Of course there were Tommy and Jessie, the young lovers, he was able to free them of the path that they were forced upon. He liked Tommy, his wit, and fearlessness in the face of whatever. In their times together on the road he always proved to speak to every person he met with in the exact same way, nobody was above anybody else to him, he had once explained that they were all people, why would one person demand a tone that they had not earned? Cristiano had never thought about it that way before, and thus made a conscious decision to be that same way from then on, not that he had an opportunity to speak to many people, but the sentiment still stood. He missed them, they had brought an air of, something, was it honesty? Innocence? Normality? Perhaps that was it, the fact that the organisation could not affect them as it had done the others. Some of them were from a different time entirely, a different generation, they all allowed themselves to be under the old man's spell, to follow him wherever he took them. Cristiano had always felt like an outsider from it all. Yes he did as he was bidden, but all the time he ached for kindred spirits to work with him to get rid of Hoxton, which was where Tommy came in, and by extension, Jessica. Tommy was smitten by his lady, and his desire to do everything that would create a safer world for her was the driving force. Cristiano envied him to a degree, he had somebody to protect, he had a mission in life, a point.

As the lammergeyer emerged from its feeding and continued its journey into the horizon, Cristiano turned and lumbered into the cabin, pulling an Estrella Damm from the refrigerator, ripping the lid from its lips and gulping it down, emptying the thing in seconds. He pulled another one from the shelf and turned into his living space. On the whole he was happy with his home, it had everything he needed. His huge bookshelf ran from wall to wall and was filled with items to occupy and feed his mind. The LED television which filled another wall was only ever used for viewing *Herederos* or when he was blasting the hell out of anonymous strangers on Call of Duty, muttering profanities when cheats came online and ruined his gaming experience. On the decking outside sat his hot tub, where he had spent many a night charming the pants off hookers he had arranged to visit. They didn't require charming to get their pants off, but it made Cristiano feel good to put his moves on them, lean across them with his huge, and defined biceps, lift them out of the hot tub with one arm, and carry them to the bedroom where he would spend the whole night snorting cocaine from their buttholes, fucking them until they were sore, and then paying them handsomely for the privilege. A man had needs. As far as the cock was concerned they were being fulfilled regularly, but a niggle entered his mind only occasionally, but had been appearing more often recently, sometimes a man also had needs as far as the heart went. A good woman to provide that feeling of being needed. As he sat in his armchair he sighed once more. He conceded that the truth of the matter was that he was bored. A man who was officially dead, wanted by police, journalists, Ada and her gang of ass licking puppies. A man like that was one who must lay low in order to keep the easy life, but the easy life could be boring sometimes. He craved action of some variety. A burglar to beat into submission, or somebody taking a pot shot with a pistol, but most of all, he just wanted a woman. Flicking the button of his television remote he sat back into the soft padding of his armchair, placing his beer on the small table beside him. Literally seconds later he felt a firm cold metal press into the crown of his skull, and heard the click of a bullet entering the barrel of a gun. It was like the Gods had heard his plea for action, like they just knew what he needed to put some meaning back into his life, because the next thing he heard was:

"Alright dickhead?"

He didn't move an inch. Just sat, his eyes on the TV, he could hear the dialogue but it filtered through his mind like white noise, a smile shone in his eyes as his head rotated to see his ambusher.

"You sneaky motherfocker, Tommy, I missed you man."

Every Day Is A School Day

His muscles squeeze tight around our heads, pulling us close to his chest, his booming laughter ricochets from every wall in the cabin, he sounds utterly delirious, like we're the first people he's seen since, well, us. He's got bigger since then, if that's even possible. We're released from his grip and he heads straight to the fridge, still laughing with delight, and pulls out two beers. Tom takes it from him with one hand, offering an appreciative smile mixed with a pained look as he rubs the back of his cricked neck with the other hand. I want to kiss it better. He hands me a beer which I have no intention of drinking but I want to delay the inevitable bear hug when we break the news for as long as possible. He's lovely but he reminds me of Lenny from Of Mice and Men sometimes, ever so strong but unaware just *how* strong.

"How's tricks then Mr Beefy? Long time no see." Tom says as he chinks his bottle against Cristiano's and settles himself on the arm of the chair.

"Tricks? You think I am a magician Tommy? What the fock is with the tricks?" And he flashes a wink at me. He's a real wind up merchant sometimes, and Tom falls for it every time.

"No, I mean, it's just a phrase you fanny, how are things?"

"I know what you are meaning Tommy, you are the fanny, you are way too easy!" His huge shoulders heave as he laughs again before beckoning us out onto the vast decking outside the cabin, pointing Tom and I to a padded sofa swing that's facing the valley that drops ever so deep below us, it's a truly breath-taking view. He's going on to explain what he's been up to, telling us how he's been bored, but he's become an expert in keeping his own company, devouring the written word, feeding his brain and imagination. I admire him for it, I really do. I couldn't stand so much time alone, I would go crazy. But no matter how much he tries to sell the lonely life, I can see genuine warmth in his eyes, like he is over the moon to see us. He's going to great lengths to tell us about the books he's been reading. I have to admit that he does seem a lot wordier, talking about the things he's read up on with a great authority, throwing daft little facts out to prove he knows what he's talking about, it's kind of fun to watch though, I know that every time he gives us a pointless fact that Tom's just itching to say "Thanks for the info-nugget, I'll keep that in my back pocket for a rainy day" or "Every day's a school day." He does it to me every time I tell him about something new I've learned. It used to be one of those things he didn't even realise he was saying, like when he starts every bloody sentence with "For sure", now he does it to affectionately annoy me, the git. It's as if he can tell what I'm thinking, because when Cristiano reveals, as he points to a bird soaring above us, that there are twenty three species of vulture, there's this mischievous look in Tom's eyes that smiles at me as he says "Well Mr Beefy, I did not know that, for sure, every day's a school day." He puts the bottle to his lips as Cristiano considers this for a second, and nods in appreciation.

"Every day is a school day," he says, rubbing his chin, "there is a lot of truth in that, I like it!"

Tom smiles again with affection as our in-joke flies so fast over Cristiano's head that I swear I can see his hair twitch as the velocity disturbs it. He mutters the phrase again and seems genuinely pleased with it. Tom's free hand strokes my thigh and I feel a light buzz between my legs as my crotch awakens to his touch and I gasp slightly, which he seems to pick up on because he gives me a naughty wink and squeezes the flesh a bit, I stifle a giggle and clear my throat, bringing my left hand out and resting it on my knee, looking from Cristiano to the ring that sits proudly upon it. Tom spots what I'm up to and takes his cue. "So yeah, the reason we came to find you, we've got good news."

Three hours later and the boys are making a real racket in the lounge of the cabin, and I'm still outside on the swing. They're pretty hyped up, I know for a fact that they're doing coke but it *is* a special occasion, so I'm leaving them to it. On the drive up here Tom was blabbering like he'd already been on it but I know it was excitement, going on about names and everything. If it's a boy he wants to call it Justin, after his friend who died, and if it's a girl he likes Natalie. I like Henry and Lucy. We'll see. I get up and walk closer the edge of the cliff, and perch myself on a rock, cuddling myself to preserve my body heat. The mountains are incredibly serene, and the moon is providing just enough light for me to see it reflecting off of a snowy peak out in the distance. It's really cold outside, and I'm shivering like anything, but I feel so content right now, staring into the dark, my mind settled by the twinkling specks of the moonlight bouncing off streams and lakes, and the snow. I love it. A wolf nearby startles me by yelping into the night, and I'm suddenly unnerved by the night, and get up to move inside the cabin. I can see the silhouettes of the boys, still lively, play-fighting like drunken hyper shadow boxers. They're clearly in their element, and I know that Tom is loving it. He can tell me I'm the greatest thing on Earth, and that I'm all he needs 'til the cows come home, but, looking at him, and hearing his laughter echo out through the air, he has missed male interaction so badly. I want him to enjoy it. I want him to ignore me for a while, to let me alone to think about how our lives have changed and how they will

change in the future. I want him to forget that we'll be on the run forever, bound together by a mutual love, and of course mutual enemies. I want to watch him being, well, *normal*. This is something we have both needed. I got my taste earlier today in the boutique, this is his release, and I wouldn't dream of denying him that. I stand silently watching the window, a smile on my face as the smaller shadow boxer says my name, and then calls it out. I head inside to see the boys. Tom cheers as I enter the lounge, and approaches me with open arms, welcoming me into his embrace, he's rapidly muttering that he loves me, telling me I'm his angel, and that he never wants to be apart from me, and that he can't wait to be Mr Me. I know it's the drugs, but I'd be stupid to think it wasn't borne from true feelings. I tell him I can't wait to be Mrs Him either, and I endure a long wet kiss on the face owing to his delight. Wiping the saliva from my ear with my sleeve I pull away and smile at him. His eyes are like saucers, and his teeth grind together as the drugs work their way through his system. He gets like this. Like an affectionate wild animal. Like a lion that learned to kiss, and cuddle, but no less dangerous if his pride was threatened. I do love him though. I kiss his cheek and give him another smile. "Have fun baby, be careful, I'm going to bed."
He stumbles a little over his own feet and leans into me, declaring his undying love, he holds my face in both of his hands, firm but at the same time entirely tender, his glazed eyes do their best to look me directly in mine, but they're all over the place. We kiss our departing kiss, and I say goodnight to Cristiano before heading through to the bedroom that he advised as being ours for as long as we wanted. I know Tom will want to stay here for a while, and I think I'll be happy with that for now. The place is

secluded, secure, and it is the epitome of the word luxury, I love it.

    I sink into the king size bed, and although the weather outside is freezing the cabin is really well heated, and I find myself dragging the duvet from my legs. I love it when I can do that, like, keep the duvet bundled around my body, but leave my legs uncovered, it's a really nice sensation, the air licking at my feet. I'm tired but my head is still swirling. I'm going to get married, and have a baby. There's a niggling doubt that floats about my atmosphere. How are we going to raise a child when we lead the lives we do? How do we possibly get married when we've officially disappeared from the face of the Earth? I know Tom will work his arse off to make it work, I *know* he will, but the doubt is still there, what kind of upbringing might our child have? Being dragged from country to country, city to city? No family except Tom and I, how would our child end up? Then my mind flips to the other side of the coin, there are children out there with far less options than ours could hope for, children dying every single minute of every day. We have a lot of money, he or she will want for nothing. We won't spoil them, but they will never, ever, want for anything. I *know* that Tom will be an unbelievable dad, he's childish and daft a lot of the time, but only to entertain me, and he's so fiercely protective that when he says he'll die to protect us, well, in his words, *for sure* I believe him. This thought soothes me and my brain begins to shut down, my thoughts gradually slow in their regularity, and I can feel myself dropping into a slumber. My final conscious feeling is the mixed up idea that the unconditional love and protection for me and my unborn baby is drinking booze and doing drugs downstairs, but it doesn't scare me, far from it, he's my rock. It's how he works. And I fall to sleep knowing that the sounds of Tom and Cristiano will go on for a few hours yet.

Chapter 3 - January

A Minor Inconvenience

The game had changed. It had to. The world was a vastly different place to when Hoxton ran things. It was becoming smaller. Technology was evolving, and people were evolving with it. Communication technology had become an all-consuming monster, and the power had shifted greatly to the hands of the people, everybody was permitted to give their opinion on everything, and when they were not permitted they forced these opinions out regardless. Families had the ability to connect within seconds, no matter where on the planet they lived. Photo recognition software allowed nobody to hide. Paedophiles could ply their sickening trade, exchange pictures and connections with other equally disturbed wretches across the globe. The time-proven methods of securing players, and gamblers, were now beginning to show cracks. People talked to each other far too much. Increasingly able, and cheaper telephones, and social networking had been entirely instrumental. The world's dependency on them had become critical, and had become a more suspicious place. Shadows were forever questioned for their motives, and for a woman that lived in the shadows, Ada was more vulnerable than she had ever been. The game *had* to change.

    The meeting after South Africa served to highlight the cracks within the organisation. Cristiano, the treacherous scum-dog, had been left to destroy not only the man who created all of them, the man to whom they owed their previously meaningless lives, but he had also destroyed the wire-thin trust that they held between each other. At

the meeting they had shouted and threatened each other. Yannick, with his low French growl, and his workmate Lukas, openly mocking her and her ability to take over the organisation. Dietmann, with his irritating brown-nosing. The new girl, Liezel, brash and reactive, had entered their realm and begun to ask questions. If it was not a *what* then it was a *why* and if answers were not forthcoming then she behaved like a petulant child, causing yet more rifts between them. Liezel had flagrantly abused the responsibilities she was tasked with. Instead of researching their targets, following them, and assessing their suitability, she could not seem to detach herself from her job, and had begun a one-woman vigilante mission, leaving behind her trail of corpses. A trail of corpses that Lukas and Yannick had refused to clear up. The girl had not become a liability, she was born a liability. She had every intention of simply wiping her out, burying her, and getting on with her own life, but the fact was that Liezel had her uses. Ada intentionally sent her for the tasks that would keep her out of the way whilst she performed her own jobs, all the while grooming her to perform what would be their crowning glory. If she were to be caught, or killed whilst out and about, then that would be a minor inconvenience, but it would not harm the work that Ada had put in on her own time. It would merely dictate that she would have to find somebody else to be her dancing monkey. Her personal project was one borne of vengeance, and of humiliation, and it would be-
Her telephone vibrated in her pocket, it was Rufus, she excused herself from the table and answered.
"Tell me good things Rufus."
"The couple spent the day in Barcelona, and arrived at a cabin in the Pyrenees at approximately three

o'clock in the afternoon. They are now with a man who appears to reside at the cabin. He is huge. They have been in and around the building since they got here, and are currently all inside. Do you have any requests?"

"Not as yet, Rufus, stay there and continue the surveillance as usual, keep me abreast of any developments."

"Of course."

As Ada ended the call Rufus' words reverberated around her skull, her mind was giddy with possibility, the man who appeared to reside at the cabin. Huge. *Cristiano.* Perfect. She returned to the table and flashed her host a smile as he pulled her chair out for her, allowing her to seat before he returned to his own.

"I do apologise, a matter of urgency." She said, brushing the material of her dress down over her bare legs.

"Oh darling, it's absolutely fine, I don't doubt that I may have a few of those myself, let's call it a professional courtesy to one another that we may take our leave to attend to matters of urgent business, agreed?"

She smiled at Isaac Charles

"Agreed."

Isaac Charles reached down below the table and brought a glossy black briefcase to its surface, laying it flat before him, and flipping open the lid, and sliding the usual envelope her way.

"This gem is perfect for your girl, an absolute rotter, I'll allow you the pleasure of reading up on him in detail but take it from me, the things he has done, he will last about a minute in the company of your little renegade once she clicks as to his MO."

"Which is?"

"Honestly darling, it isn't for the dinner table, believe me. You should try the foie gras by the way, to die for." Isaac Charles purred, placing another bite of toast into his mouth, his eyes rolling dramatically as he savoured the taste, then gulping down a generous mouth of his wine.

"Not my, cup of tea, I'm afraid, but please, enjoy on my behalf." Replied Ada to her companion, placing her recently acquired envelope into her bag, and turning her attention to her own starter. Drawing the asparagus soup to her lips she felt the hot liquid smother her taste buds, feeling them delight in the sensation. She was not a vegetarian, nor was she particularly carnivorous, but the whole idea of foie gras concerned her, the treatment that the animals must endure in order to provide people like Isaac Charles their culinary treats. The irony of her own feelings toward cruelty was by no means lost, but nevertheless she did not condone the creation of foie gras. Keeping the thought to herself she ate in silence, allowing herself brief glimpses of the former PR man sloppily devouring his own food, moaning orgasmically now and then. Ada did not for one second believe that the man was any different behind closed doors. He was a pantomime in himself, but it did not detract from the fact that he had a brilliant mind, one which Ada found to be most useful, she'd been using it a lot since Hoxton's death, and would be using it a great deal more in the near future.

There's A Bad Moon On The Rise

He dropped his bag onto the thin bed and sat beside it with laboured effort, taking the time to absorb his most recent surroundings. A basic hotel room. An attempt at a wardrobe stood in the corner, no doors, just a dark wooden rectangle with a bar to hang clothes, two weak spare pillows sitting atop it. The chest of drawers at the end of the bed housed a small travel kettle, with two cups, a jar filled with drinks sachets, and a tiny flat screen television, its remote control sitting snugly in the plastic grey holster glued, or screwed, to the side of it. The light linen curtains fluttered softly in the breeze of the open window, fetching with it an eerie rumble from the highway in the distance. Roda de Isabena. The latest in countless villages and provinces he'd encountered on his slow, and uneventful surveillance mission, following this young couple across Europe for reasons unknown. How the woman Ada could afford to pay him all this time, or why she allowed it to go on for so long, he didn't even try to speculate, but he would happily watch the money mount up in the bank whilst he embarked upon this unlikely road trip. However unorthodox this current job was, he remained a consummate professional, he put his receipts in every month, and kept his every transaction above board, doing his utmost to remain as transparent to his employer as he could, there was no way that he would do anything to jeopardise this cash cow that had fallen into his lap. Of course there were downfalls, the most prominent being Charley. He spoke to her every day, saw her on the video calls all of the time, but he had not felt her press against him since May, he hadn't filled his nostrils with her scent, feasted upon her lady garden, looked down to delight in watching her tiny arse pushing back onto his cock, in eight months. He missed her. The talking was all well and good, and seeing that gorgeous smile on the computer screen was great, but there was only so much joy a man could obtain from pounding his cock with his fist, and firing his muck over his own

stomach before wiping it away with yesterday's undies. The image of her leaning back, her hands resting upon his thighs as she pushed herself hard onto his cock, eased its way into his mind, and he slowly fell backward onto the bed, his hands snaking around his belt buckle. In his mind's eye she was going round the world, spinning on his member and-
"I see, a bad moon rising, I see, trouble on the way." The Ada woman beckoned as John Fogerty sang out from Rufus' mobile phone, lurching him immediately from his fantasy like a swamp rock juggernaut, Charley disappeared into the ether, leaving him to consider what the Ada woman might want. He always allocated the CCR doomsayer theme tune to any employer, at one point he thought that this might reflect on his own personality more than anything else but it was *his* phone, he could use whatever he wanted.

"Rufus." He barked, feeling just slightly put out by the interruption to his getting his rocks off.

"Any news?" The pleasantries generally kept to a minimum, they weren't friends, this was business.

"I left them about an hour ago and checked into my hotel, it seems they're content to sight tight just now, nobody left or arrived since they got there."

"And do you have any intentions of returning tonight? I do not pay for you to spend your nights like you are on your holiday, in hotels, Rufus." And so it began, he had learned over time how to firmly placate her without antagonising her, but she loved to play the role of ball breaker, whether it was a front or if she really was such an uptight cunt he wasn't sure, but while she paid him as she did, he was happy to play the game.

"I appreciate that, but that car is armed with the tracker, and it seems like they're pretty comfy with the fella they're visitin', they ain't leavin' tonight." A moment's silence stretched into what felt like minutes, almost to the point where he fancied that she might be twitching on the floor, spazzing out with an embolism at his sharp tone, a notion quickly dismissed as she spoke.
"Fine, be sure that you do not waste your time in the morning, do you understand?"
"Loud and clear ladyboss, loud and clear."

And that was that. Sometimes it just felt like she needed to flex her authority muscles, remind him who was boss, as if he could forget. He'd been in this game long enough, and met enough people like her to take it in his stride, but at the time they were always a royal pain in the arse. He had no doubt that she had enough in her to make things even more difficult for him, but he hadn't made it this far in life by being a soft touch, and if she stepped too far out of line, then by Christ would she know about it.

The couple didn't seem spectacularly corrupt, or troublesome, by any stretch of the imagination, he had been following them for eight months, and for what it was worth all they did was indulge in a spot of sightseeing. They cruised through Europe, visited the usual cities, Amsterdam, Bruges, Berlin, Paris, Prague, Florence, Krakow, and the rest, spent maybe a few days in each one, then stopped in rural areas to lay low for weeks at a time. What they had done wrong to the Ada woman he wasn't sure he wanted to know, but she put a hell of a lot of importance on keeping tabs on them. Anybody else that he had worked for would want the job done immediately, wipe out the enemy and move on. In his experience allowing people to live longer than necessary only served to caused more trouble in the future, and if you had no intention of letting them live in the long term, kill them when you have the chance. Ada seemed to have a plan though, so good luck to her, and as long as she continued to pay, then Rufus was happy to go along for the ride. Besides, he was mildly intrigued to see how all of this would pan out, and there were always benefits available to your friendly neighbourhood mercenary when you were prepared to keep your options open. Right now, Rufus was keeping his options as open as a whore's legs when the sailors came back to port.

Throwing Shit At The Situation And Seeing What Sticks

Dietmann glanced from the papers before him up to Ada. She faced away from him, hands behind her back, watching the sea from the window. He reflected sadly that she had changed since Hoxton's death. She had become colder. Back in the old days he found her to be approachable when she was away from the watchful eyes of the rest of the team, she would act like she had his best interests at heart, in her own way. She seemed to value his opinion, and encourage him, as one of the youngest members of the team to come forward with ideas of how to improve their part of the operation, to save time and so on. When the operation became jeopardised she placed enough trust in him to take the helm in her absence, and with the esteem that she had appeared to hold him in, it was enough for him to gain a drip of respect from Mr Hoxton. Now, however, she was cold. She was impatient with him when answers failed to materialise immediately, when he approached her to discuss his ideas, she would sigh, and tell him to come back at another time, and that she would speak with him when she could. Of course, he was well aware that since she had taken over the organisation, admittedly of her own accord and that there were not any nominations taking place, that she had placed herself under far more pressure than she was ever under when Hoxton ran things, she had some very large boots to fill, and looked like she was determined to do a great job of filling them. The most hurtful aspect was that she was now far more secretive than she had ever been. When Cristiano and the others ripped them off and killed Hoxton she became withdrawn, would leave the room to make telephone calls to, well, whoever. Dietmann knew that she had irons in several fires, and based on past experiences she did well to keep her cards close to her chest, but had he not proved himself to be worthy of unreserved trust? Had the last seven years been for nothing? She treated him like a weak younger sibling who had become more of a hindrance than a help, and his declining sense of worth gnawed at him like a vulture on the bones of some fallen beast. He performed the tasks requested of him with aplomb every time, but it was without any sort of recognition. Returning to Ada with news of a job well done was received with ice cold nonchalance, and an uncaring sniff. These recent feelings, and the increased secrecy with regards matters of operations now meant that he no longer felt at ease with offering his opinions. If people's importance were ranked on a need-to-know basis, then Dietmann would be firmly rooted below sea-level, below even the kinds of fish that did not even need eyes because the visibility was so poor. Nevertheless, he clung on to the hope that his stock may rise in the future. He would go out of his way to impress Ada, and her impeccable standards, and

continue to develop new ways and means of improving their operating systems on his own time, and essentially throw as much shit at the situation and hope that eventually something would stick.
She turned to face him, registering the look in his eye.
"Is there something you wish to say, Dietmann?"
He opened his mouth to speak, but faltered, doubt in his mind, what was the point?
"No Ada, nothing."
She accepted this and turned once again, briefly glancing out of the window and then strode from the room.

He *did* have something to say, however, and it was about the file that lay before him. The contents of it, and more specifically the man that they related to. He was the highest profile target that they had ever looked at, and his actions meant that Leizel would never allow him to live. He hoped that Ada knew what she was doing, because whatever she had planned had the potential to blow their lives apart if it went wrong. She was not only placing Leizel at risk, she was placing herself, Dietmann, Lukas, and Yannick at risk.

William Walters, also known as Will Thunder, one half of Thunder & Lightning, Britain's foremost comedy duo, their rise from children's television to primetime stardom was as rapid as it was spectacular. He and his colleague, Johnny Lightning had become the highest paid television presenters in their country, and had become synonymous with the channel they worked for. The go-to guys for the most watched shows in the country. Their circle of influence was not exclusive to the UK either, and their antics had become the stuff of legend across Europe, their iconic *That's not my dad!* routine had been viewed millions of times on YouTube, ripped off

and homage paid to with various versions surfacing over the internet, and they had a host of awards to attest to their popularity. Walters surrounded himself with an entourage of hangers on, users, security, and guys who ensured that he never needed for anything, and that truly meant anything, and this was the trouble. This was the reason he had fallen onto the organisation's radar, which directly placed him into the firing line of Leizel and her vigilantism, and Dietmann was very well aware that she would stop at nothing to ensure that justice was served. With this in mind he picked up the telephone, tentatively nudging the buttons, and let out a long sigh as the tone rang out.
"Yes?"
"Leizel, we have a job for you."
"Surprise surprise, I shall be there tomorrow, goodbye."
And he was left cradling a telephone which sounded out the disconnected tone, until he replaced the receiver. He looked back at William Walters' file, and hoped to God again that Ada knew what she was doing.

Chapter 4 - February

We Push Our Evolution Back By Over A Century

"In my eyes, she is a hero to the people, you only have to look at the overwhelming opinions across the social networking sites to see that the public have no sympathy for Will Thunder, he is a predatory paedophile with access to anybody he wants. Parents have *paid* to get an audience with him for their children-" The right wing politician was cut off by his left wing counterpart.
"But have you no idea of the human rights laws we are infringing upon if we allow her to continue with her plan? Of course the social networking sites are awash with people calling for his murder, but we do not live in a society where the law dictates an eye for an eye, no matter how popular that option may be." she countered. The audience applauded, and the host directed his attention to a man in the third row, a full ginger beard and vast bush of curly hair atop his chubby face, his maroon and green striped jumper fitting snugly over his gut.
"The bearded man, third row." Directed the host. The man cleared his throat, and waited for the boom microphone to be hovered over his face.
"Um, yes, a question for Steven Mallinson."
The right wing politician smiled.
"Wouldn't it be better to allow the authorities to deal with both of these criminals in a court of law? Surely letting one murder the other and then arresting the killer leaves blood, and the stench of hypocrisy, on the hands of the justice system?" The audience applauded once again, which seemed to irritate Steven Mallinson, a staunch supporter of the return of capital punishment for crimes less than murder.

"This man, and others of his kind, are a stain on our country, there are more and more of them coming to the surface, and what do we do? We jail them for a few years, and then allow them to go back underground to ply their vile trade, and the criminal checking system is ridiculously flawed. I'm sick to the back teeth of stories of people being permitted to work with children who are convicted sex offenders, and SHE," he pointed to his opposite number, "almost condones it with her incessant defence of human rights, is it really Will Thunder's right as a human to touch up whoever he wants to?"

More applause from the audience as their attentions turned to the socialist representative.

"Daisy Beckford, what do you have to say to that?" the host gave her cue.

"Of course I don't condone his actions, but the issue is not whether he has a right to *touch up* as you so eloquently put it, the point is does he deserve to publicly die for his actions or should he be tried in a court of law for the crimes he has committed? I fully appreciate that the man has flagrantly abused his position and deserves to be punished to the full extent that the law will allow, but if we pander to public opinion and allow an open and televised execution for his crimes then we push our evolution back by over a century."

More applause.

The host, Gareth Bennington-Lane smiled to the camera.

"Now let's hear from our viewers, we should have Brenda on line one, Brenda are you there?"

The host, his guests, and the audience stared off into space, expectantly waiting for the voice of the ghost of Brenda to boom into the studio, Gareth Bennington-Lane watched himself on the monitor,

noticing that his turquoise tie was slightly crooked to the left, or the right, he couldn't quite tell with the angle and the reverse image aspect of the camera, so was hesitant to shift it in case he moved it further askew. For what seemed like an age there was nothing. Wayne Cooper, the show's director-cum-producer, considered cutting the call and allowing another faceless pleb an opportunity to say their piece, until suddenly the voice of Brenda echoed through the studio.
"Hello?"
Gareth Bennington-Lane smiled.
"Hi Brenda?"
"Am I on TV?"
"Hi Brenda yes you're live to the studio, what's your question and who is it for?"
"Well, I just wanted to say that I agree with Steven, Will Thunder deserves whatever he gets, hanging's too good for him. He needs his bits cutting off and putting into a blender, and what about Johnny Lightning? I bet *he* knows what his mate's been up to, even if he's kept his willy in his pants he's as much to blame as the other, the dirty little Herbert."
The audience applauded once more, their whooping led by a boisterous Steven Mallinson, on his feet, geeing up the crowd.
"That certainly seems a popular opinion Brenda, do you have anything else to say?" Gareth Bennington-Lane's twinkly eyed smile gazed out into the world through the lens of the camera.
"Can I say a few hellos?"
"Make it quick Brenda we need to go to adverts soon."
"Hello, hello, hello, hello, hello."
Laughter erupted in the studio as the penny dropped at Brenda's joke. Steven rocked back in his seat and

clapped, Gareth Bennington-Lane grinned in a complicit manner, appreciating the humourous interjection by Brenda. Daisy Beckford still fumed at the low brow turn the programme had taken.

"Thank you Brenda." Laughed Gareth Bennington-Lane, turning to his guests, "She does have a good point though, you'd have to think that *somebody,* Johnny Lightning or anybody, would have an idea of what he was up to? Worth a thought that," shifting his attention to the adoring lens of the camera he spoke to his audience, "And after the break we'll go back to Alex Green from London where a masked vigilante has taken Will Thunder hostage in his Kensington home, and is streaming his humiliation live to the world, how will it end? Stay tuned!"

Every Cunt Has An Opinion

Wayne Cooper watched the arse of the young production assistant as she crossed the studio to speak with the make-up people applying fresh licks of war-paint to the faces of the panel guests. She was a lively intern named Sophie, and was the latest addition to the bevy of girls in his wank bank. She had a shagger's glint in her eye when she spoke to him, twisting the ends of her plaited hair, pulling her head to tilt to the side. If she would ever let him climb on top of her and get his cock inside her, only time would ever tell, but for now he was content to let his mind do naughty things to her, if he ever got time anymore. He watched her speaking with Gareth, the mummy's boy prick, pulling that same tilted head move on him, a pang of jealousy rose within him until his attention was snatched by Simon Theaker, the video editor he'd been given for this gig, straight out of uni, a decent kid.

"Cutaway to the house after his intro, cool?"
"Uh, yeah, then on to the Will Thunder piece with the voice over, then back to the studio, pretty simple mate."
"What do you reckon to maybe getting Danny to pan over the crowds too?" The kid eager to impress with a couple of little ideas, he wasn't being overzealous so Wayne indulged him slightly.
"I dunno, maybe."
"Shall we get a shot now just in case?"
"Yeah, can do, it can't hurt."
Simon gave the order to the cameraman on location and turned to Cooper.
"Do you think he's done it?"
"Probably, you just told him to."
"No, I mean, Will, do you think he did what she says he did?"
"You can't argue with the evidence mate."
"Who do you think she is?"
"I don't fuckin' know mate, what's with all the questions?"
"Sorry, it's just mind blowing, he just always seemed so, *wholesome,* I've seen the footage she put out but I just can't get my head round it, I mean, *Will Thunder? A paedo?* That's just messed up."
"It takes all sorts to make a world kid, some of 'em are bound to get made a little bit wrong in the head, he's just one of 'em, the latest in a long line of shitheads in this industry, you'll get used to it believe me."
"Everybody on my Facebook's saying she should kill him, get it out of the way."
"Yeah but that's Facebook, every cunt has an opinion, put any of 'em in front of the guy and they'd shit it, big celebrity man in the room, don't matter if he's a kiddy-fiddler."

The kid looked doubtful. He'd never admit it, but Wayne didn't really believe himself, the mob was after Will Thunder's blood. They didn't care how it was spilled, or even when, just as long as it was spilled.

Is That Intentional?

"What's Will Thunder's favourite thing about twenty-five year olds?"
"I don't know, tell me."
"There are twenty of 'em!"
Mike Rotch (real name Barry Pratt) was on fire tonight, delivering near-the-knuckle jokes to the grimacing presenter as the audience, here to see the comedian in his first exclusive interview since a recent rape allegation, of which he was entirely cleared by Judge Peter Wise. He had been uncharacteristically quiet throughout the trial, pushing himself underground and hoping to ride the storm out when he *did* appear on television as other comedians made him the target of their jokes on topical panel shows, doing his best to take the stick with the greatest of grace, but he had been cleared and was now firing on all cylinders. His publicist, Isaac Charles, had arranged a warts and all interview with Sir Clarence Watson, to publicly air his side of the story, talk about his childhood, and generally show that he wasn't the ogre that the media had recently portrayed him as. Sir Clarence was eager not to allow his interview to descend into the vulgarity for which Rotch was known, and attempted to rein the comedian in.
"So the trial, tell me what was going through your mind when you were in the dock."

Rotch sat forward in his chair, composing himself, leaning over and staring at his praying fists, before looking Sir Clarence deep into the eyes with as much sincerity as he could muster.

"Well, I were thinking, how can this girl honestly stand there and say those things? She seemed to genuinely believe what she were accusing me of, I tell you what, she were an hell of an actress."

"Did any part of you feel like maybe, regardless of your innocence, that you brought the attention upon yourself? I mean, if it had been anybody else that had come into the firing line, you would have been at the front of the queue to tear strips off of any of your peers."

Rotch felt his eye twitch involuntarily, and considered his answer. Isaac Charles had briefed him on potential questions, but Sir Clarence was notorious was throwing curve balls now and then.

"Well, I was innocent, I *am* innocent. I didn't feel like I deserved anything like what the papers said about me, I'm not Will Thunder, there's no videos on t'internet of me doing owt but stand up. There's no sixty page dossiers been sent to every paper, TV channel or internet site in the chuffin' country!"

"You seem preoccupied with Will Thunder and deflecting everything toward his plight, is that intentional?"

A Cool Authority

"As you can see the police have set up their cordon about twenty yards behind me, and aren't letting anybody from the public or the media any further than there. The crowd is growing by the second, and the police are struggling to contain the increasing numbers. I spoke to a senior officer in the last thirty minutes and understandably he wasn't giving much away, given the extent of Will Thunder's captor's seeming omnipotence. Also, in line with your caller's point, Johnny Lightning was seen for a short time, but has since disappeared somewhere, I'll keep you posted if he shows up again." Alex Green spoke to the camera with a cool authority, hands in the pockets of his designer jeans, his weight rested on his left leg, with the crooked right leg, showing a hipster edge that he gained from his experience in youth television. Now he was attempting to gain a more credible status within the later night political arena, the natural step being to here, as field reporter slash pundit on *Politickle My Funny Bone*, an irreverent and topical look at the week's events, it was a hit with the student population and had scored him several stints at fresher nights across the country. Gareth Bennington-Lane spoke into his ear, which to the audience, would appear that they were having a direct conversation via the ever advancing technology of television.

Behind him, the crowd was swelling further, an increasingly alive sea of heads in hats, limbs in gloves, a variety of banners and placards damning Will Thunder to hell, protruding at all angles from the swell.

"What's the vibe you're getting from those crowds Alex? I bet it's absolutely electric, I'm a little bit jealous that it's not me down there."

"Well, I'm actually freezing my nuts off, but it does promise to be a very interesting evening."

Behind Alex Green a pair of hooded youths wandered in and out of the frame, much to Gareth Bennington-Lane's annoyance, and amused themselves by making guns with their fingers are pretending to shoot Alex in the back of the head, and falling into each other with the apparent hilarity which they found their actions to have, they then disappeared from the frame once again, only to return as Alex spoke.

"As far as I can tell the police are content to allow Will Thunder's captor to sit tight, to maybe, I don't know, gain some sort of false sense of security. Maybe they're hoping she becomes complacent and drops her guard before they make their move, who knows? All I know right now is that if *she* doesn't kill Will Thunder, then this baying mob almost certainly will!"

Chapter 5 - January

Working One Eyed

I feel Jess moving about in bed beside me, shuffling and sliding herself out from under the sheets. I'm going fucking nowhere, my mouth feels drier than a nun's cunt, and I'm pretty sure I'm still pissed. I open one eye and reach out to grab at her arse before she disappears from arm's length. Her arse is immense. "Mornin' baby." I mumble gruffly, my one good eye peeking at her, a poor attempt at a smile itching my face. She turns and kneels back onto the bed, kissing my forehead.
"Good morning my love," she whispers into my greasy fringe, "get back to sleep you pisshead." And she disappears from the room, off to wherever, probably a shower, maybe a bit of breakfast and a mooch about the place.

  I don't know what time me and Mr Beefy finally went to bed but it felt brilliant to cut loose with him, like, properly shake the cobwebs off my party self. We just sat up listening to some tunes I brought in from the car, playing Fifa, and hoovering up a great many grams of party powder. I could tell that Cristiano loved having some company, he was like a big Spanish pig in shit. For sure, when you feel like it there's no better feeling on Earth than just kicking back and getting hammered with good friends. But then I suppose when you feel like something there's nothing better than anything. I mean, for sure, if what you fancy is egg and beans on toast, when you get that egg and beans on toast in your belly you're gonna love it aren't you? But that feeling of totally giving in to the booze, and the drugs, when you feel like *that,* there's no greater feeling.

Don't get me wrong, some people might get high on religion, daft cunts, others might buzz off some jittery half-buffered man on man action while their PC gets gradually more and more riddled with viruses, lonely boys. Jess, she just digs life, she loves everything, she doesn't generally have a *thing* as such. She really does just dig everything, she's that easy going. Nah, for me there's not much better than getting wrecked now and then.

So now I'm awake I can feel this twinge in my bladder, but I have no intention of going anywhere, I'll ride it out and hopefully get back to sleep. I roll over onto my belly and bunch the pillow up under my heavy head, patting it down and trying to make it comfy with my cheek, and l lie there for a while longer, but that twinge, it keeps me just awake. I hate these times because no matter how often it happens I never learn. I *always* lie for at least an hour, fooling myself if I think I'll ever get back to sleep before I've gone and had a piss, so eventually I relent, and roll over onto my back, twisting myself across the bed in the process, and feel my legs leave solid ground, hovering out of the side of my scratcher, and lowering slowly to the floor. The hard floor cools the soles of my feet as I hit it, and I slither from under the sheets, rising to stand beside the bed, a slight wobble as I realise exactly how pissed I might still be. With one eye open I lumber toward the en suite bathroom, my every step feeling so heavy that it makes the room shake, honestly, I'm not even that fat, I just feel like my whole body mass is resting in my feet, transferring into the foundations of the building.

In the bathroom I'm still working one-eyed, staring out of the angled window to the mountain range on the horizon, which takes me aback slightly because I'd totally forgotten where we were. With a hand pressed against the wall as I pull my cock out and direct it into the bowl, a fat rush of dark, stinking yellow piss froths up the water. I know it's a big piss because the pitch of the contact between me and the water is very deep, like it's coming out at a good level of pressure. Sometimes when I'm in public toilets I hate it when the guy in the next cubicle is knocking out this deep manly sounding piss, and I'm just squeezing a tight one out and it sounds like I'm a five year old boy in my cubicle. Don't ask me why it bothers me so much, it just does. The relief running through my very core is brilliant, my balls tingling with the hot liquid gushing from me, and my face involuntarily raises skyward as my mouth drops open and I let out a "Gaaaaaaaaaaaah!" and then that weird tickle runs up my spine, culminating in that spasm of the neck and I shake my face, the insides of my cheeks slapping against my teeth. As my face lowers to look out of the window again I spot a bear moving about in the trees, a fucking bear! This is mad as fuck, I've only ever seen a bear on telly and at the zoo, my eye that was previously crusted closed opens and I give the pair of them a rub, picking pale green sleep from the corners of them, rolling and flicking them away before I turn my attention back to the bear outside. What's weird about this bear though, is that it's standing upright, wearing a brown fluffy deerstalker hat. It's not a bear. It's a bloke. And it's a bloke with a backpack and a handgun, and by the way he's creeping through the trees toward the cabin is telling me this kid is definitely not out for an early morning ramble. Fuck. Without shaking my cock I turn to run out to the bedroom, but smack myself in the head, right against the corner of the door frame. As the stars sparkle into my vision I'm unconscious before I even hit the ground.

A Minor Compulsion

"I see, a bad moon rising, I see, trouble on the way" He sighed at the vibrating phone on the bedside table, as he pulled his boots on. She'd called him three times since six o'clock, and the time on the display of his mobile read *06:38.* Last night she was her usual huffy impatient self, but there was something colder, abrupt, and just downright pissed off about her this morning. Somebody had definitely pissed on her chips overnight, and she was now taking it very much out on Rufus. He answered the phone.
"Rufus here, how can I help you this time?" He sighed, not a little impatience coating his words.
"You do not sound as if you are outside Rufus, do you think I was joking when I asked that you get straight back there and finish the job?"
"No, I don't think you were joking ladyboss, but how much quicker do you think I'll go if you call me every five minutes?"
"Are you being a funny man?"
"You know what? Leave me to it, I'll call you when it's done."
"Who do you-" He hung up, placing the phone back onto the bedside cabinet, then lifted his left knee to his chin on the bed, and finished tying his bootlace.

Before he fell asleep last night the Ada woman was content to pay him to follow the couple around Europe, but now something had happened at her end, maybe orders from above, maybe she had read his thoughts and realised that there was no point keeping somebody alive that she was going to have killed anyway. Whatever her reasoning she called him at six on the dot and pretty much told him the holiday was over and to get his game face on. She wanted them dead, and she wanted it done quickly.

Striding to the window Rufus pulled the curtains closed, even though he was on the third floor it was force of habit. Masking himself completely from the world so he could retrieve the backpack from beneath his bed, and empty its deadly contents out onto the duvet without prying eyes feasting themselves upon them. He checked that everything was present and correct and made his move, all to the soundtrack of Creedence Clearwater Revival from his vibrating telephone on continuous loop. *Fuck her* thought Rufus, the bitch had been getting right on his tits, she could sit and wait, the next time he spoke to her it would be to give the good news that there were three dead bodies and a whole lot of rubble.

He checked out under his usual assumed name John Fogerty and dumped the tools in the back of the rented Megane, before sitting calmly in the driver's seat, checking his watch, six fifty seven. He placed a CD in the player, tapping out a steady beat on the wheel to Captain Beefheart, and watched the clock tick over, fifty seven, fifty eight, fifty nine, then turned the ignition the second it flipped over to seven o'clock, shifting it into gear and powering out of the small hotel car park, and onto the road, directing the car deeper into the mountain range. The cabin that his three targets were staying at was about half an hour away, if he parked at a safe distance he could get up there and make a big boom at eight. Rufus enjoyed working his life out in thirty minute increments. It helped him to remember the past, and to organise the future. There had been times he'd sat for twenty six or twenty seven minutes, patiently enjoying music, and his own company, until the clock rolled back round to that ever so important thirty minute mark, and he could get down to business. It was a running joke between he and Charley that he had to give her at least thirty minutes of foreplay before he could finally put his cock inside her, not that she ever complained, she could happily let him stay down there for hours.

He killed the lights as the car rolled up about a mile from the cabin, pulling it between a pair of oak trees, noting the time at seven thirty three as he pulled on his hat and gloves, and threw the backpack over his shoulder, he needed to get a move on.

The morning's sun began to rise behind the mountains as Rufus ascended the rocky ground toward the cabin, pulling himself further uphill using the thin bare bodies of the rows of seemingly fresh tree saplings in their plastic coiled homes, snapping and bending them as he went, his thighs feeling tighter the higher he got. His head rose above the brow of the hill to bring him into plain view, at which point he felt more than inclined to pull his Type 77 pistol from the backpack, and slow his pace. The grounds of the cabin were a lot larger than he originally thought, the previously unseen side and back filled with a wide hot tub and chopping area with a massive axe standing by a chopping block that was half as big as he was, which stood as a testament to how big it's owner was. Rufus felt extremely glad right now to be dispatching the gargantuan bastard with some good old fashioned explosives rather than a dose of hand to hand combat.

He crept to building as stealthily as possible, removing his toys from the backpack, and began planting C4 around and under the structure, the ever present buzz of the incessant Ada woman calling his mobile pressed against his leg. The bitch badly needed fucking or something, it was like she had nothing better to do. Once he had his toys in place he withdrew from the cabin and dropped himself back below the brow of the hill, and removed the remote from his bag. His watch read seven fifty eight. It was these moments that he hated himself and his minor compulsion, this two minutes where anything could go wrong, and sometimes did. The seconds thumped around the face so sluggishly that they threatened to stop. Even in the brisk cold of the clear morning he felt a bead of sweat leak from beneath his deerstalker, and tickle the side of his face as it meandered down his cheek. The minute hand lurched over to fifty nine, and began a new journey from nought to sixty seconds. His hand squeezed over the ignition release trigger, and he waited. Time ticked over, forty six, forty seven, forty eight. He felt the spring loaded trigger press back against the palm of his hand, aching to be released, begging him to allow to it to blow something up, to destroy everything in its path. *Hold steady young un* he thought, *five seconds.* As the minute ended its long journey he slowly released the detonator and all hell broke loose. The C4 released its nitrogen, and carbon oxides, and the sound-waves of the explosion rocked the ground beneath him. A cloud of dust and wood billowed out above him. As the echo rang further and further away from him into the mountains, setting off an avalanche over an unsuspecting sleeping couple on honeymoon, who would not be discovered for six days, his head raised above the hill brow to admire his work. The cabin was decimated, taking everybody inside with it. Rufus smiled, and only now was content to speak with his paymaster. The impatient bitch could now hear the good news. Rather than scrolling through his contacts he simply clicked on the eighty three missed calls he had ignored. She picked up immediately.

"You do not ignore me Rufus, I pay you well for a reason, I fucking own you."
"Yeah yeah, cool your fuckin' jets, the job's done yeah? You fuckin' pay me well because I do a fuckin' excellent job."
She went silent.
"The job is done?"
"Of course the job is done, I told you I would speak with you when the job was done. It's fuckin' done."
"Excellent. Get out of there, I shall call you later."
And that was that. The young couple that he'd followed over Europe were dead. Their hulking monster of a pal was dead. And Rufus was a half a million quid richer.

He placed his tools back into the bag, and turned to leave, to drop back down the hill and head back to the Megane. Taking one last look over his shoulder he grinned again. This time the grin lasted less than a second, as from the corner of his eye he spotted the girl. The ginger girl he had been following with her fella. She stood, motionless, her mouth dropped open and tears in her eyes, watching the mess that Rufus had just created, she hadn't seen him yet. *Fuck* he thought, pulled the gun back from his bag, and headed toward her.

You Should Have Been In There

My world has gone. My Tom. The dad of my baby. Gone. I'm frozen on the spot and my head is spinning. I don't have a clue what I'm supposed to do, I want to rip the wreckage apart with my hands, I want to find my Tom, I don't want the last words I ever said to him to be *Get back to sleep you pisshead.* I want to go back in time. I want to drag him out of bed and go down to the lake together. I'm not even thankful that

I survived. That I climbed from my bed, kissed his head, and then went for an early morning walk, to clear my just-woken mind. I left the cabin and went to watch the sun come up by the lake, to think happy thoughts about my future, with Tom. I sat and came to terms with the last few weeks. Tom, he asked me to marry him. I said yes. I'm pregnant, oh God I'm alone. I don't know what I'm going to do. Five minutes ago I was the happiest I had ever been. I had my man, I had my future mapped out, I had everything I could ever want. I sat by the lake, my feet swirling the ice cold water around, watching the pink sky, the silhouettes of the mountains framing my world. I had come to terms with the way that my life was going, I had names. I saw us as an old couple, sitting at the seaside, that old cliché, eating ice creams and holding hands. Our baby all grown up, with children of their own, running up and down the seafront, chasing seagulls. Now I have nothing but heartache. Awful awful heartache. My eyes are filling up and the smoking mess before me becomes a blurred smoking mess. My Tom is under there somewhere. It's unlikely, but he might still be alive. If he's not I refuse to let him stay here. I don't care anymore if the authorities catch up with us. I need my Tom. I need to do something. The rubble is smouldering, and flat. Oh God it's so flat, how can he have survived? I can't see an answer to that. I can feel my mouth scream, I can hear the screech come from within me, and I feel my knees hit the floor. My face is wet. My swollen eyes are streaming. I don't know what to do. A branch snapping to my left grabs my attention and I look, is it Tom? *It has to be Tom. Oh God please let it be Tom.* It isn't Tom. It's a man with a gun and he's pointing it at me. Like I care anymore. I've lost everything that means anything to me and I

want to be with him. Through my sniffling, and my tears I watch as he approaches me. He's taking steady steps.
"You should have been in there." He says to me, and I wish I had been, but I have nothing to say, this man clearly killed Tom, he has killed Cristiano, and he wanted to kill me. And my baby. Oh God my baby.
I'm on my knees and he's almost where I am. The gun aimed at my face. I wish he'd kill me already. But my baby. *Our* baby.
"You should have been in there." He repeats, he's faltering. I'm willing him to pull the trigger. But our baby. But I want to die. But I don't want my baby to die. His gun is in my face and my mouth is trying to say something. My mind *is* saying it but it will not translate to actual physical words. He says it again "You should have been in there." His eyes squeeze shut, he's going to kill me and my baby.
"I'm pregnant." I whisper through my tears, looking down the barrel of his gun. My eyes raise to meet his. He looks confused.
"What did you say?" He's now holding his gun away from me, waiting for me to speak. I say it again, and he rolls his eyes. The hand holding the gun falls by his side.
"Seriously?"
I nod. He shakes his head.
"For fuck's sake."

Un Hombre Fuerte

At least one of his ribs was broken, and his left hand was crushed under, well, something. How long he had been under there he couldn't even guess, nor could he guess what time of day it was, he was entirely surrounded by rubble. Cristiano had no intention of staying much longer. He needed to get himself from under this pile and find his friends first, and then he needed to find the motherfucker that did this, and break every single bone in their body. He knew exactly who was responsible, that cold little bitch Ada. Tom and Jess had led her to his door but they weren't to blame. They had done exactly what he should have done, and stayed on the move. Ada would have tracked him down eventually, he wasn't exactly the "melt into a crowd" kind of guy, at six feet seven and built like a tank he would always draw attention, he remembered a young boy tugging on his mama's dress in the town square when he ventured down there to buy provisions, and the kid was just pointing at him excitedly and repeating *"él es un hombre fuerte, mama mama, él es un hombre fuerte!"* and Cristiano bristled with pride, thinking, *You're right kid, I am a strong man* and it had made his day. So he felt that it was the best way to keep an easy life by settling down here, out of the way. Or so he thought. It wasn't hard to know what had happened, or who was responsible. He certainly hadn't fallen asleep with the ceiling of his home broken into a million pieces all around his body, no, he had passed out after an eight hour bender with his old friend Tommy, and no matter how wasted he was, there was no way he could have crawled under the mess he was under without noticing, and there was nobody else on the planet as vengeful as Ada. She had proved that when she killed the poor journalist motherfucker for even thinking to disrespect Eastern Europeans in an article he wrote. The bitch was unhinged, no matter how much of a professional she claimed to be, she was crazy, like a dog with a fucking bone.

    He tried to move his left hand, but there was nothing he could do, it was stuck fast, probably ground to dust beneath the metal girder which held it. He reflected that it was probably the mattress which saved him when the bomb, or whatever it was, hit the building. It was a good quality pocket sprung number, fat as hell with a sweet feeling latex pillow top, and definitely cushioned him as the debris fell. But now was not the time to go blessing the pushy salesman for feeding off of Cristiano's taste for luxury. Now was the time to get out of here.

There was little space around him but just enough to swing his right arm against the shit around him, so swing he did. There was pretty much nothing to lose for Cristiano just now, he could lay here and die from suffocation, hunger, thirst, whatever, or he could fight against this heavy mass of brick and wood and metal. So he fought, with his eyes closed and his breath held he put everything he had into pushing upwards, to dislodge the layers. His knees thumped against his previously much higher, and intact, ceiling. It broke further from his heavy but limited blows, his right arm continued to pummel from a short distance, but eventually the resistance began to relent. The weight of his tomb began to lessen, and his fist was able to push deeper into the belly of the rubble. Still his left hand was trapped but he was determined to cross that bridge when he got to it. If he could free himself from the shit he was surrounded by then he could lift the girder away. Like a baby on its back on a changing mat, kicking and waving its arm aimlessly he continued to break the tomb down. Shards of light began to pierce the darkness before his eyelids, he was winning, but he still refused to stop, there was still resistance against his legs. He wormed up and down heavily against the mattress, kicking up with every cycle, smashing planks against his shins until they were dust. Burning light pressed against his eyelids as fresh air became his to suck in at his leisure, no longer a murky luxury in the dusty dark unknown. Cristiano roared as he finally freed every limb except the trapped one, filled with a renewed vigour he pushed through the pain, upwards with his left arm, and forward with his right, and dislodged the girder to release his wounded blackened, bleeding hand. It looked like he would imagine a zombiefied claw reaching up through the dirt of a fresh grave might look, gnarled and eaten by decomposition. There was no pain for Cristiano just now, only relief at his redemption from the dusty cave, and even then there was no time for that emotion. He needed to find Tommy and Jess. He strapped his hand as best he could and surveyed the mess, trying to figure out where they would be, then he became a rubble removing machine, pulling planks and bricks, throwing them behind him indiscriminately. It didn't take long to hit pay dirt. The mess of a body of Tommy lay, deliriously murmuring the name of his beloved, at least he was still alive. Cristiano heaved him up over his shoulder, and carried him from the wreckage, dropping him heavily onto the grass. The kid screamed with pain, and as consciousness took him over he began to lick at the grass, he must have been dehydrated to hell. Cristiano retreated from Tom's prone frame, to a burst pipe spraying ice cold mist into the air, and collected a drink for his friend in a crushed metal cup, returning to hand it to him. The kid gulped down whatever he could get into his mouth, and clearly more, because he choked it back up over his face, spluttering into his sleeve. Cristiano hammered the palm of his hand against Tom's skinny back, easing the water out of his lungs. Once the choking had eased he stood over his friend, as the kid's gaze wandered from his feet up to Cristiano's beaming face.

"Tommy man, you look like shit."

Tom smiled back at him wearily, and nodded to him.

"So do you ya big cunt."

Chapter 6 - January

Where Did You Sleep Last Night?

From the corner of the room he could see her watching in silence as Leizel absorbed the information presented to her, her eyes flicked him so Dietmann nervously stared at, and pulled at the hem of the sleeve of his sweater. He almost jumped out of his skin when she cleared her throat violently, looking as if she would say something, but then continued to read the file. They had omitted nothing, and Leizel was intent on reading every word. Ada sighed impatiently, arousing little response from the South African, but Dietmann looked her way, a pained look in his eyes that seemed to be requesting action. She looked back to Leizel.
"Do you intend to take all day?" She asked, her every word coated with sarcasm, a sentiment not lost upon its recipient.
"Ada, I am more than happy for you to go and follow this guy, seriously, I would welcome it."
"That is not my job Leizel."
"Tell me exactly, what your job is." She stood, and turned to face Ada, who bristled with rage, she did not take kindly to this sort of confrontation from her subordinates. She stepped to Leizel.
"You will show me respect, as you have two options. You will do as you are instructed, or you die, and believe me Leizel, if you die I shall ensure that I do it myself."
Liezel stood toe to toe with Ada, as they silently sized each other up, barely mustering a sniff of a blink between them. The atmosphere dipped below freezing, and a bigger man might have stepped in and taken control, but Dietmann would never dare in all

of his life. So as it was he watched the pair eyeballing each other. Eventually Liezel sniffed, and shrugged nonchalantly, and turned from Ada, returning to her seat, and the paperwork before her. Without looking up she spoke.

"That is fair enough Ada, but if you want to go down that path you'd better finish me quickly, because I will fucking tear you apart."

Dietmann winced as his superior visibly murdered the Afrikaaner with her eyes, she looked at her like she had slowly raped and beaten her entire family, starting with the aged members, and then shit in her breakfast bowl for good measure. She evidently had never ever been spoken to with such audacity in her existence. Dietmann had himself a new heroine, she was so flagrantly brazen in her disrespect of Ada, but at the same time he didn't blame her. The Hungarian threw her weight around like she owned the place, as if she had a *right* to take over the organisation. He had rolled over, and allowed her to do so without argument, but only because he had hoped that she would offer him some degree of responsibility, but no, and now her own perceived power had gone to her head and she treated everybody like shit. She had not *earned* the respect which she demanded, and Liezel appeared to be very much a woman who required her respect to be earned. Dietmann would always keep this opinion to himself, because as much as his respect for Ada was on the wane, his fear was at a consistent high. She was more of an alpha male than he was. If he spoke out of turn he was likely to receive a back handed blow to the mouth.

Ada's stare continued to bore into the back of Leizel's head as she read the file on Will Thunder, her eyes involuntarily squinting in anger as she read of his exploits, her fists clenching on the table. He was barely aware that he was doing it until Ada's attention switched to Dietmann and seemed appalled to note his glowing look of admiration of Leizel. His cheeks flushed red and he immediately lowered his head, tears welling in his eyes, as he could feel the burn of her wicked glare now upon him. He dared not to raise his face for fear of that look. Ada was not a woman to lose control of a situation, she was always so cool and so, well, *in control* of her environment, and now was faced with not only an outspoken and threatening Leizel, but a silently mutinous Dietmann, and she appeared to be focussing her rage on the milder of the pair. He would *not* raise his head, no matter how much she might will him to do so. His heartbeat quickened, and grew heavy. His whole body felt as if it were rocking to the beat of his pulse. He would *not* raise his head. He could hear it, the bass drum of his heart against his ribcage. Between that there was the cymbal of his breathing, growing heavier too, the exhalations powering their way through his nostrils. He felt faint.

BANG!

The gunshot noise rang out. He almost leapt out of his skin. He felt for pain. Nothing. He looked at Leizel, expecting to see her skull opened up, but no. Nothing. He looked at- She was gone. The bang was the slamming of the door behind her as she had stormed from the room. A mass of emotions washed over Dietmann. Anticipation, awe, relief, but mostly fear. His fear of Ada and what she was capable of massively overrode the admiration for Leizel right now. If she was unnerved then Leizel was struggling to show it. Dietmann, cleared his throat and stood, before rushing from the room, to follow his mistress.

He found her in the kitchen, gulping down a large glass of vodka, judging by the opened bottle beside her, and then slamming the glass onto the Formica worktop to refill it with the neat spirit. She was physically shaking with rage, bringing the glass to her lips once again.

"Ada?" He whimpered, scarcely audible even to himself.

"Oh, here comes the big loyal man, come to stab me in my back," she turned away from him, "go ahead, you know you want to."

"No, I do not want to. Ada I'm sorry." He stepped closer, as she stood, seeming almost vulnerable, he wanted to hold her. His hands hovered by her side, but he hesitated and pulled back. She turned to face him again.

"Yes you do, I saw the way that you looked at her just now. You admired the way that she disrespected me. You should be ashamed of yourself Dietmann." She gulped down the last of the vodka in the glass, reaching immediately for the bottle. For whatever reason, be it recent events, or the vulnerability he saw in her at this moment, Dietmann felt moved to speak frankly.

"But why should I Ada? You speak to me like I am a piece of shit on your heel. We used to be close, but you continue to treat me with utter contempt. You make me scared to speak and it should not be the way. You used to respect my opinion, but no more."

"Do you want to fuck her?" She asked, ignoring his point entirely.

"What?" He stuttered, incredulously.

"I asked if you wanted to fuck Liezel, are you hard of hearing?" She had begun to slur, she was drunk.

"No, I do not, what do you-" She pulled him to her and kissed him hard on the mouth, their teeth clashing.

What could Dietmann do but kiss her back? He would not dare resist her. She pulled her face away from his and spoke, the stench of alcohol on her breath.
"Do not think that this is anything more than sex, I want you to fuck me until I bleed."

The Cold Dark of Day

She awoke with a start. It was still dark outside. Her mind was clouded by flashbacks to the night before. *Him,* and *her.* The tender way he attempted to make love to her but all she wanted was filthy animal sex. She wanted him to pull her hair, to bite her, spit on her and make her feel like a dirty dirty bitch, she wanted to have the rage fucked out of her. As he lay on his back, his eyes wide like a deer caught in headlights, she dug her nails deep into his chest, ripping chunks from his flesh, she pushed herself down hard onto his cock. She had never seen it before and was pleasantly surprised to see that it had a nice size, so she used it for all she was worth. She had no intention of pleasuring him, this was about her. As she rode him violently, she continued even after he had shot his load inside her, bringing herself off to a shuddering and massive orgasm, but even then she was not finished, she shifted herself further up his body and sat hard on his tongue, barely caring that she was unloading his own muck back onto his face and into his mouth. When she was suitably appeased she sent him on his way. He tried to kiss her as he left the room but she turned away, his wounded animal look serving to turn her on even more, leaving a lingering temptation to fetch him back in and fuck him further, but she was tired, and the effects of the alcohol were wearing off, self-loathing already working its way into her system.

That scratching feeling at the back of her mind, spreading infectiously into the flesh at the top of her throat, she could physically *feel* the hatred in her mouth, and it was leaving a bad taste.

Now it the cold light of day, there was a darkness that consumed her, in her bed she curled into herself and pulled the linen sheet tight around her body. Yesterday she had been humiliated by Liezel, her authority shot to pieces by the upstart and her attitude, and for the first time since she could remember she felt like the inferior one in a room. *She* was the reason this organisation was still alive, *she* was the one who single-handedly dragged it from the ashes, and *she* was the one who arranged the South Africa game, in honour of Hoxton and the land of his birth. She deserved respect. Dietmann with his whining had threatened to derail her carefully constructed cold exterior. She accepted that maybe he had something of a point, but she treated him the way she did to toughen him up, to make him a harder man, he showed a lot of potential for greatness, but his sensitive bullshit needed to be beaten out of him. In the cold dark of day she had a realisation that she had allowed Liezel to get away with far too much. The bitch had grown too big for her boots. She would get her comeuppance soon. For now Ada had to reassert some sort of authority, to show the organisation that she was still the force to be reckoned with that she always was. She lay fantasising over walking into Liezel's room, and filling her sleeping body with bullets, spitting on her crimson corpse, dragging it from the bed by the hair and hanging her in the courtyard as a warning to anybody who might have ideas above their stations in life, but there was always that niggle at the back of her mind that she needed Liezel. For the time being. Who she *didn't* need, however, were the three parasitic thieving scum bastards that she had kept tabs on for so long. She would have them killed, then she would parade their deaths before Liezel and the rest, and inform them that while they had been sitting with their fingers up their butts, or on vigilante quests against pederasts and perverts, she had tracked down and destroyed the trio of disloyal scum without their assistance, that she could do the same to them if they ever dreamed to replicate their actions, there was no hiding place from Ada Birzcek. She called Rufus.

"Good morning ladyboss, what can I do you for?" He had groaned, obviously just awoken by her call. Here was another one who felt it acceptable to speak to her, he boiled her piss with his attitude.

"Rufus, kill them, and kill them quickly."

"What?"

"I want them dead, kill them."

"As you wish, gimme half an hour."

Before she could tell him that half an hour was too long he had hung up. If he thought he was getting the final pay off he was dead wrong. All she had bought with the thousands of Euros she had already paid was ignorance and cheek, the least he could do to repay her was kill the trio. If he would take exception then she would personally kill him too. She redialled.

"Rufus."

"Thirty minutes is too long Rufus, I want them dead now."

"Now huh? Well, given that I'm standing here with my tackle out trying to get dressed I'm not sure *now* is too possible but leave it with me I'll see what I can do."

And now was her turn to hang up. *The fucking English* she thought maliciously. They were a law unto themselves.

Ryan Bracha   Tomorrow's Chip Paper

Jou Maaifoedi

Ada had not spoken to her since their altercation yesterday. Big shame. Her threats succeeded in nothing. The *doos* that she was. The reprieve from her constant yammering and weight throwing came as a welcome rest. It allowed Liezel to concentrate on the latest job they had tasked her with. The celebrity. She had read his file all of the last evening, every single sordid detail pored over, and over again, all to the suitable yet hilarious soundtrack of Ada wailing like a banshee and the pained yelps from Dietmann with every thump against the ceiling of the study she sat in, as they fucked long into the night. The photographs of Will Thunder and his cohorts filling every hole of a prostitute with their weak dicks, the images of his snorting cocaine from the curve of her back, then the photographs of her bloody and bruise face after they had finished with her, and then the paperwork showing the healthy financial settlement for her to keep her mouth shut, "*Jou Maaifoedi.*" she repeated after every new level of deviance that was uncovered in William Walters' personality, each different slice of evidence coming in its own card folder. Her stomach turned somersaults when she was faced with the grainy black and white images of his *fixer,* a sleazy looking hard man by the name of Stew Taylor, sunglasses on despite the rain, a shit eating smile as he took money from some nondescript middle aged gentleman, happy look on his plain face. The next photo showed a young teenage girl emerging from the man's car, a Thunder & Lightning t-shirt worn over the top of her existing outfit, clearly only recently purchased from the live recording she had just been a witness to, excited apprehension on her face. The next photo displayed

Stew Taylor with his arm around the girl, leading her through a door, Liezel didn't need to see the rest to know where this was going, and briefly skimmed the flip book photo story of the celebrity man receiving head from the teenager, then signing her t-shirt. A satisfied glow about the man, a shamed hangdog vibe around the young girl, him patting her on the ass as Stew Taylor escorted her from the room. The photographic evidence grew worse and worse, and culminated with Stew Taylor and an unknown man carrying the body of a girl, in the dead of night, throwing her into the back of a blacked out Range Rover, and dumping her in a field. Liezel felt her breath become shallow, and her head faint. Her heartbeat clattered quicker and her throat constricted, she suddenly felt the need for air and stumbled to the window, ripping it from its hole, and leaning into the sea air, gulping it into her lungs *"Jou Maaifoedi!"* She gasped into the night. The sounds of Ada getting fucked all ways by Dietmann echoing out above her. The cunt would regret that in the morning no doubt. Which cunt she meant she didn't know, probably both of them. Will Thunder was the worst human she had ever had the misfortune to be aware of, he needed to die. If there was any meaning to Liezel's life then this was it.

She had never been the perfect example of morality, she had made a living by feeding from the greed of others. The World cup ticket scam, for one, was a perfect example. Selling tickets to matches at hundreds of Rand cheaper than the actual legitimate ticket prices, to people who could hardly believe their luck, people who must have never paid any attention to the phrase *too good to be true.* She, and her brothers Zander and Wian, had made a fortune, and then disappeared for a while. Then she was broke, and robbed tourists of their jewellery, and cash, at knifepoint. It wasn't a particularly proud point of her life but survival was her only priority.

Then she was introduced to this, well, organisation was what they called it, but the operative part of the word was *organised,* and organised it was not. Ada always appeared to have her mind on other things, like she didn't have enough fingers for the many pies she was juggling, so everything seemed half finished. She would start some new project, only for it to fall by the wayside once she started another, but she would expect the full cooperation of everybody til its bitter end. She did have some consistency with regards sending Liezel on these little adventures against sexual deviance however, oh yes, she would *always* have time to send her to some piece of shit nowheresville to find a beast to destroy, and save countless futures. But the question for Liezel, was *why?* What did she gain by shipping her off? Something was very *very* amiss, and tonight's confrontation signalled the beginning of the end for somebody, and if it was to be Liezel, then she would sign off in the most spectacular of fashions.

The cool evening air relaxed her overworking mind, as her heartbeat slowed to normal Liezel stepped back into the room, and turned to the file. Pulling the papers from each folder she pored over them again, and began to put a plan into place. If she was going down then this whole piss poor house of cards was coming with her. Dismantling the organisation, its connections, and the disease that was Will Thunder, that was the easy part. The difficult part was to ensure that she was still standing as the last brick crumbled.

Chapter 7 - January

Was It Worth It?

For the last twenty minutes neither of them had spoken. What was there to say? *I'm sorry kid, I blew your old fella and his mate up, I had every intention of blowing you up, but now you're here with a fucking baby inside you. A fucking baby with no daddy 'cause of me.* Nah, it wouldn't cut it, he just had to let her come to terms with everything in her own time. She would blame him, of course she would, she would probably be the end of him, however she did it. When he was back home, wandering through Ikea with Charley, looking for new furniture for the house that the Ada woman paid for, he'd feel a sharp pain in his back. He'd turn to see the now empty hand of this girl here, a look of pure defiant determination on her face as he would fall to the floor, Charley would scream, and drop to her knees, crying his name. He would quietly succumb to the blood loss, and he would blame nobody, he would know that he had earned it, and she would melt back into the crowd that by then would be a perfect circle of gawkers. This was the worst possible outcome. His stupid thirty minute obsession. If he'd done the deed that few minutes earlier he would have been out of there and in his mind there would be three dead bodies, job done. Kerching. Half a million in the bank. Thank you very much Ada. It was what it was, however, and he now had a problem to deal with. He had all manner of options here, and they all led to an almighty pain in the arse. One, cut the girl loose now, just kick her out of the car and hightail it out of there, tell Ada the job was done and not worry about it any further until the aforementioned Ikea scenario. Two, kill the girl, and her unborn baby. Three, tell Ada what had happened, accept that she would instruct him in that way she did, that unless he killed his unwitting hostage then he would be walking away from this empty handed, which could not happen. He had been on the road, away from Charley, for far too long to accept that option. The thousands he had skimmed, from forged receipts and mini scams he had pulled off with conspiring shop keepers, were not enough to consider allowing Ada to fuck him over, it wasn't just a few bob she owed him, it was half a million quid, and even if he *did* have this girl to worry about, he had pretty much done the job, and very well. Then there was the stern but gloating voice she was bound to have when she told him that she *had* told him to get up there quicker. No, it was more trouble than it was worth. The only option he could seriously consider was the first one. She knew his face, but not his name. But she knew his face.

He had spent nights in hotels all over Europe. It wouldn't take long to track him down. *You're in one cunt of a bind old boy* he thought *Fucked if you do and fucked if you don't.* He looked to the girl, she was a beauty, huge sad eyes and long red hair that dropped by her neck into loose curls. Her lips were full and pouty. There was a flicker of a reaction in her eyes when he turned his head, but she couldn't bring herself to face him. Who could blame her? The silence wasn't altogether uncomfortable, as if it was mutually agreed that neither had the words to define the feeling within the car, and were both lost in their own thoughts, so it came as a surprise when she spoke. "Was it-" She started, but had to clear her throat "Was it worth it?" She hadn't turned to him, she just spoke to the clear windscreen before her. He didn't know what to say, just watched the side of her face through those curls. Was it worth it? *Not yet*, he could tell her, *got to wait for this Ada bitch to come up with the readies.* He could maybe tell her that until she wandered onto the scene that *Yes, I was reasonably satisfied with the arrangement.*

"What?" Is what he actually said.

"Was it worth what she paid you? To kill us?"

"Who?"

This time she turned to face him, her bright red eyes glowing from her light face.

"Give me some credit you fucking cretin, unless you won the game you're being paid by Ada"

"Won what game?"

The girl frowned.

"So she's paid you to kill us then, brilliant."

The girl was gutsy, no question about that, the hardened look she held him with was one of something of experience, there was this deep knowing inside her. It was like she had been through hell and back, probably on more than one occasion, and this was just the latest in a long line of events in her life that had challenged her, and for some reason he didn't doubt that she'd come through this too. His feeling that she would be the end of him suddenly felt that little bit stronger. Nevertheless she was in shock right now, so he was inclined to let the cretin comment slide, and he might as well take a good bite of the bullet, she deserved something.

"Look, I was doing a job, it wasn't personal right? Some chicky phones me up and says follow people, I follow people. She says kill people, I kill people. It's my job."

"Your job," the girl said, her attention turned to her passenger side window, something ticking over in her brain, before she looked back at Rufus, "so how much did she pay you?

"You really wanna know?"
"I asked didn't I?"
He hesitated. She was asking how much three lives were worth to him. He could lie, tell her three million, one for each of them.
"Half a million quid." He said, resigned to the fact that he was not gonna sit and lie to the kid. Her eyes welled up again, processing the information that had just been presented to her. For the first time in his life he was faced with that question, *how much is a life worth*? He had never given it a moment's thought before, he was a cold hearted cunt with a job to do, and generally did it very well, present circumstances excepted. He didn't know how much a life should cost.
"So was it worth it?" She asked again. She wasn't letting this go.
"Honestly? You'da died I wouldn't have given it much thought, I'd collect my money and go home. You sitting here quizzing me on it I'd have to say no, it wasn't."
"Tough luck, some people really can't catch a break."
"You got some mouth on you, you know that?"
"Yeah, you just killed the father of my unborn child for money, forgive me my sins."
He couldn't respond. The kid was right. He sighed, and they sat in further silence for a few minutes, both lost in their own personal concerns. The girl chewed her bottom lip, and her tongue explored the back teeth, the twitch of the skin of her cheek bumping out catching the corner of Rufus' eye. He sighed again. He was so close to getting home, to seeing Charley, to fucking her hard. Now her sweet pussy seemed further away than ever. *Fuck's sake* he thought. He was midway through his third sigh as she spoke.

"So half a million," she started, her tone said she was going to continue, "is that how much it'll take to kill Ada?"

Half A Million Carrots

I watch his reaction carefully. He told me he was just doing his job. That won't do. I can't let him get away with it. I'm utterly devastated, I've lost Tom. I'm doing everything I can to think of how he would be, what he would say. He has, had, that cheeky way with words, always throwing caution to the wind, taking a chance with how he said what he did. And it *always* worked. He got away with saying some outrageous things to important, and dangerous people. I need to be the same to get through this. I'm absolutely crapping myself, and I want to cry. But I need to be strong for my baby. He finally looks at me, apprehensive, his eyebrows raised.
"You serious? That's a lot of money you're talking there."
"Why do you think Ada sent you after us?"
"I dunno, it's not my place to know."
How could he be so *cold?* She pointed him in our direction, dangled half a million carrots in front of him and said "kill", and he's just done it, no second thought. Then a sadness takes me over again. Tom. That's basically what *they* made him do. The reason we're here. We went on the run because they gave us no choice. Tom killed people because they gave him no choice. But *he* killed Tom. For money. For his job.
"I can afford it." I hear myself say.
It's funny, not funny haha, but for all of my telling Tom, *Tom, w*hen we were with Hoxton and his cronies, I always said violence wasn't the best way of getting revenge, that there were other ways of

making somebody pay for their crimes. But here I am, about to order the man that killed my fiancé to do the same to the person that paid him to do it, and I really don't care. Tom and I used to lay in bed together, me on his chest, running my fingers through the curly hairs and listening to his heartbeat, and his voice booming through his ribcage while he stroked my hair, every night we would come up with a daft topic, Tom would come up with ones like *You're on a desert island with your five favourite celebrities, which do you fuck first and what position?* The dirty git. Like, I remember one time we had been bickering about how I said there were better ways of getting revenge on somebody than violence, and we played this game, I would come up with five imaginative ways to get revenge without resorting to killing somebody, and he would try to trump my answers with horribly violent methods. I don't remember all of our answers, but my favourite one of mine was to drive by their house every night, on the hour and ring their doorbell, and run off. We used to do it when we were kids. We called it Thunder and Lightning. Knock like thunder and run like lightning. For obvious reasons I'm reminded of Will Thunder and Johnny Lightning. Tom says that when he was a kid they'd do the same thing but they called it Bobby Knocking. For the rest of that week I called him Bobby Knocker. He would correct me and say we weren't well enough acquainted, in this posh snooty voice, and tell me to address him as Mr Robert Knocker. His gratuitously violent manner to counter that was to drive *to* their house at night, wake them up and tie them down, and then proceed to pull every single hair out of their head and body one at a time, and then put them in a bath of aftershave. He said I wouldn't understand,

that it was a man thing. I miss him so much. I look back to his killer.
"So?"
"So this is a new one on me."
"Join the club. Look, half a million, I want you to go to that bitch, and I want you to slowly kill her, I want her to know that it was me that sent you, and I want her to know why. I know you work for her, but now you work for me too, and don't think for a second think that you don't owe me that much. I shouldn't even offer to pay but if I don't I'm afraid you'll finish the job on me and my baby, and I don't care if you know I'm afraid. I don't know you, and you don't know me, but I do know that you'll do anything for money so I'm offering you money to spare mine, and my baby's lives, and to return the favour to Ada. She's-" I stop. I hate the word. But it's true. "She's a cunt."
His eyebrows raise again. A strange look in his eyes. "You finished?"
"Yes."
"You're right, she's a cunt. She gets on my tits. And I'll do it. But I'm afraid you're gonna have to come with me until I say so, and I know we ain't gonna be buddies, but you're gonna have to live with what I did for the time being."
Live with it? Is he for real? And of course I'm going with him. Because as soon as Ada is gone then he's next.
"Okay." I say, and I look forward, expecting him to start the car, thinking that this is it, this is the start of a chapter of my life that I would pay to not start. I would give up every single penny we took, to go back and start in a small flat somewhere with Tom. Maybe with a guinea pig. A ginger one. But no, this is the start of I don't know what. I'm seeing it through to

the end. On my baby's life I'm going to make them all pay. The killer has still not moved. He's just looking ahead.
"What are you doing?" I ask.
"You don't wanna know." He says, looking at the clock, but I do, I really do, but I'm not pushing it, he's not my friend. A couple of minutes pass and while he watches the clock again he suddenly turns the ignition, and sets off. The clock reads nine thirty. As the car accelerates he turns to me.
"The name's Rufus, by the way."
I say nothing.

This Time It's Personal

Cristiano is talking to the woman on the front desk of the hotel in Roda de Isabena, putting the feelers out for the shithead that blew the cabin up. Me and him, we ripped the wreckage apart piece by piece, looking for my girl. Even when there was nothing left to rip apart I dug deeper, I was convinced I'd find her dead, my hands were ripped to the bone, but did I give a fuck? Did I fuck. I just needed to find her. But we didn't. I don't know if I'm relieved or not, I mean, for sure, if she wasn't in the wreckage then she must be alive. And if she's alive then he's got her, because if he didn't then she woulda been sat there by the wreckage, the bobbies and firemen woulda been battling to rescue us. Or they've got her. And if any of those things have happened then I can't be sure of how long she'll be alive. My head is a fucking shed. I was only under the rubble for about four hours. I must have been delirious to think I'd been under there for three days. I'm a proper fanny. Love, man, it knocks the alpha male out of you sometimes.

Reminds me of that Johnny Cash tune, A Thing Called Love.

Mr Beefy comes back to me and I'm hopeful, but he starts shaking his head.
"There has been nobody here, the lady, she says they have had nobody for three nights here, she says to try further up at the Tomaso, that he might have stayed there."
My heart sinks.
In the car toward the Hotel Tomaso Cristiano's driving one handed, his mangled paw wrapped in a T-shirt we managed to salvage from the cabin. I'm the same but both hands are wrapped. We look a right pair. He's talking revenge, and even though I'm hearing him I'm not listening. I'm trying to figure out how the fuck they found us. Have they been watching Cristiano for ages? He stayed in the same place, eventually they could have tracked him down, watched and waited and all that. Then we rock up and hey presto, they have their three biggest enemies in one place? Fuck knows. I can't stick all the blame at Beefy's door, they could have been following us, maybe Beefy had the right idea all along, just sit tight in a secluded area and get on with it. Maybe us, Jess and me, maybe we got too cocky, strutting our stuff all over Europe and eventually one of Ada's contacts came up trumps for her. Maybe we brought a shitload of trouble to him. He was just chilling out, fucking hookers and drinking beer, and then less than twenty four hours later his home is exploded on top of me and him, and my future wife has gone missing. Either way though, there's no getting away from the fact that we've been found out, and we've had our boots rattled, and we've got to stand up for ourselves and fight. I can't see Cristiano shying away from that like.

My girl, my kid, that's what's at stake, the old team's back together and this time it's personal. Fuck me, I just thought that. *This time it's personal!* Too many films that. Still, it doesn't take away from the fact that it really is personal. My girl is alive. I just *know* it. I can feel her. Sounds gay but it's true. Cristiano's still talking angry when we pull up outside the hotel, and his words finally come into focus, aurally speaking. "When we find her I will pull her arms and legs from her body like the wings of a fly, and then I will crush her skull." His one good fist pounds the steering wheel, which shits us up as the horn sounds out. A cat scuttles from behind some bins in the street and rockets into a bush. Shaking my head at the big bastard I get out of the car, and face the hotel, for some reason I just *know* this is the one. My fists clench and pains whip up my arms as I forgot just how fucked my hands were. The hotel's a big rustic looking thing, like the rest of them round here, all pale stone and greenery. Mr Beefy joins me and we head inside.

      Just like the last place I stand back and let Cristiano do his thing, he just calmly walks up to the concierge and schmoozes her, gives it the Spanish charmer act, and the girl is putty in his massive hands, she's laughing and throwing her hair back, then she leans in and squeezes his bicep, and makes baby noises as she rubs a scabbed up lump on the bridge of his nose. Fuck knows what he's telling her but I can guess, and he is definitely the hero of the piece, and he's purring as she fawns over him. I clear my throat that doesn't need clearing to get him to speed the whole process up. He gets the message, and carries on, then nods to me, beckoning me to come over. Jackpot?

"An English man was here Tommy, he checked out at about seven o'clock this morning."
"We got a name? A description? Car?" I'm sounding somewhat impatient here.
"Okay okay, he calls himself John Fogerty, Matilda here says he is tall and good looking, older than the thirty years and has a full head of the blond hair which is slightly shaggy and hangs before his eyes, she says that she enjoyed his smile, because he smiled with his eyes, he was not talkative but he was definitely from your country. She also says that he was no match for me and my muscles."
John Fogerty. Sounds familiar.
"Course he wasn't, she say owt else?"
"Yes, perhaps the most important parts, he has a long scar on his cheek, Matilda remembers because she tried to touch it but the John Fogerty man became less friendly, and did not want to be friends any more. He drives a Renault Megane, which is blue. This is all she can tell us."
John Fogerty.
"It's enough, we need to go, say goodbye to your girl, tell her cheers."
Where the fuck do I know John Fogerty from? That's gonna wind me the fuck up.

Chapter 8 - February

Kill, Kick, or Mercy

The vibrations of the bass of the tunes coming from Kenny's room rocked the loose bubbles of wallpaper beside his face, the half smoked spliff danced around the circumference of the ashtray, the ash inside the tray leapt for joy, and the lake of white cider lapped against his pint glass. Despite the pounding music Jake couldn't hear a thing. The headphones embraced the sides of his face, feeding the sound of the streaming video directly into his brain. His yellow fingered hand reached toward the spliff, pulling it to his mouth and having it's green filled brains sucked out by the bearded twenty something. The vibrations from his flatmate's music tickled at his balls through the padding of his leather seat, bringing an involuntary and unusually unwelcome hard on. Frowning at his own aversion to it his focus returned to the screen, the girl's face paused, dimmed behind the seemingly everlasting buffer circle, Kenny's music coming to prominence. Jake thumped the wall between them, bellowing for his flatmate to turn that shit down, and was rewarded with a *Fuck ooofffffffff!* for his efforts. As his internet connection caught up with itself the action recommenced onscreen. He had missed a few seconds of her speaking but got the jist. This girl was fucked up, but he was utterly besotted with her, it wasn't sexual, she was just so, fucking, cool. Her eyes were mesmerising. To be fair, her eyes were all he could see, but he knew the rest of her would be just as hot. She said some of the craziest shit he had ever heard, and half of it he was repeating as part of his own verbal repertoire, and aside from Alan Rickman's pantomime villain accent in Die Hard he had never enjoyed a South African accent so much. The way she said *Jou Maaifoedi* as she stuck another boot into Will Thunder's shivering body, it was a joy to behold. *You Motherfucker.* He loved it, and took great joy in repeating the phrase as a greeting to his friends.

It had been a day since the story broke, but he had been glued to his computer from the off. Every few hours she would do a live video link for half an hour, to let the world know her hostage was still alive, and to give them an opportunity to vote on the fate of Will Thunder. She called the event *Kill, Kick or Mercy,* and it had gradually gained a real following, it was all they were talking about down the pub, everybody of course voicing their own opinions on it. Several Facebook fan pages had been created, the most popular being *Hang Will Thunder*, there were even fake versions of the girl on Twitter, all gaining thousands and thousands of followers. Spoof accounts for Will Thunder were removed as quickly as they were created. The premise of *Kill, Kick or Mercy* was self-explanatory. Voters were encouraged to decide whether they wanted the mystery lady to kill the guy, kick him, or spare him any further humiliation, at least until the next time round. Jake's vote went on kick, without fail. It wasn't due to any favour toward Will Thunder, not by a long shot, she could do as she pleased to the seedy fucker, he just wanted to prolong his exposure to her. To watch her in action. Thunder was still alive by now, the votes had started out offering him mercy, but as more evidence was leaked by the mystery girl to the public the tables were gradually turning, and the percentages were shifting with every vote they were allowed. The majority was now into giving the guy a kicking, but the mercy votes had dropped to less than twenty per cent, and the kill votes were up to about thirty, it was only a matter of time before she was given public permission to bury him for good. Of course the left wing brigade were asking how or why the police didn't interject, but their hands were tied, she had taken their power away from them, and given it to an almighty entity. Public opinion.

He watched her intently, she finished her spiel, and again the country had voted to kick him. Her eyes smiled through the mask wickedly, a satisfied glint, before she turned from the camera, and tipped the bloody and bruised celebrity, tied to a chair, over on to the ground. She turned back to the audience and winked. "I'll make it a good one eh?" The hairs on the back of Jake's neck stood to attention, the girl was awesome, the anticipation was almost too much, and as the bass from Kenny's room thudded into his body, he leapt into the air in delight as the mystery woman's boot connected with the stomach of Will Thunder and roared at the top of his voice at the same time as she did.

"Jou maaifoedi!"

He didn't hear it but from the next room Kenny bellowed once again that he could fuck off.

Feeding The Nation

Click.

She shut the webcam software down for the time being, and turned to her hostage.

"You are a great sidekick William, truly great, the audience love you."

The celebrity wept in agony.

"Sorry, did I say *love?* They can't fucking stand you! It's fucking brilliant! Here, do you want your update on what your public have to say about you?"

She scrolled the cursor over the screen, restoring the previously minimised internet browser.

"Listen to this, Lisa says I ought to put cigarettes out on your cock, good idea Lisa, that *would* be funny. It looks like twenty thousand, three hundred and sixty eight people would agree because they have the thumbs up to that, maybe next time eh? What is this? Kevin says you can rot in hell for what you have done, oh Kevin, he'll be in hell a few times before I allow him to *actually* go and rot away, would you like me to continue?"

She looked to her hostage, even though the question was entirely rhetorical. He said nothing. He had started this whole exercise declaring his innocence, demanding to know who she was, who sent her, telling her he could have her killed if he wanted to, he was *that* powerful, and all of that shit, but soon became the submissive piss ant that he truly was. The slow dismantling of his defiance was a joy to behold. That first live link, he sat there, informing the world that he had been taken hostage by a crazy fan, telling the police to get in here and shoot her, a bruise forming around his eye, a scabbed crack in his lip, asking what he had done to deserve this in tones that reeked of the kind of guy who would ask unwitting bouncers if they knew who he was when they dared to obstruct his path into high class nightclubs whilst wearing sneakers, threaten them with their jobs, tell them he earned more in an hour than they did in a year. In essence, a really nice guy.

      Between that first link and the second, Liezel had begun to leak the evidence online, and to the media, starting out with the mildest photographs, ones where everybody had their clothes on but hinted at something much darker. The horrified shock in her hostage's face at being finally exposed.

That fear of the unknown. Of what else she might have up her sleeve. He had demanded that she show what other malicious material she had on him before she started throwing ridiculous accusations round. By then a small crowd had begun to form around the building, a smattering of police officers keeping them at bay, the quickly created banners held aloft in support of Will Thunder filling the back drop to the increasing number of news reports live in Kensington. It was perfect. Liezel could not have planned it better. The media vans had begun to roll up, and she was gaining a great captive audience. In the living room of her hostage every television program she flicked to was gradually being interrupted to bring breaking news of the situation at hand. It promised to be a very exciting few hours, or days, or weeks, depending on how it all panned out. The second live video feed, Will Thunder spent declaring his innocence, calling for his fans to trust in him, that he could never do what Liezel was accusing him of, that the photographs were false. By the time the third live feed went out she had revealed the imagery of the young fan, forced to suck his cock whilst Stew Taylor watched on, she hadn't held back either, there was no organisation that could censor the material she put out online. Obviously the material would be censored by the time it hit the news reports, but by then the damage was done, a race had begun to find that girl, to get her exclusive story, unbeknownst to Liezel at that point one the tabloids had already begun a smear campaign against the anonymous father of the girl, offering the opinion that he was actually in on the whole thing. Others were printing pleas for her to come forward, asking anybody that knew her to name her, so that they could get help to justice for her and the ordeal she went through. The tide slowly turned against Will Thunder, the number of signs showing him support diminished, gradually replaced by those condemning him. She chose the third feed to set her stall out, and to speak to the world. She lay down the rules to what was happening. The police were warned that if anything untoward happened then the whole place was rigged with explosives that were just itching to blow, that she would ensure that her piece was said before she would allow them to intervene. She gave the public their first chance to decide upon the fate of her hostage, with her unimaginatively titled yet no less effective Kick, Kill or Mercy, she told them that he was *their* celebrity to judge. He was *their* property. The outrage they were displaying was nothing short of spectacular, every man and his wife had employed themselves as judge, jury, and executioner of the rapidly waning star of one William Walters. Aside from a few human rights campaigns she had become some sort of saint to these people, they loved her and everything she seemed to stand for. It was perfect. Over the last day or so she and her hostage had become the only thing the country was talking about. She was feeding the nation, and like a starving town centre pigeon it was eating right out of her hand. Eventually the meal would change, and it would blow their fucking socks off.

What the Fuck Are We Going To Do Giles?

"What the fuck are we going to do Giles?" John paced the room, his red baby face engraved with worry, and panic. From behind the chrome and glass desk Giles was filled with a resignation that he had not experienced since he finally admitted to himself that he was never going to finger Jenny Robins at school.

"I don't know."
His visitor ignored the response, and continued to pace, his overworked mind almost at breaking point. His world had collapsed over the last few days, and everything he had known over recent years had been tarnished by accusation and doubt, his fuck-up of a friend and colleague had single-handedly destroyed everything they had worked to build up. The wholesome image they had so carefully constructed was gone, wiped out in a sea of inequity. They were broken.
"Giles, what the fuck are we going to do?"
The older man pinched the bridge of his nose beneath his wire-rimmed spectacles, his eyes shut tight, and exhaled sharply, his breath catching the shield of his hand and fogging up the lenses, creating that ever-so-blurred vision of John, still pacing the room before him.
"I told you, I don't know."
"Really, what the fuck are you gonna do to put a positive spin on this? How can you possibly polish this turd?"
Giles didn't answer right away, he didn't even know if there *was* an answer to his client's questions. They had only been involved with each other for a few months but he and his controversial partner had already involved him in more crap than the rest of his clients combined. Of course, he felt for the one pacing up and down to some degree, but there was only so much that William could have done without John suspecting *something,* although Giles felt that perhaps now was not the time for divulging that particular doubt.
"I don't know, and you walking my carpet to the bone really isn't helping, sit down for Christ's sake, I can't think."

"Okay, okay, sorry, my head's all over the place, I haven't slept in two days."

Giles was well aware of this fact, given that the guy had called him countless times throughout those two days. He guessed that he hadn't called his solicitor as often. Knowing him as he did he doubted that he'd even called his own mother as much. John was a predator as far as his own success went. To the public Johnny Lightning was that wholesome clean-cut, butter-wouldn't-melt hero, the relationship, and chemistry between he and Will Thunder was coveted by every comedy duo in the business, the likeable pair at home whether it was on one of their multitude of Saturday afternoon family shows, or fielding the ever so risqué questions on the flamboyant vehicle of everybody's favourite gay, Jack Knapton. Behind the scenes however, John Thorne was known as a shark, who stepped on everybody that dared to get in his way. A raging sycophant in the company of his paymasters, and the bane of the lives of those beneath him, and for as intentionally awful as he was behind closed doors, what scared him most was the loss of that fiercely guarded public persona, and it was most definitely under threat, hence the ridiculous number of calls to his Public Relations Manager.

John seated himself, his hands wedged firmly between the chair and his arse to try to keep his already shot nerves under control, his right leg going hell for leather beneath the lip of Giles' desk. Indeed he had spent the last couple of days without sleep, having initially gone to ground, but then been subjected to a variety of intense inquisitions at the hands of the police, and then the media in a hastily arranged press conference, refuting all claims and accusations that he and Will had been in cahoots. His brain felt fried. Never in his life had he expected his showbiz partner to have been unveiled as the sleazy kiddy-fiddling drug fiend that he had been. He could honestly say that he did not know, nor suspect, that much was true. He did keep company with some unsavoury characters but the business was filled to the brim with unsavoury characters, every one of them was out for themselves, and now because he was now exposed and vulnerable, the knives were out. That fat cunt Mike Rotch had led the firing squad, and everybody else followed suit, it was a feeding frenzy on his integrity. John would have the last laugh though, because he knew he was innocent, he knew the heavy shit would die down, and he knew that when it did, he was going to hit each and every one of them with the biggest lawsuit they had ever seen. Giles remained silent, watching his client intently, the nervous twitching, the sad look of a puppy left for days by its owners as they embarked upon a weekend away, sitting by the front door, lonely, starving and forgotten, awaiting salvation, not so much demanding pity as quietly and tentatively requesting it for fear of upsetting anybody. This was *not* the John Thorne he had become accustomed to, this one was defeated and vulnerable. Eventually Giles spoke.

"Look, John, your only option right now is damage limitation, and as far as I can see your only way of doing that is to distance yourself from William, from everything. You have to do everything in your power to be seen to cut all ties with him. If you want to support him then do it in your own time, but *do not* do it in public, they'll eat you alive. Everything you've been through in the last two days will come at you again ten-fold."

"I know this."

"I haven't finished. You need a cause. Something to raise your stock with the everyman. They're your bread and butter. Without Mr and Mrs Saturday Night Telly you're nothing. My suggestion is something in line with what William is embroiled in. I don't know, *Save The Kids* or *Murdering Hookers Is Bad.* It can't hurt to get involved in *Africans Who Need Shoes* or some such, but you need to be seen to be actively campaigning. I'm afraid your professional partnership is effectively over."

"You're forgetting the contract."

"Fuck the contract, you think William is ever going to work again? The channel won't touch him, he's a rapidly sinking ship and you're going to have to save yourself."

Chapter 9 - January

Basically A Boy

We've been driving for about six hours before the Marseille sign comes into view. Six hours. Rufus seems to have this weird lack of self-awareness, or at least awareness of what the situation is, because he's being really obtuse, like he thinks I should relate when he tells me what a bitch he thinks Ada is. Yeah she's a bitch but come on Rufus, don't tell me what you really think of the woman that paid you to kill me. I don't give a shit. He's a curious man. I don't know if it's a nervous thing or something but when we stopped for petrol he started acting all cool, and mysterious, his walk changed and everything, but when it's just me and him he starts to talk rubbish again.

    So for the last six hours, give or take, I have spent my time staring out of the window, watching the backdrop change from the mountainous crags to flatter ground, through Carbonnes and Toulouse, Rufus talking to try to fill the silence between us but I'm making no effort to listen to him, my mind is just swamped with thoughts. A couple of times I broke down, crying quietly to myself, as the enormity of everything came gushing back to the forefront. Thankfully he made no effort to comfort me, but he did shut up, his hands gripped just ever so slightly tighter on the wheel. He did have *that* much awareness. We left the motorway near Carcassonnes so he could call Ada, to arrange a meeting in Marseille so he could claim the cash he was owed for murdering my everything, which is partly correct I guess, but he has a new job now. I think. I know I can't trust him, he could be leading me to her so that she can finish the job herself, but the way he was speaking about her in the car, when I couldn't zone out, it did feel like a real dislike, and that he might take pleasure from completing what I'm paying him for. For the first two hours or so of the journey his mobile kept blaring out from the drinks holder with the first verse of a song I don't know but sounded vaguely familiar, before stopping, then starting up again.

"If you're not going to answer it why don't you put it on silent?" I asked him.

"I like the song." He stated, matter of factly, like it was normal to keep listening to the first verse. The lyrics were quite apt in all fairness, but it didn't stop grating on my nerves. He paid attention eventually and messed with the settings, and from then on the phone acted like a faulty dildo, as my Tom might say, on and off vibrating.

Near Carcassonnes, whilst he made the call to Ada I stood by the car, he was making these gestures like he was irritated by her. I could see him starting to speak, and then stopping, his chin jutting to the sky in exasperation at the inability to get a word in, tapping his head with a curled fist. He looked my way and tried to appear calm, his hand shot into his pocket and he turned away, kicking a pebble in the dust just a little too hard to be cool. The stone flicked up and sailed above the ground, cracking firmly into the side of a bin, the impact creating hollow but really loud clang. The weirdo pulled his hand from his pocket and made a subtle celebratory fist, clearly pleased with himself. He didn't notice that I'd noticed. When he came back we just got in the car and carried on, the next stop being here, Marseille.

Us on the motorway:

"So what's happening? Is she in Marseille?" I ask him, taking the time to turn and look at him. His eyes stay on the road.

"No, but that's where I'm meeting her, gonna be tomorrow now." he says, looking at his watch, like it made a difference, tomorrow is tomorrow, it doesn't need a glance at a watch.

"What did she say when you said we were dead?"

"Does it matter?"

"Well, I guess not, but you didn't look too pleased with yourself, if there's a problem you ought to tell me."

"There's no problem, I just don't like the girl, wants the moon on a fucking stick and she wants it yesterday."

I roll my eyes, he still thinks I'm supposed to empathise with him. I say nothing. Sensing that I'm not going to say anything yet but that we're in discussion for the first time since forever, he continues.

"When we get to Marseille we're gonna have to get checked into a hotel, if it's alright with you I'm gonna book you in under the name Susie Quentin"

"Why?"

"You never hearda the song Susie Q?"

"No."

"Don't know what you're missing, Creedence Clearwater Revival, you know them?"

"No."

"Proud Mary? Bad Moon Rising? You never hearda those?"

"No."

He reaches toward his phone with some misplaced eagerness, he thinks I care. I feel moved to stop him.

"Look, I'm not that interested, if you want to call me Susie Quentin then do it, I'm not here for a holiday.

You murdered Tom, what part of *we are not friends* do you not understand?"
His phone goes back into the drinks holder and he sits in sulking silence like some scolded child. He's got this totally different character to when we first met, me thinking he was some cold-hearted killer, but he's basically a boy. A murdering idiot of a child, who doesn't seem to feel he's done anything wrong, and if he does then he's not acting like it, and I will *not* feel sorry for him. We drive on for a few more miles, and he speaks without turning to me.
"You stop being a dick and I'll kill her for free."

The Cuntarian

How's this for a turn up? Beefy's only got her fucking number! All this time and the big daft bastard's had it memorised. He says he would sometimes sit in the hot tub, coked up to the crab's eyeballs, looking at the number in his phone, thinking about calling her up and giving her shit. For sure, there's a chance that she's changed her number by now but we've not got much to lose have we? Maybe a few Euros for a couple of chuckaway mobiles and top-up cards, and a few minutes of hope, I can live with that. The gain far outweighs the risk. So we're in a mobile phone shop in Barcelona, I'm wandering about, looking as English as I can, to try ward off the hovering shit flies that work here. These shops man, same everywhere, never known a species of person like your mobile salesmen. Like right now, this one kid is yammering at the speed of light at Cristiano and waving the phone around, showing him all the cool features that he'll never use. It's getting just slightly on my tits so I head over and whisper at him.

"Beefy, tell him to shut the fuck up and sell us some fucking phones man, I swear you're doing it to take the piss."

He laughs at me, and turns to the salesman who's stopped talking and is now watching me with this gone out expression. I'm sure he can tell by my tone, and the universal language of the word *fuck* that I'm not here to join the party. Cristiano says something to him and they both crack out laughing. Fucking hate that. We need to get the phones, get out of here, and get onto the Hungarian cunt. Cuntarian? I like that, the Cuntarian. Yeah, we need to get onto the Cuntarian and find out what the fuck she's done to my girl. I really need to calm down so I head out of the shop, pushing past one of the shit flies who gabbers on in Spanish as I slam the door behind me, I turn and eyeball him through the window, the eyes bulge out of his caramel coloured head as I blow him a kiss in fury, but Cristiano's placing his hands on the kid's shoulders to calm him down. Fuck him. He wants to fucking dance then I'll dance. I'm suddenly aware that the whole shop is looking at me, and I realise what the fuck I must look like. Dirty, scratched up to fuck, and two hands wrapped is scabby cloth. I look like a tramp, and I'm bringing a hell of a lot of attention to myself. Whilst Beefy sorts the phones out I seat myself on a bench and watch the shop. The shit fly is giving me the daggers through the window, his wounded pride still itching for a fight. Fuck him. I'll kill the cunt if I have to. I've got miles bigger fish to fry than that prick. I need my girl back. She grounds me, she calms me, she controls me. Not in any way that you'd construe as being, like, possessive or owt, I just mean it's the effect that she has on me. She's like a spliff for my temper. I need her. I'm a self-destructive loose cannon when I don't have her around. I've been the calmest I've ever been in the last couple of years. Before her I made daft decisions, I got into fights, destroyed my own relationships with others, and I got one of my best mates killed. With her I had a reason to chill out, somebody to look after, and all that. Now she's not around I can feel the shit head in me coming back out, and while I'm scared of it, I think I need him around. I need to be that cunt again, to find my girl, but then again, that cunt will draw attention to us, we need to get the phones and get out of here.

I stand again, and walk to the window, Cristiano's paying up and turning with a bright red bag, bulging square with the phone boxes. Boxes for phones, that is, it'd be pretty daft if he had a pair of actual phone boxes in his bag. Still, he's hard enough, if he wanted to he probably *could* carry em. I digress.

"What the fuck were you playing at?" I hiss at him, instantly feeling slightly bad that I'm taking it out on him, the big daft fucker's saved my life, and he's got his hands held up, palms to me, in that universal apologetic gesture.

"Heyyy, Tommy, I'm sorry man, but we can't be making no trouble for the people here you know? They so quick to be calling the police when you English cause the trouble, you get arrested we can't find little Jessie, you know? Calm yourself."

He's got a point, and it's well made. I consider some sort of response but he's already on the move, back to the car. How's that then? Shut your mouth Tom, behave yourself, and come on. Cased closed. Fair enough pal, let's do it.

About half an hour later we're sitting in the car, and my palms are feeling properly sweaty. Cristiano's tapped the number in, and he's looking at me. His eyebrows raise, like to say *Are you ready?* and

I nod. He brings the phone up to his ear, and we wait. His eyes tell me that it's ringing. It's fucking ringing! I wait. He waits. The anticipation is crackers, like life slows down for a few seconds, your heartbeat rattles against your ribs, and the questions that run through your mind, is she gonna answer? What is she gonna say? What is Cristiano gonna say to her? We've not really talked about what we'll do if she does answer, like the unspoken agreement is that we're gonna wing it, play it by ear, because I don't think any of us actually expects that she'll pick the phone. I'm forgetting to breathe right now. Suddenly he pulls the phone away from his ear and presses the disconnect button.

"What happened?" I'm asking, as I let out this *whoosh!* of an exhalation.

"It was her, she answered the telephone." He says, calm as you like, I suppose it answered my question, but it goes no way to explaining why he just hung up on her.

"So?" I ask, hoping my tone also asks that question.

"So, I did not know what to say, you know? I froze." It's hard to imagine the big daft get freezing at owt, but fair enough, at least he was honest. I'm gonna have to do it. I hold my hand out as if to request the phone, she's answered once, she'll answer again.

I hit redial and I wait. That long foreign ringing tone meeps in my lug hole. Fuck knows what I'm gonna say. The tone clicks to stop, and we're connected. She says nothing, I say nothing. We're listening to each other say nothing. I turn to Beefy and he's staring back, anticipation twinkling out of his eyes.

"Who is this?" That voice. I've not heard it in about two years. Just from those three words, she sounds colder than I remember. Harder. Fuck it.

Ryan Bracha   Tomorrow's Chip Paper

"Hello madam, my name is Tom, I'm calling from the Society of Vengeful Pricks, and I'm wondering how you felt about having your arms ripped off and then being beaten to death with them?" I'm saying, but I'm thinking *Smooth,* and Cristiano's in silent stitches beside me, holding his hand over his mouth to stifle the sound. Ada says nothing. You can almost hear the cogs whirring, and the penny dropping. I feel inclined to continue.

"Here at the SVP we're more than happy to allow you to live in exchange for the very reasonable price of my fiancée returned without a hair on her head touched, how does that sound?"

<u>Really Fuckin' Cool</u>

The car rolled down *Rue de la Republique,* the tall department stores and fashion shops creating a darkened and cool shade for the pair as they silently moved toward *Quai de Belges,* Marseille seafront opening itself up to them, the sun forcing the girl beside him to visibly squint, her hand coming up to her forehead to create a shield. Rufus reached up in front of her and brought the visor down to help her. Despite herself she looked to him gratefully, offering a thin smile before her eyes darted away. The marina before them, filled from left to right with private boats and yachts that seemed to stretch for miles, the sunlight bouncing from each and every one of them to create a dazzling whiteness that surprised even Rufus. From a small holder above his head he retrieved his favourite aviator sunglasses. He would never wear any others, he loved to catch glimpses of himself in mirrors and windows. He was never really that vain in himself, but something about those shades made him feel really, *fuckin' cool.* He swung the car onto *Qaui Rive Neuve,* the hotel was a standard Radisson Blu, but made all the more special and expensive by its incredible location. There were reservations in the names of John Fogerty and Suzie Quentin awaiting them, but Rufus was happy to slowly cruise along the sea front, hoping that the serene view might defrost his passenger's already slowly thawing demeanour. After he'd made the offer to switch allegiances once and for all, and perhaps more importantly, for free, on the condition that she lightens up just slightly. She hadn't so much begun to offer smashing conversation, but had been less abrasive toward his own attempts at conversation. Her attitude had shifted from hatred toward him, to her own sadness, and the atmosphere became somewhat less uncomfortable. What hit Rufus the hardest however, was that he had finally been faced with the effects of his work. He had killed so many people in his lifetime, all of them for payment, it was his job, and it was a job that could only be really undertaken by a certain, cold hearted person. He had always been that kind of bloke, he could detach himself from the task at hand, but this time, he had been sitting in a confined space with the human effects of what he did. It remained to be seen whether it would change him as a man in the future, whether for the better or the worse, but at the present he felt something that might even be recognised as compassion for the girl. He wanted to ask her about this guy Tom, what made him so special, why *he* was the only bloke for her, but he knew in his heart of hearts that it would be so spectacularly insensitive that he couldn't bring himself to ask the questions. He turned the car off onto a back street and found the car park, sliding the car into a space, and killing the motor. He turned his attention to the girl.

"You ready to rock and roll Suzie Q?" He asked, trying to keep his voice from slipping into over-friendly.
"I suppose I'll have to be." She said, turning to him but still unable to look him directly in the eyes, even if she couldn't see them behind the lenses of his aviators. He gave a brief sad smile, and- noting the clock flip over to six o'clock -he got out of the car, shifting round the front in order to open her door, receiving a barely audible (but audible nonetheless) noise of gratitude.

The doors of the Radisson swished open to reveal the open foyer, and Rufus bade the girl to go and take a seat whilst he did the job, which he did with relative swiftness. Watching her from the desk she was sitting quietly, the grandeur of the foyer was all but lost on her, such was her own self-absorption. Her red hair sparkled bright as the light of the sun hit it. That hair, physically speaking it clearly defined her. It wasn't an orange ginger, more a rich dark red, maybe part of it came from a bottle but it suited her, like you couldn't ever imagine her with any other colour but that. Her pale complexion, turned darker by the Mediterranean sun, matched it perfectly. She was a good looking girl, no doubt about that, maybe in another world he could have been the man who was allowed to love her. In this one he was the last man she would ever dream of being with, and besides, he had Charley. Charley. He hadn't called her in a couple of days. She'd be climbing the walls with worry. What concerned him most by the situation was the fact that he'd not even thought to call her to put her mind at rest. He did love her, he really did, but it had been so long since he'd actually seen her there in front of him that she had begun to feel like a distant memory of a relationship he'd once had. A sword of regret stabbed him in the heart, before the concierge handed him the keys to their rooms, and thrust reality back upon him.

He left the girl at her door with instructions to be ready for a knock at nine thirty, and walked on to his own room, that familiar silence cloaked him as he entered, but he wasn't ready for it at all. The girl had only been with him today, but he had become accustomed to her company. Dropping his backside heavily onto the mattress Rufus had to concede to himself that something was changing, *he* was changing. Was it old age? No, he was only thirty five. Depression? Hardly. He needed a drink, he needed noise, he needed not to be alone, he needed to consider what the hell he had gotten himself involved in, he needed to work a plan out for tomorrow, he needed to be entirely sure he knew what the hell he was gonna do with himself once it was over, because he sure as fuck wasn't gonna carry on with the path most trodden any more.

In a bar around the corner he sat on a stool, a cold pint of lager lubricating the thoughts that whirred around his head, his phone began to glide toward him across the marble top of the bar, the introduction to *Bad Moon Rising* starting up with that tell-tale guitar riff. He didn't notice it, but one bloke seemed to appreciate it as he exited the toilets, his hands both wrapped in the fresh cloth of stolen towels, leaving the bar and meeting up with his giant Spanish friend.

The Society of Vengeful Pricks

Ada didn't know what the fuck had hit her, it was hilarious, she totally didn't expect to be hearing from me! It was brilliant, she defo weren't acting surprised when she finally responded to me. SVP. The Society of Vengeful Pricks. Just thought of that there and then

when I rang her. Sometimes I think that's the best way, you can come up with your classic funnies when it's spontaneous and off the cuff like, get your best laughs off your mates and all that. She'd sat on the other end of the phone all quiet like, working out what to say, and I was happy to leave the ball in her court. I'd made my threat, no point keeping on cause then she can smell that I need a response from her, like I'm desperate to know that Jess is alive, I just told her outright basically, you've got my woman and if you don't give her back I will rip you to fucking bits. So when she finally spoke she tried to be all cool.
"Tom, it has been too long, how are you?" She said to me.
"Just ever so slightly pissed off to be honest Ada, cunts trying, and failing, to kill me, my woman, my mate, you know? So you'll probably forgive for cutting to the chase, you or your fucking silly mate have got Jess, and I want her back."
"You want her back?" She sounded slightly surprised, like honestly surprised, that I would want her back.
"Course I fucking want her back you daft cunt."
She didn't say much for a short while, then she said "Then you will meet me in Marseille, give me your number."
So I spat out the number of the other mobile I've got in my pocket, and tell her we'll be there in the morning, and that we weren't fucking about. Before I could hang up Mr Beefy hollers in the background:
"You are nothing Ada!"
And we fire the car up, and get on a full speed race to France.

In Marseille I'm reminded just ever so slightly of the last time me and Jess knocked about with Ada, the South of France, full of boats and money, wankers in white trousers, women whose fingers sparkle more than the glass clear water with the sun licking its back. It's a whole other world to what I was used to in my old life. The people in my old life wouldn't know what to do with themselves. The dull dirty banality of existence creating this cynical society that blames the next man for its own shortcomings. Down here the kind of people I used to mingle with would have a fucking meltdown when faced with the creatures that lurk here. For sure, drop some benefits cheating, chain smoking family of nine, undeservedly minted on the back of an inevitable lottery win, on the seafront of Marseille and they would prowl the place as if they were on some sort of safari of luxury, observing The Money in its natural habitat. The Money would turn from the sun-kissed cafe bar windows to witness the trousers and trainers oiks, horrified by the scabby open mouthed looks of gormlessness foisted upon them. As a part of The Money's natural defence mechanism, it would attempt to *tut* the Trousers and Trainers to death, to no avail, the Trousers and Trainers complete lack of self-awareness being more than a match for the disdain. For sure, turn the tables and put The Money in my old stomping ground and it would be ripped apart within seconds by jackals and desperation, its own self-perceived superiority the cause of its downfall.

We're rolling around the marina, Cristiano in the driving seat, me picking at the scabby shit I've got wrapped around my hands, feeling entirely at odds with my surroundings. With my hands looking like they do I'll draw more attention than a fiver in a whorehouse, so I get Beefy to pull up on the main road at an Irish Bar, and get myself inside quick sharp. The place isn't too full, just a few expat builders around the pool table, drawn in probably by the English speaking barman, who's chatting to some girl at the end, and then there's a guy alone at the bar, who seems to be in his own world, staring at the pint he's got in front of him. They're all side-tracked enough to allow me to slip quietly into the bogs unnoticed. I love these kinds of places, they'll have a Guinness sign outside, giving themselves a name like *O'Shannigans,* or *Shamrock* and then underneath they'll have a subheading like *Le Pub,* and the tourists will rock up thinking they're getting a home from home experience. They aren't. In the toilet I pull the shitty cloth from my injured hands and have a look, the bruising's defo coming in good, and raised crystallised scabs bridge the gaps between the dark purple and yellow swollen skin, for sure, they're a fucked up mess. Ah well. I dump the manky cloth in the bin beside the sinks, and help myself to a couple more towels from beside the basins. Gripping them tightly between my teeth I wrap them as best I can around my paw, the sharp pain shoots up the arm, into my chest, and as I grip the side of the basin my other hand cracks open, it hurts like fuck, but it needs done. Eventually the whole operation is finished and my hands are both taped back up, fresh as a fucking daisy, as they say. I cover the old scabby towels up with some tissue from the dispenser and get myself out of there. The pool players have gone, but the guy at the bar has a fresh pint, and as I ghost past him his phone kicks in and I'm pleased to hear his ringtone is *Bad Moon Rising,* good tune it has to be said, and I know I'm gonna have it in my head for the rest of the day.

    I get back to the car feeling a lot fresher with my new wrapping, it looks less grubby, less conspicuous, it's a lot easier for the naked eye to ignore I reckon. Me and Beefy drive along the

seafront, and I'm humming the tune, and I really want to listen to it now, in my old life I had their greatest hits, for sure, it was a soundtrack to stoned and coked up sessions with my mates, sitting round a TV playing old school Xbox all night and getting hammered. Great band.
"There's a bad moon on the rise." I mutter to the tune, Beefy looks to me.
"What?" He asks, he thinks I was talking to him.
"Nowt, I was just singing." I say, my eyes jumping from boat to boat, boats with names like *Florence,* and *Tallullah,* personal tributes to the women in the lives of these millionaire sailor men, a bloke is pulling at ropes on the deck of his yacht, his dark skin testament to the time spent on the ocean. If I could stand being on the sea I'd say was a great way to live, but nah, it's not for me. Water is too dangerous, man.

    We get back over to the other side of the marina, on our way to our hotel, deeper into the side streets, a little more under the shade of the buildings around us, off the beaten track, if you will. It has a little four space car park, of which one of those spaces is- John Fogerty. John Fucking Fogerty. Creedence Clearwater Revival. This is fucked.
"John Fogerty!" I exclaim, to Beefy's surprise.
"What?"
"Fucking John Fucking Fogerty! The bloke in the bar, his ringtone, Creedence Clearwater Revival, it's John Fogerty's band. They're here Beefy, they're fucking here!"

Chapter 10 - January

Mutinous Seeds

She listened to him intently, his lying snake mouth spitting words that meant nothing more than noises, but she wanted to know how far he would take his deceit.

"Did you see their bodies?" she asked, more out of the desire to piss him off than anything else.

"Sure did, twitching bleeding hands poking from the wreckage" he responded, the lies that poured from his mouth, so natural.

"And nobody saw you Rufus?"

"No, no-"

"Are you sure of that? Are you sure that you are not being followed?"

"Ladyboss, it was the first thing in the morning, there was *nobody* around, they're-"

"Will you go and get a photograph of their dead treacherous faces so that I may look at them?" Of course he would not, but it couldn't hurt to ask.

"Ladyboss, I'm in Carcassonnes, ain't no way I'm heading back there to take some fuckin' photos, I just wanna come and claim my-"

"You will speak with respect Rufus, I am not a whore that you can speak to as if I am a piece of shit, you have ignored my telephone calls for hours, now that I finally have you, you will listen to me, do you understand?"

He didn't say anything for a short while, then finally let out on exasperated sigh.

"Yeah ladyboss, I understand."

"Good, get to Marseille, I will meet you in the morning at eleven fifteen, I will call to tell you where to meet."

"Quarter past eleven?" The hit man paused as if thinking something over.
"Do you have a problem with this?"
"Can we make it half past?"
It didn't matter what time she met him, the lying snake would be dead whatever time they met, but, again, out of a desire to piss him off she repeated.
"I will meet you at eleven fifteen"
How could the snake be so flagrant with his lies? He was on his way to Marseille- possibly with the girl, since she was not with the other idiots -and was going to attempt to take half a million from her. The idiots were also on their way to attempt to take the girl from her. Things had taken a very interesting twist so far. The snake, Rufus, had called her to arrange the collection of his money, yet had somehow failed to kill a single one of his targets. The biggest falsehood that stuck in her throat was the possibility that he might now be in league with the girl. The thieving *Alattomos disznó* that Ada brought into the organisation. It was she that helped to murder Mr Hoxton, which meant that by extension, Ada had helped to murder Mr Hoxton. It was she that would feel Ada's wrath the most, she would torture her before her *Picsa* boyfriend, and the hulking dope Cristiano. She would take her eyes, and her ears, and her tongue. They would watch, helpless, and they would see Ada dismantle the girl tiny piece by tiny piece, and then she would put bullets into the skulls of Thomas and Cristiano. Rufus was simply a *Szarházi* who was going to find himself dead in a gutter, his death was going to be fast, meaningless, but no less fun.
The telephone call with Thomas played her in her head. She thought he was dead. Rufus had already *told* her that he had finished the job, so it struck her

as a voice from beyond the grave. A voice that she never ever thought she would hear again. His stupid foul-mouthed rant, thinking he was a comedy legend or some such, he had never been as witty as he thought he was, he was merely an irritant. She had taken him to be extremely loyal to start with, but his true colours were shown before long. He was loyal to nothing and nobody but himself, he bit the hand that fed him, that offered a new lease of life, a new direction. He was the one who put ideas into Cristiano's tiny mind. He planted mutinous seeds. They worked together too much, Cristiano was content to amble along, and be told what to do, he was nothing more than a muscle-bound drone, a tool, a sheep. If she wanted to she could quite easily turn him against the others, she may even do that, allow the lumbering oaf to do her dirty work, whilst she sat back and enjoyed the fruits of her labour, the pitch black parts of her mind even taken by the idea of shooting him in the face whilst she rode his tiny cock. She smiled at the thought of his face, a mixture of orgasmic stupidity, and that fear that people have when they're looking down the barrel of her gun. She found herself aroused by both the dirty thoughts *and* the murderous ones, barely aware that Dietmann had entered the room. She shifted uncomfortably on the seat she had been perched upon, lost in herself, until he cleared his throat behind her, Ada swung round in her chair to face him, torn between taking his cock in her hand and bringing it to hardness, pulling it from his pants and forcing him to fuck her, and punching him repeatedly in his weak face, to take out the frustration of the day's events. She did neither.
"Yes Dietmann?" She asked, inviting him to speak, the guy watched the floor, unable to make eye contact with her. The rising bile in her throat at his weakness

killed any urges to fuck him, now she wanted to pull him apart. She wanted to slap him around the face and tell him to grow some balls. All around her people were proving themself to be worth less than she had ever given them credit for. Far less. Jess and her *morals*, Thomas, led by his penis and the allure of the redheaded *Kurva*, Cristiano, merely an imbecile. Now Dietmann, incapable of being a man, she had used him for his tool, and now he looked at her differently, through the eyes of a lost lover, he could not detach sex from emotion. A pussy man. To her credit, Liezel was the only one living up to original impressions, she refused to bow to any kind of pressure, she did the job and she did it her own way, but she was petulant and disrespectful, and for that she would die. As much as they would perform the tasks they were given, Lukas and Yannick were non-entities, ghosts, they flitted in and out of her life upon request, and for financial gain. She was running the operation, and she was running it alone. These people, Thomas, Rufus and the rest of them, they would think that Ada's world revolved only around them and their petty issues. No, no such luck for them, or her. They were merely a side-track from the main event that she could quite easily do without. Dietmann's eyes finally raised to meet hers.

"I was wondering..." He trailed off, unable to finish his sentence.

"Yes?" She asked, with not a little impatience.

"I am not doing anything of interest right now, I was wondering..." Again he trailed off.

"Dietmann finish your fucking sentence you little pansy boy, spit out your words!" She snapped, the German flinched, his eyes saddening, his head lowering once more to where it had begun.

"It does not matter Ada." He whispered, skulking silently from the room, *Köcsög* she thought to herself, turning back to the desk, her eyes back upon the telephone before her, she wanted to toy with Rufus, perhaps make great promises of more money, but no, she would let it lie for the time being, she had far too much going on than childish games designed to antagonise mercenary hit men. She had a new game. She had the biggest challenge of her life, far bigger than anything she had ever embarked upon before. If things went right she could get out of this, away from incompetent employees, and idiots looking for revenge. Ada picked up her telephone, and scrolled through the contacts, searching for his name, there were others she could have called but she had chosen him, he would be the one. She dialled, and waited. He answered, as enthusiastically as usual.

"Ada, darling, we're having a whale of a time down here, you really ought to join us, what can I do you for?"

He was really quite eccentric, and the relationship was entirely professional, but it really was difficult not to warm to him when she spent any great length of time with him. Today, however, she was in no mood for pleasantries, and needed something done.

"I need a favour." She said, and then spent the next twenty minutes explaining exactly what she needed done.

Blood And Semen

The door slammed behind him and he rushed to his bed, throwing himself dramatically onto the duvet, his face buried into the pillow to drown out the sobs that emanated from his heaving body. His sinuses filled with mucus of sadness, evidence of the fact that this was a *real* sadness, no crocodile tears to be seen. *Real* tears. *Real* emotion. How could she not see what she was doing to him? They had spent an incredible night together, he did not know that sex could be so good. In Germany, back when he was officially alive, he had only ever been with one girl, Greta, and it had been an awkward affair. They would meet to hold hands, and walk together, he had never even built up the courage to try to kiss her. He was scared to. He had heard from his other friends that she had ended previous liaisons with boys because they would attempt to be too forceful with her, they would try to get their hands into her pants and she would pull them away, and slap their faces. They were only after one thing, but Dietmann liked her, he *really* liked her, and he did not wish to spoil things between them. He wanted to talk with her, to absorb the things that she had to say. For a while she played the game, but she herself had become frustrated that he did not try to kiss her, she wondered if he was not attracted to her like the other boys were, but he *was,* he would spent night after night masturbating into his bedclothes with thoughts of only Greta. For him he was fearful of scaring her off, so would never dream of leaning into to kiss her lips. Then it happened. They had got drunk on schnapps one Friday evening, when her parents were out in Cologne, and she had become aggressive, asking what was so wrong with her that he did not wish to be intimate with her. He tried to explain how he felt but the words would not come out, through the drunken schnapps fog he could not tell her that he had spent so many nights dreaming of finally being with her, of taking her in his arms, carrying her to bed, and slowly making tender love to her. Through the stuttering he took the plunge and kissed her hard on the mouth, pulling her face into his, fumbling with her blouse buttons, and grabbing roughly at her small breasts. She reciprocated his actions, and they ended up on her living room floor, their inexperience becoming a tangle of limbs and fluids, discarded underwear, clashing teeth. His fingers clawed between her legs, one finger poking around for a hole, he knew there was a hole for peeing from, so he avoided the top one, his digits guiding themselves down to the lower one. As his finger entered it she yelped, pulling away, and informed him that he was trying to invade her anus. The red-faced shame of his error put a slight dampener on the situation, but she was not to be put off, she grabbed his hand and placed it on the top hole, using his hand to bring herself to wetness, before pulling him on top of her. She guided his cock to the hole, and he felt her lady bits grab a hold of it, the feeling of it being pulled inside her was like nothing else on Earth, it felt nothing like when he did it himself. He moved himself awkwardly up and down, his hands groping at her breasts, pinching the nipples to hardness, causing her to gasp with the pain, but she was not for stopping either, they were becoming adults, finally, at seventeen they were fucking, they were making love, and with no former experience to set the benchmark, they were enjoying it. Afterwards they had lay together, for a short time, naked on her parents' living room floor, no words spoken between them, an uncomfortable cloak began to descend upon them. They had broken all barriers between each other, and it appeared that there was nothing left to learn. The pressure, and the tension was gone, and all that was left was loathing, for themselves and for one another. The silence had grown ever louder. He stared at the top of her head and wanted to smash it in. When any of them moved even slightly the other flinched. It was only when her parents returned from Cologne that they moved, as quickly as they could, pulling on clothes from wherever they could find them, his socks ripped onto his feet inside-out. His sweater on back to front. Her stockings halfway up. Her parents walking into the living room, full of laughter and beer, to see them both half dressed, that tell-tale panic in their faces, and the huge gloop of blood and semen in the middle of the pure white carpet. Dietmann never saw Greta again. For a man as meek as he, it was enough to put him off that kind of thing for a long time. It did nothing for his confidence around women, and began to hang over him as heavy as lead. Into his twenties he was *still* telling stories to his few friends, of liaisons with non-existent women. He fell in love on a daily basis, with the girl at the butcher shop, the girl on the train, the woman who smiled and thanked him for holding the door open. He even fell in love with the stern traffic warden who gave him a parking ticket. He was a romantic. Then, when he got involved with this organisation he found himself surrounded by hard men. Men who could kill people with their bare hands and think no more about it. A sex addict who was so easy with women, who had been to bed with thousands of women. A man who would order the deaths of hundreds of people in the name of morality. *Morality!* Men who would chop up and bury the corpses of all of those people. He could never do anything like that. He was the very definition of a fish out of water. Ada had always been the closest thing to a kindred spirit within the organisation, she was a hard woman, but she spoke to him like a person. Once upon a time. Now she was who she was. She was not the woman he once knew. But he still *loved* her. He *knew* he loved her. His heart pounded with aching for her to take him again, but she had reverted to treating him like a dog. *Worse* than a dog. She spoke to him with such contempt. He rolled over on the bed, wiping his red eyes with the back of his sleeve, and gasp slightly to get his breath. He watched the ceiling behind the tears that continued to build in his eyes, and his mind turned to darker things. Like ways to end this misery. But he was weak. He would never have the courage to end it. But the pain. The pain was so bad. Dietmann sat up on the side of his bed, and looked at the light fitting in the middle of the ceiling, sizing up the weight it could take with his eyes. He was only slender but could it take his dead weight? There was only one way to find out. The belt ate into his skin, gripped his oesophagus, crushed it. His legs twitched as he swung. The light held him up. His eyes rolled into the back of his skull as he embraced an end to the pain. She could go and fuck herself. She had lost the best thing that could have ever happened to her, but had spurned. Dietmann had won. He was so, *so* close to being pain free. His heart smashed into the inside of his ribcage, trying to force blood into his face but it could not, the belt took care of that. A whiteness filtered into his vision. A door opening. Somebody standing in the doorway. His consciousness declined. His mind was clear. The pain disappeared.

Chapter 11 - February

Died A Little Inside

"Day three of the Will Thunder situation. As public opinion of him declines ever further the stock of his captor is rising. A deranged masked South African woman is fast becoming the most famous person in the country. Only in Britain. My guests today are the ubiquitous Mike Rotch, and Thunder's former showbiz partner, Johnny Lightning. Mike shot to fame with his controversial sketch show *Sit on Mike Crotch,* gaining plaudits and complaints in equal numbers, his record breaking tour of the UK was sold out for two hundred and fifty six nights straight, and the DVD of that tour has been number one in the comedy chart since before Christmas. Let's have some applause for Mike!"

The audience whooped, and hollered for the larger than life comedian, and the host turned his attention to Johnny.

"And my other guest, Johnny Lightning, is equally celebrated in other arenas of showbiz, a multi award winning light entertainment legend, he and his partner Will Thunder have enjoyed success at almost every endeavour they have had a hand in, the disastrous *The Music of Thunder & Lightning* Christmas Special of two thousand and nine notwithstanding. Their shows have been enjoyed by families for over eight years. The relationship reached breaking point when this masked woman, whoever she is, took Will Thunder hostage at gunpoint with evidence that he was a drug addict, rapist, paedophile, and possible murderer. Much like the rest of the entertainment industry then!"

Cue much laughter from everybody in the studio except Johnny who displayed a thin smile. He remained tight-lipped and composed. Giles had told him this would happen, and that he needed to take everything with a pinch of salt. What pissed him off was that the producers had thrown him a curve ball. He had been booked under the pretence that he would be featuring opposite Kari Watson, whose band were doing the rounds promoting the latest album, it would have been a light-hearted affair, he would get the chance to distance himself from Will, show the world that he was whiter than white, an angel compared to his former friend. Sitting opposite the tubby bastard he felt more than just slightly vexed at the ruse. They wanted fireworks, they wanted a fight, they wanted it live and exclusive, and he was determined not to allow them the pleasure. This was his chance to redeem himself in the eyes of his public. The laughter and applause died down, and Gareth Bennington-Lane continued.

"Welcome to *Politickle My Funny Bone*, both of you!" The pair nodded their appreciation to the host and the applaud kicked in again.

"So for a third day in a row, the police have done absolutely nothing to stop this mystery woman from doing anything she wants to Will Thunder, and the public have voted to kick the absolute hell out of him, every time. Mike, why do you think that is?" Gareth Bennington-Lane asked the rotund funny man, who shifted himself round to face the host, his face reddening in preparation for the inevitable rant.

"Cause he's a dirty bleedin' twat who needs more than a kickin'! The coppers are doing shit all because they're enjoying it. They're not rushing cause this mystery bird is doing the job for 'em! I've voted for her to kill the slimy shit every time but people are enjoyin' his torture far more."

Gareth Bennington-Lane looked perturbed, and felt moved to ask.

"You've voted *to kill* him? Harsh don't you think? Let's be fair here, if she kills him and you voted for it aren't you going to feel in the slightest bit bad? It *is* murder after all."

Mike Rotch saw it coming, and countered. All the while Johnny watched his fat face twitching in irritation.

"An eye for an eye, that's what I say, we've seen proof that him and his cronies," the comedian made a point of looking at Johnny Lightning "have killed a young woman, so what's the difference?"

Johnny doubted that the fat bastard realised the point he was trying to make was lost in the question. *What is the difference?* It essentially made him *the same* as Will. An eye for an eye. Were they living in the dark ages? He *so* wanted to ask this but he would be seen as sympathising with his former friend, instead he swallowed hard, and prepared for the attention to turn to him. Gareth Bennington-Lane did indeed swing around to face him.

"Johnny, what do you think? Have you had a vote yourself?"

Every pair of eyes in the building were upon him, his carefully constructed responses to everything over the last view days meant nothing here, he had been thrown to the lions. Live television. Live, comedy, controversial television. Opposite Mike fucking Rotch. He could kill Giles for this.

"Erm.. well, no, I'd prefer that the police dealt with the situation." He said, quietly, scanning the production crew, the audience, anywhere, for anything that might be construed as a friendly face, his eyes finally resting upon Giles, whose grimace said it all. He had to get people on side. He commanded millions of pounds in golden handcuff deals for people to listen to what he had to say. He was *never* lost for words, so what was different now? It wasn't scripted. It hadn't been rehearsed so much that any comedy he saw in it was entirely exhausted. It was him against the world. That's how he felt. They, everybody, had tarred him with the same brush as Will. What could he say? What could he do? Other than stand and condemn Will to burn in hell there wasn't much else he *could* do. So that's what he did. "I mean, yeah, I'd prefer that the police did their job, but let's look at the real issue. Right under my nose, and I swear on my own mother that I did not know it was happening, right under my nose he abused women, children, and who knows what else? Animals probably!" He wondered if Will could feel a knife in his back right at that point, but he was on a roll now, he was even drawing vaguely approving looks from Mike Rotch.

"I promise you, I never saw chicken feathers sticking out of his fly, or heard distressed cows in his room, but I can't promise he never abused any farm animals!"

The audience roared with laughter, Giles smiled and nodded out of approval, a subtle thumbs up. From then on in he continued to rip his former friend to shreds, the crowd lapped it up, Mike Rotch was even beginning to change his opinion of him, and in the green room after the show he'd acted like they were bosom buddies, or peas in a pod. It was that fact alone that made Johnny feel like he'd died a little inside.

Rubbernecking Jackals

"Next stop Kings Cross, where this train will terminate, Kings Cross is your next station stop." Announced the conductor, stirring the scruffy youth from his slumber, the last track on Black Keys' *Rubber Factory* album played and ended a good hour earlier. His feet explored beneath the seat in front of him as he performed a full and dramatic stretch, the backs of his dry hands rubbing the scum from his eyes, a long squeak-cum-yawn emitting from his mouth to show how much he enjoyed it. He recovered from the stretch, and curled his neck, dinosaur-like, his greasy hair spiked up on one side where it had rested against the seat, over the back of his seat to survey the rest of the carriage. It wasn't so busy that he'd want to worry about getting up now to beat them all to the punch it terms of getting to the door first, a couple of Laptop-and-BlackBerries still hammering away on the keyboards of their computers, trying to finish whatever was clearly miles more important to the world than anything Jake had ever embarked upon. He had once been on *Calendar News* for painting a fence with school, hardly millions of pounds worth of, whatever. Beyond them there was a pretty blonde student type, maybe coming back to London after a weekend back home, a large blue rucksack above her head that hinted at a foreign backpacker, probably been on the train since Glasgow or York, there was no way a continental backpacker would be visiting Doncaster, and he was pretty sure she was already on the train when he boarded. He slowly roused himself, and shuffled out of the seat, reaching up to grab his scabby bag, full of nothing but pre-rolled joints, prawn flavoured Skips, underpants and socks. He'd taken everything out of the bank, both the money that was his, and the few hundred pounds overdraft that they'd been stupid enough to allow him. Jake didn't really know what the plan was, it just started out as a daft discussion about the girl with Kenny over a few bucket bongs, and, once the seed had been planted, it grew. He had grown fixated with her. Her eyes invaded his dreams, that voice of hers, he'd watched the videos of her on YouTube over and over again. He needed to see her in person, be so close that he could touch her, and breathe the same air as her. The crowds that were already there, they were just rubbernecking jackals, to be a part of the frenzy that surrounded her. They wanted to get their stupid faces on TV, to hold up their badly made signs dedicated to whoever. He wanted her.

He exited the train station and took in his surroundings, Kings Cross, it was awful. Doncaster wasn't exactly paradise but he could feel himself getting even scummier just standing there, and wanted to get out of the hustle of the station entrance, the businessmen and women, the tramps, the students, the everything. He was shoved out of the way by an impatient commuter with a briefcase as he approached the front of the line of black cabs, the commuter taking his own place in the taxi that Jake had earmarked for himself. Without worry he simply ambled toward the second in line, climbing into the back, and directing the driver to Kensington. As a seasoned stoner Jake was relieved that the man up front did not want to talk, strangers generally upset him, and put him on edge. He hated having to come up with inane conversation, about the weather, or politics. Fucking politics. He hated politically minded idiots. He didn't know or care enough about politics to form his own opinions, but he felt that at least he was being honest about it. There was no bigger buzz-kill than the ill-informed opinions of imbeciles blaming whoever for whatever, it was always blame. Nobody ever got praise for anything anymore.

The taxi ride passed quietly and without issue, other than the stop-start duration of the journey, the cyclists that never failed to shit him up when they rushed past the window he was staring out of. His faintly stoned awe of the great old city occasionally dampened when the paranoia kicked in. What if he got there and it was all over? If the police had taken her away from him? The panic built up, but then would be replaced by some new awe when he passed a busy market, or some monument he'd seen on the internet. As the car rolled by Hyde Park he asked the driver to stop, and let him walk from there. He wanted to see the famous park, the venue for so many historic gigs that he'd love to have been at, the most recent being the Red Hot Chili Peppers, supported by the legendary James Brown. He'd heard from friends that had been that the Sex Machine was awesome. Wandering through the park he lit up a joint and guided himself toward where the driver told him that Kensington was. He'd been smoking weed for so long now that it took a good few joints to make any kind of a difference, and he packed them to the end with the good stuff. He loved being stoned, that fuzzy high he got when his blood was full of THC, it made the world a nicer place to live in. Nothing was too much trouble for him, unless it was confrontation, he hated confrontation. He was a lover, not a fighter. Weed made him this way, for that, weed was his best friend. Three spliffs later he decided he was ready to face his heroine, the woman of his dreams. He wanted to get there, float through the crowds, stumble past the police and the cameras, walk up the stairs of Will Thunder's house, and knock on the door, a big dopey grin on his face, waiting for her to open it, and when she did she would invite him in, sit him down in the living room and fetch him a great big slice of pizza, with brown sauce for dipping. She would stick Herbaliser's *Something Wicked This Way Comes* on the CD player, and they would smoke the biggest joint he had ever rolled, whilst they laughed at Will Thunder, strapped to the chair. Jake really did not like violence, but when *she* did it was cool, it felt like she only did it because she had to. It wasn't gratuitous. Then when they'd finished smoking, she would kick Will Thunder over on to his side, they would switch the webcam back on, and they would stream themselves making sweet stoned love to the world, and it would be beautiful.

The crowds came into view a lot sooner that he had expected, it was crazy, a sea of heads, funnelled into the narrow avenue, spilling out around the mouth of the road and clinging to the causeway, the honking of cars narrowly avoiding the stragglers who found themselves on the road. There was no way he was going to float through that crowd. No easy way of ghosting past the police. He joined the back of the crowd and became just another one of them. Another rubbernecking jackal. He craned his neck to get a better view of the house, beyond the thousands of people, beyond the police cordons and beyond the media vans, it was just a house like the rest of them. But inside it was his girl. The light of his life. She was so close, but so far. He resigned himself to the fact that he wasn't going to get anywhere near her just now, but people would *have* to go home at some point. The crowds would surely dissipate the later it got, so he turned around, and scanned for the area for somewhere to sit, where it was warm. There was a coffee shop, the kind that offered flavoured world famous coffees, free wireless internet and a loyalty card program, it would have to do. Inside, he ordered his coffee, with a sweet pastry item of some description, and took a seat, in some leather bucket seat before a low wooden table covered with magazines and flowers. It was pretty busy, and Jake just about managed to avoid eye contact with the rest of the clientele, his attention taken by one girl with her back to him, she had a mass of red hair cascading from her head down her back, and sat in front of a laptop. He did like red hair, it was just the epitome of different to him. So many browns and blondes around, a nice redhead was just different, they always attracted admiring looks. At school they were vilified by bullies, in adulthood however, they were coveted, so many girls dyed their hair red nowadays. It was just a shame that, with all the information available to her online, she chose to spend her time on Facebook.

Chapter 12 - January

Running Scared

I can't sleep. Every time I close my eyes I see him. I wish I could hear his voice just once more. Nothing I own smells of him. I've spent the last three hours throwing up. Whether it's pregnancy sickness or grief I can't tell. It's probably both. Everything has happened so quickly and I got swept along with revenge, and what Rufus is doing, and now I've had time to really think it hits me again just how alone I am now. I have to be strong. But I'm not sure I can be. I need Tom. My guardian angel. Nobody ever made me feel safe like he did, he protected me from everything bad in this world. If it was sadness that he needed to protect me from then he would cuddle me, doing everything he could to make me laugh. Whilst he held me he would tell me that his favourite animal charity was the *Cuddle You, Cuddle You, Eff,* and his favourite letter was *Cuddle You,* he was daft in the best possible way. His mind worked like nobody I have ever met before. He was sharp, and witty, and he made me smile with some of the silly faces he pulled. To strangers he probably came across as a bit of a dick, but I knew those little gestures and idiosyncrasies were all part of the plan to keep me smiling. Even now, just remembering them I feel a little bit better, I'll never forget him, the things he said, the things he did. If I have a boy I'm going to call him Thomas. And if it's a girl she'll be called Natalie, the name he chose for her. I don't know why I'm here. In a room paid for by the man who killed Tom, on a road trip with the same guy, to kill the woman who paid him to do it. It's so messed up, I don't know what I'm doing. I can't do this, this revenge thing isn't for me. There's been too much death in our lives, and I'm going to bring a new person into this world, *alone,* and I'm making plans with a cold-hearted bastard to end somebody else's life. What am I becoming? I wish I could get out of my own head for a while. I can't do it, but I have to. If she gets wind that I'm alive she'll come back for me again, or worse still my baby. I can't go on in life running scared, always looking over my shoulder for Ada or one of the others, or another Rufus, I need to end this now. But how can I? I can't trust Rufus, but I have to. I can't kill Ada, but I have to. This is so messed up. I'm in the worst place ever mentally to be dealing with all of this, I just *know* I'm going to meltdown before all of this is done.

I've not moved since I got into the room, just laid on my back, staring at the ceiling. I want to bawl my eyes out but I'm just feeling numb. I only know I'm crying because I can occasionally feel a tear tickling the sides of my face. My hands rest on my tummy, the fingers clasped together, and my feet are crossed over each other. I haven't got the strength in me to get under the covers, I just want to lie here, and sleep, but sleep is eluding me, my mind can't shut off. How will I feel when I'm looking at Ada's dead body? Will it be a relief? That I'm not running anymore? Will I want to spit on her corpse as I finally have revenge for my Tom? What if she doesn't go down as easy as we're expecting? I've been going along with this like it's going to be simple to walk in there, kill her and walk back out again, I haven't even considered that she might finish the job she started. Oh God, I don't want my baby to die. My only connection to its dad. This is so messed up. What would Tom do? Tom would tell me to calm down, to go and wait for him to do what he had to, and then he would come back and say something funny, to put me at ease. No matter what had happened he would tell the story as exaggeratedly entertaining as he could, and easy, it wouldn't make a difference how much danger he might have been in, he would have strolled in and bullets would have been whizzing past his head, but he would have walked in and said 'something cool' before doing what he had to, and then coming back out without a scratch on his body, declaring that the situation was *sortabix*. Sortabix. His daft way of saying it was *sorted*. It would be partly through his natural bravado, but mostly to put me at ease about it all. God, I love him. I'd give anything to have him back, to hear his voice. For him to just phone me up and tell me he was okay. I'd even accept a simple dream about him, just to see his face again. I wish I could sleep. I'm so tired. I need to do something to occupy my mind, to kill the thoughts, questions and doubts that are racing through it so fast that I can barely keep up with them. My hand reaches for the TV remote on the bedside, and my fingers explore the raised rubber buttons, looking for that tell-tale round one at the top, which they find with ease, and I robotically switch on the television, some French chat show is on RTL, discussing issues with the slums of Paris, and what to do to help the people that live there. I flick the channel up again, and there's a soap opera on. The character's wife has left him for the maid, and they have run off together, so the wife's sister is here to tell him that she has always loved him, that he should forget the wife and get with her. He looks off in contemplation, considering switching his allegiance and love. They're the same in any language, everybody has such short memories. A husband can die in a horrific accident, and his wife will be in the bed of another man within weeks, the husband no more than another character that once lived in the fictional area. I hate it. I know that they're supposed to be exaggerated versions of real life and the writers need to keep their audience gripped but I can't get into them. The next channel is BBC News, the ever rolling feed of what is or isn't happening around the world. The next channel is back in French, and I'm no longer actually watching anything here, it's just back to colours and noises designed to occupy my mind, and they're failing. A rising wave of nausea rolls from my stomach and up my throat, and I have to swing from the bed quickly and make the short journey to the toilet. I've already thrown up everything I have inside me, so I dry retch over the bowl, my stomach is in agony as the retching just will not stop. My forehead is cooled by the porcelain, as the nausea subsides slightly. I feel awful. The life I had before me is gone, nothing is going to be the same, and to top it all off I'm looking and sounding disgusting with my red, slobbering, puffed up, all-cried-out face in a toilet. There's a quiet, almost polite, knock at the door. I'm not answering it looking and feeling like I do. Rufus can go and screw himself tonight, I need to be alone. I need to get my head around my life, if I can. That same knock again. "Leave me alone." I squeak, my throat raw from the effort of trying to throw up.

Rufus knocks again, he's not giving up easily.

"I said leave me alone!" I call out, slightly firmer than before, hoping he gets the message, but no, another knock. I drag myself up from the floor using the towel rail, and labour to the door, and the room spins as I think I got up a bit fast. Another knock, I could throttle him, I told him to leave me alone, if he's playing games then he's playing them with the wrong person. I swing the door open and yell "I told you Rufus, to leave me alone," and the mystery man at the

door looks at me gone out, his eyebrows raised, and then this ghost, his features take on a familiar form, his eyes smile at me, out of relief, and joy. I'm obviously hallucinating. His face is overjoyed to see me, but I can't be happy, I thought I would be but I'm not. He isn't real. I burst into tears again, and he enters the room and his arms surround me, they take me in and I feel warm. I'm imagining his smell filling my nostrils as I snort up the phlegm from my crying, it's almost a good job he isn't real because I'm a mess. My face is pressed firmly into his chest, and what should be his hands stroke at the back of my head, they aren't his hands though, they feel like a teddy bear's hands might feel, soft cloth surrounding them. He's talking to me but I don't know what he's saying. I pull away and look at him, and he's looking back at me, a smile on his face.
"Alright gingerbonce?" He says, his padded hands rub against my chin, wiping the snot away, and his face takes on that familiar cheeky form, like it does when he's going to say something I might laugh at.
"Looking fit baby, for sure, I've never fancied you more."

Alright, Silly Bollocks?

The barman filled his glass up for the fifth, or was it sixth time? Seventh? He wasn't sure, every time he checked the clock to leave Rufus was always just too late, and ordered another large one to while away the time until the next thirty minutes. It was good beer, but it wasn't offering the clarity of thought that he originally considered that it might, and his brain was a muggy, hazy cloud by now. Whilst he was still somewhat sober he had spoken to Ada, told her that yes, he had landed in town, and would expect a call in the morning to confirm a location. He had tried once again to get her to agree to eleven, or half past, but the awkward bitch stuck to her guns and told him quarter past. He couldn't be arsed to argue, and the more drink that passed his lips, the better an idea it became to just show up at eleven thirty anyway, *fuck her* he thought, for what was probably the fourteen thousandth time since they'd first met. For all the years he'd been in the business there was nobody that infuriated him more than her, she acted like he should be grateful of the business. Should he fuck, he was one of the most feared names in his field, he was expensive because he was the best, that Eastern European cunt from the back of beyond should feel privileged to have acquired his services. It was only because she had come to him with Isaac Charles' credence that he had given her the time of day in the first place, now she had become the bane of his very existence. She called his phone incessantly with the most inane of queries, or just to tell him to do something he was already doing, it got right on his tits. His morose pissed was fast becoming angry pissed, and he knew himself well enough to know that he needed to get back to the room, because he was prone to do something he might regret if he stuck around in public for too much longer, like the time the bravest one of a group of local kids in some outback town in Australia decided he was easy pickings, and literally came over to him in a bar and pointedly picked his own pint of lager up, and drank it down in one go, before turning back and taking a seat amongst his jeering pals, staring him out, almost daring him to make a move. He had wanted a quiet night so he let it slide, simply getting another pint, and eyeballing the youth, who returned the stare. Leaving the bar they had followed him out, and that same ringleader came up in his face, told him that the English weren't wanted round their parts, to fuck off back to where he came from. Rufus had said nothing, just sized up his foe, placed the others behind him, assessed the situation, before laying his forehead on the bridge of the kid's nose, exploding the spotty thing all over his face. Before the others could make their moves a local copper appeared, who'd seemingly witnessed the scene in the bar earlier, and to Rufus' relief he ordered the youths to go one way and Rufus the other, and watched the hit man as he wandered off into the distance, no doubt putting an alert on a potential trouble maker. After the incident anybody that would care to look would see that John Fogerty checked himself out of his hotel and had to check into one fifty miles down the road. Stupid Aussie shitheads.

  Clocking the time, eight twenty seven, he slid his arse from the stool, and downed his pint, reasoning that he could easily squeeze a piss out and be able to leave the bar for half past. The walls rocked from left to right as he took a step-wobble-step approach to the men's room, the scouse barman watching his progress with amusement, nodding the girl he was talking to in his direction. He felt a lot more drunk now he was mobile, but he had been drunker before, and he reached the piss hole without incident. Rufus step-wobble-stepped to a urinal, pulled out his dick, and sprayed the back of the porcelain, emptying his full bladder, gracelessly allowing the splash-back to coat the backs of his hands with a fine yellow mist. He didn't mind so much, even pissed he took pride in his hygiene, and punched the soap dispensing button with one hand to drop some jizz looking gloop into the palm of his other hand, and scrubbed them thoroughly, ripping several rough grey hand towels from the unit on the wall. He'd seen enough of those to last a lifetime, the kind of hand towels that are stacked stupidly inside their holders, and you had to pick at the edge of them to try to pull one from it, only to pull about twelve, wasting thousands of trees in the process. He preferred the ones like fag rolling papers, the ones that you could at once, take the one you want, and leave the end of the next one ready to be called up to the war on wet hands. Discarding the towels to the small bin he noticed some dirty towelling balled up in there, his upper body wobbling on feet that seemed glued to the floor, squinting and looking through one eye to gain some sort of focus on the towelling, he noted that it was covered in dirt and blood, and had he been sober he might have thought that kind of thing suspicious, especially in a town where at least two murderers were expecting a showdown in the morning, but in his drunken state he simply frowned, and checked his watch, the second hand was bringing time back round to half past the hour, and he step-wobble-stepped out of the bar. The light of dusk welcoming him to the outside world, the smell of the ocean, and the noise of gulls reminding him where he was. The part of town he was in was lively, and although he was definitely the drunkest man around, he was able to melt into the bustle, and coast along on the tides of the public, jumping onto another jet-stream in the directions he needed, ending up on the main strip, his feet once again glued to the floor, whilst his body wobbled at the waist, his eye squinting to confirm that it was indeed the Radisson he had arrived at.

He not so much coasted as clomped through the lobby, disregarding the stares of disdain by the clientele and staff, apart from the point-nosed receptionist Khadisha, who was phoning up to room Four Twelve, and stood before the elevator doors, his looking-eye doing its level best to focus on the floor number he needed, before his finger tried to communicate with it and press the button he needed. Inside the lift a middle aged couple joined him, and began muttering a self-conscious conversation between them, as far as he could tell they were bickering over his behaviour in the restaurant earlier, but he couldn't be sure. They left at the second floor and allowed his passage to the fourth undisturbed. At his own door he waited, considering with the mind of a drunkard, that he ought to go and check on the girl, try to maybe get some conversation out of her, see what she was all about. The angry drunk in him had subsided, and the talkative friendly drunk had appeared, ready to try to make friends with the one person on Earth who was least likely to reciprocate. To a pissed mind every idea seemed like a good idea. Rufus approached her door, and hovered there, weighing up the potential outcomes, he so wanted her to let it slide and be herself, and right now he had every intention of telling her so, in a friendly way, of course. Eventually he allowed his hand to knock on the door, which, to his confusion, swung open without any resistance. A sober Rufus might have also found this to be somewhat disconcerting, but drunk, he frowned and pushed it further open with his forearm, bimbling into the darkened room, curtains drawn. He scanned the room, his hand grabbing in the dark for a light. In the newly illuminated room he looked for the girl, she was there, standing in the corner, but in Rufus' fuzzy vision, she had taken the form of her dead boyfriend, and she was holding a gun in his direction, and as she spoke she spoke as a bloke.

"Alright silly bollocks? Sit yourself down lad, we've got some talking to do."

Chapter 13 - January

Optimistic Crumbs

He thanked the woman for her help and replaced the receiver, his friend's face filled with hope and expectation, only to deflate with a shake of Cristiano's head. It was the fourth hotel they had tried in the area. Tommy had wanted to head straight back to the bar and find the guy, but Cristiano had reasoned that the roads were a mess in Marseille, with the upcoming year of it having the honour of being the *European City of Culture.* The authorities had decided that they would rather cause chaos for the locals for over a year in order to cater for the impending tourism boom, so it would take them an age to get back round, so they should continue to their own hotel and check in, and take it from there. The kid was anxious, though. He couldn't get into the room quick enough, an excitable air about him, his girl was in town and he wanted to find her, his anxiety was understandable, but he needed to see reason. Ada had arranged to meet them in Marseille, the very same place that they had possibly discovered the guy that she sent to kill them. Something was going down and they should not rush in, all guns blazing, if there was a chance that they were being ambushed. Cristiano promised him that he would find them, if Tommy would agree to put his trust in his friend. They needed to be smart, they needed to find them quickly and quietly, and then decide on their next move. So whilst Tommy racked up two generous lines of cocaine, made all the more generous courtesy of his distinct lack of grip of the bank card with his wrapped paws, Cristiano set about locating all hotels within a mile radius of the bar that Tommy believed their man was drinking in, calling them up one at a time, and getting nowhere. The first one he called he came up with back story about having had his phone stolen, and could they tell him if Mr John Fogerty was residing at the hotel, and they came back talking about security and the rest, so after that he simply asked the second receptionist for Mr Fogerty's room, and would be told that, no, sorry, there was no Mr Fogerty staying at the hotel. The third and fourth yielded the same results, and as the cocaine fizzed into Tommy's brain he was becoming more antsy with every fresh hope that was shot down as quickly as it arose. He held the CD case with a healthy line of coke for Cristiano, who sucked it into his nostril with minimal effort, and allowed the white crystals to crackle in his throat, that familiar and great bitter taste attacking the back of his tongue. He sniffed up any optimistic crumbs that dared to cling to his insides, and swallowed them loudly, and the rush hit him instantly, they were good drugs, no doubting that.

The next hotel, the fifth so far, was the Radisson, he doubted that the hit man would choose a location so blatant and open, but then considered that maybe that was the exact logic that the guy had followed, maybe it was too obvious. He dialled the number.

"Le Radisson Blu Marseille, you are speaking wiz Khadisha, 'ow may I 'elp you?" The young female's nasal voice reverberated so much that he felt his eardrum physically wince, and his right eye twitch slightly.

"Hello, can you put me through Mr John Fogerty, s'il vous plait?"

"One moment monsieur."

The line went quiet, to be replaced by some French language reasons to choose Radisson, Tommy was

sitting on the edge of the chair opposite him, his knees twitching, and his jaw rutting from left to right. The kid was high as hell, his eyeballs bugged out in anticipation of any kind of news. The girl came back.
"Allo monsieur?"
"Yes?" The pair of them sitting on baited breath, would the hit man be here? He doubted it, they were looking for the proverbial needle, with an alias, in a haystack.
"I am so sorry but Mr Fogerty is not in the hotel," His heart dropped, and his friend saw the disappointment in his own face. Tommy punched the air out of frustration, and pulled his head into his hands, despairing. He was about to offer his thanks for trying, when the girl continued.
"However, his colleague Miss Quentin 'as not left ze hotel, would you like for me to transfer to 'er room monsieur?"

Trisky Manoeuvres

His eyes proper bulge out and I'm sure it's not just the coke, we're making headway here, I just know it. He's smiling at me and talking into the phone.
"No, that is okay, I will call back, merci beaucoup."
And he hangs up, just like that, I'm up on my feet now and I'm looking at him with this face that's screaming *Just get me told you big bastard!*
"He is not in the hotel just now, but his colleague, a lady called Miss Quentin, has not left her room."
And this roar just rises in me, powers up through my chest and lungs, vibrating my throat.
"Yeeeeessssssssss!" My arms, and padded hands, held aloft in the room I feel like Leeds have just won the Premiership, FA Cup, League Cup, The Champions League, The World Cup, The fucking Sunday League

title and Miss World in one go, and then Ken Bates has invited me round to kick him in the chin to celebrate. I feel *that* good just now. My hand instinctively reaches for the bag of coke in my pocket and I'm racking up a couple more lines while Cristiano's working the plan out.

"He is not in the hotel Tommy, if we can get to her before he returns we can maybe leave a telephone with her, and then follow them to Ada, we can take them all at the same time."

But I'm not having any of that, the Cuntarian has tried to kill my girl, and now some piece shit wanker has taken her hostage or something so I'm going in there, I'm gonna pull his fucking head off and then I'm gonna shit down his neck hole, and then I'm gonna clatter Ada an' all.

"Mate, once we get to her I'm not letting out my sight."

"Yes, but-"

"Honestly Beefy, there's no buts here, I'm finding my girl, then I'm keeping her at my side until this is over. We don't have to disappear, but I'm not making any trisky manoeuvres when her life's a stake."

And he looks at me, like he wants to say summat else but he knows I'm not kidding about. My coat's already on and I'm absolutely buzzing, but at the same time I know there's still a shitload more to be done before I've got her safe. We only know she's alone now, the shithead might have come back before we get there. The fucking bar was about two minutes from the hotel. We drove *past* the hotel that my girl was holed up in. Now I'm wondering how she is, what she's thinking. She can't know we're alive, I bet she's in absolute bits. I never even thought about what might have happened to her, and now I feel like a wanker for not thinking about it sooner. Cristiano's on his feet an' all now, and he's telling me we need to think about it, but what's there to think about? We get Jess back, and then we tackle the minor issue of the people trying to kill us, simple as that.

In the hotel corridor I'm powering forward chatting shit, and for once Beefy is struggling to catch me up. This coke, man, mental. The doors pass me in a blur and I'm already bounding down the stairs two at a time, then three at the bottom, the *fwish* of the automatic door allows me through onto the road, bounding further on toward the car, and I'm dancing by the passenger side door, waiting for Beefy to lumber his big bad self over here and get us on the road. My girl my girl my girl my girl my girl my girl my girl. Yeeeeaaaaaah. Gonna get my girl back! I'm fucked. My whole body just wants to go without me, it's raring man. Proper *raring* to go. Hah, raring. Good word.

In the car I'm like a coiled spring, and Beefy's talking ten to the dozen too, he thinks he's in control just now, all trying to sound calm, but I don't think he realises that he's probably as wound up as I am. My eyes bug out as I watch the city roll by and start to work on cool stuff to say when I finally grease the hit man wanker.

You Should See The Car!

He walked coolly into the lobby, taking the time to notice everything, his brain fizzed with the drugs but he was alert, that was the important thing. The bar area across the way was filling up with early evening socialisers, most seemed like patrons of the hotel, couples tucked into nooks, corners and crevices, maybe some newlyweds down in the south of France for a few days in luxury, all in their own small bubbles. In the middle of the lounge there were a variety of business-types, tapping away on computers, mobile telephones and the rest. Nobody appeared to pose a threat, in that they were far too preoccupied with what was directly before them. In the lobby there was an elderly couple, sitting on the sofa, watching the world go by, his wrinkled, liver-spotted hand sitting securely atop his old lady's. A softer man might have been moved by such tenderness at their age. Cristiano simply sized up the risk they posed. Nil to low, was the assessment.

At the desk he spoke in a low, calm tone, to the girl behind it. It was that same high pitched, nasal voice that came from her mouth when she spoke, and it seemed to match her slim frame, squared fringe at the front of a well-kept bob of dirty blonde hair, a small head with an out of proportion huge and pointed nose, flanked by small blue eyes, the girl was definitely at the back of the queue when they handed out good looks.

"Good evening monsieur." She squeaked through a well-practised smile.

"Ahh, hello madamoiselle, I would like to order some flowers to a work friend of mine who is staying at the hotel, Miss Quentin, she is pregnant and is going to be married, they are to be a surprise, could you possibly tell me the room that she is staying in, s'il vous plait?" he grinned, as sincerely as he could, his back teeth grinding gently against one another. The girl looked at him through dubious eyes, first resting upon his battered hand, and then his face, and the scratches on it, which he felt moved to acknowledge.

"I was, hit by a car," he said, almost apologetically, before adding "You should see the car!"

That did it, the young girl was laughing and snorting pig-like in his direction, in hysterics at his joke, her hand slapping the top of the desk. It wasn't *that* funny, but he appreciated the response. The ice was broken, but the girl knew the rules.

"Ahh Monsieur, I cannot give you the room number but I am happy to pass on any gifts to your friend."

A pained look struck Cristiano right in the face, like he'd stubbed his toe but was holding the initial shock deep inside.

"But it must be a surprise," he already knew her name but took a long lingering look at her name badge anyway "Khadisha, you are such a pretty girl," he lied "You have such lovely, lovely, eyes."

She blushed, her fingers twisting around each other, her embarrassed but beaming smile focussed directly on them. She was only quite young, but definitely of age.

"I bet that your boyfriend enjoys looking deep into them, I know that I would." he said, his finger rested under her chin, pulling her gaze back to his own unblinking, lady-killer eyeballs, focussed on her soul, his ears already hearing the gushing that was happening right there in her panties.

"She is in room Four Twelve monsieur," She said, quietly, checking quickly that nobody was around, before returning her attention to Cristiano. "But I did not tell you that." She smiled, shyly.

"Khadisha, you are an angel, and I shall not forget this, au revoir." He purred, pulling her hand to his lips, and kissing them gently, that blush returning to her hideous face. He kept his smiling eyes on hers as he retreated from the desk, turning slowly to walk away, his friend and colleague passing him in the lobby, having heard the whole encounter seconds earlier via telephone.

A Fleet Of Bees

My hands are sweating like fuck, and my eyes feel really twitchy, like, I can feel every movement in them, the smooth sliding of my eyeball rubbing against the inside of my eyelids. The noise of the artificial lighting in the lift is buzzing in my ears, like this fleet of bees is following me around as my own musical theme tune and they've only got one note in them, and I look up to see if there's anything I can do to jolt the bulb in right so it stops, but the panel won't move so it gets on my tits as the lift rises through the first, second, and third floor. I reach the fourth and the buzzing continues with me and I'm not sure if it even *was* the bulb making the noise, maybe it's in my own head, and I'm scanning the walls for a direction to Four Twelve, which is somewhere down on the left. I stealth down the corridor toward her room, the buzzing subsides and now the only sound I can hear is a whistling in my coked-clogged nostrils, I should have blown my nose in the lift or sniffed right up to dislodge the drugs that I'd rather did not go to waste. Fucks sake. Four Twelve comes into view and I feel sick, my girl should be in there, but then what if it's not even her? All we know is that the hit man bastard has got a bird with him. What if it's Ada? I feel for the pistol in the back of my belt, it's still there, if it's Ada in the room I'm gonna have to think fast. I tentatively knock on the door and wait. There's this little sad voice behind it, I can't make out what she's saying, so I knock again, it's quiet for a time but then the girl behind the door calls out again, telling me to leave her alone. A wave of excitement rolls into my consciousness cause I just *know* that it's my girl in there, it's defo her voice. I want to call out and tell her it's me but I daren't, I need her to open the door. I

knock again, and all I'm thinking is *Come on Jess, open the door girl, please* and I'm not giving up, I knock one more time, and there's this shuffling about in the room, she's coming, I just know it, I'm gonna see my girl. The door swings open and she's there, her eyes red from crying, her face all snottery around the nose. She's still the most beautiful girl I have ever seen. She says "I told you Rufus, to leave me alone." Before her face goes all weird, like she's seen a ghost, and I wrap my arms around her and lead her into the room. I can't say anything, I just hold on to her, and it breaks my heart 'cause she's burst into tears, her tiny frame heaving into my chest, and I want to cry myself but I can't, I need to be strong for her.
"I've missed you baby, I can't believe you're here." I say, and I have to compose myself 'cause I'm on the verge of tears, she snorts up some snot really heavy so I take an opportunity to do the same.
"I'm not gonna let you out of my sight ever again." I'm pawing at the back of her head with my battered hands, before I pull her away from me and look at her face, she's a gorgeous mess, there's no denying it, and I give her my cheeky smile, to try and bring some sort of normality to proceedings, and I say "Alright Gingerbonce?" I smile again, I totally love this girl. "Looking fit baby, for sure, I've never fancied you more."
She's staring up at me, taking it all in, her big blinky green eyes squishing the tears away and down her rosy cheeks. She doesn't know what to say, I can tell, she's just absorbing the sight of my face, taking it all in. You can't fake the look she's giving me, she totally doesn't believe I'm there, for sure, I should be dead right now.
"Takes more than a bomb to kill me." I laugh, and guide her to the bed, sitting her down whilst I lean

against the shitty long table with the kettle and telly on it and that. She's still just staring up at me, and then her eyes wander down to my wrapped hands, and I feel myself looking all sheepish.

"Knackered 'em up looking for you." I say, and she leans forward and she's holding my hands, kissing the cloth that I've got around them, and rubbing them against her cheeks, and she pulls me closer and she's squeezing me, her face against my gut, and as lovely as all of this is, we've still got the small matter of the hit man, Rufus, I would assume.

"Where's he gone?" I ask, squatting down to bring myself to her level. She looks at me some more, and shrugs gently.

"Baby, I need you to listen to me here, he's gonna come back at some point, and we need to be ready for him. Has he hurt you at all?"

She shakes her head, *no*, thank fuck.

"Is there anybody else with you other than him?"

No again, brilliant. I'm looking round the room for somewhere to maybe hide, or just sit and wait, but it's quite a small room, and people pay shitloads to stay in them, hotels man, I'm defo in the wrong business.

"I thought you were dead." She whispers.

"So did I baby, so did I, you can thank Cristiano later for saving us." I say, smiling at her.

"Rufus was going to kill Ada." She reveals, and this takes me aback a bit.

"What? What do you mean?" I ask, and I'm sure she's got it wrong, but then it does go some way to explaining what the fuck she's doing here with him.

"He did it for money, the bomb, he did it for money. I'm paying him to get her, for you, he says he'll do it for free." She explains, and that last part gets me a bit, cause why would he do it for free?

"Free?" I ask, my eyebrows raised.
"He doesn't like her, he says he's going to collect his money from her and then kill her."
This is very interesting, I think I want to meet this fella Rufus, see what he's got to say for himself, he may prove very useful indeed. So me and Jess sit and talk a bit, a combination of relief and what we've been up to since yesterday. She's all over my hands, pulling the wrapping away and she gasps in horror when she sees the mess they're in.

What's most intriguing though, is the fact that Ada's supposed to be meeting this Rufus character tomorrow, where he's supposed to be popping her in my name, but then Ada is supposed to be meeting us tomorrow an' all, where I imagine she'll be wanting to kill me in Hoxton's name. I think Rufus has told her we're dead and he wants paying, but then we've told her we're alive and we want Jess back, and she hasn't told Rufus she knows he's lying, and she hasn't got a clue where Jess is. That's what I think.

About half an hour later the room phone rings, as expected, it's the walking party blower that is the girl on reception, she's telling us that Mr Fogerty is back in the hotel and is stumbling through the lobby right now. I guide Jess into the toilet, kiss her hard on the lips, my knackered hands holding her cheeks, and I look her deep in the eyes.
"Baby, stay here, don't come out until I tell you, okay?"
She nods, but there's a fear in her eyes that I haven't seen since the day I met her, and I never thought I'd see again.
"Tom," She says, holding my arms "I love you."
"I love you too baby," I say, kissing her again "wait here."

And I close the bathroom door, leaving my beautiful angel behind it, and prepare for the mysterious Rufus to show up. I need to entice the fucker in, so I open the door a bit, maybe make him think Jess has done a runner, get him off-guard like, then I turn off the light, and I wait.

Chapter 14 - January

Youth And Young Manhood

She sat by his bed as he lay naked and unconscious, his neck bruised dark purple from where the belt had eaten into his flesh, his breathing light but noticeable by the movement in his pigeon chest. Why would he do it? She knew he was sensitive but things must have got very messy inside his head for him to go this far. She should have spotted the signs, taken some sort of action, maybe got him to open up about what was in his head, but she didn't. She just let him get on with things, and now they were here. She didn't know if he would thank her for saving his life. Maybe, maybe not.

She'd only come in here to confront him, to find out once and for all what he knew about this Will Thunder situation. Ada hadn't exactly been forthcoming with information, other than telling her that everything she needed to know was in the file, but that wasn't good enough. She'd trawled the internet for more, collected every minute detail of William Walters, and his alter ego. He was born in Manchester, nineteen seventy six, to Stephen and Miriam Walters, had two elder brothers, Warren and Wayne, the latter having succumbed to heroin addiction and then death in the late eighties. Other than that his youth and young manhood passed trauma free, he joined a local community performing group, organising and hosting open-mic comedy nights for his friends to perform in front of the residents of the council estate he was brought up on. His thirst for entertaining led him to a degree in performing arts at Edgehill University in nineteen ninety four, where he met John Thorne, his future comedy partner, but they didn't work together until a few years later. Again he began to promote and host comedy nights, in the student union, notable performers that he worked with included the controversial tubby funster Mike Rotch. He gained quite the reputation for his tenacity, he was noted as a hard worker who would stop at nothing in his quest for success. He worked for free most of the time, his love of entertaining being the driving force behind the work. The disconcerting part of his history was that there was nothing to suggest a taste for the darker things he would get up to later in life. His record was relatively blemish free, other than a few fallings out with colleagues, underlings and publicists, but that sort of thing could be found on *anybody's* record in life, they didn't necessarily need to be a part of the celebrity culture. Another but, was that despite the apparent lack of clues as to his future endeavours, it wasn't exactly a guilty pleasure of stamp collecting that he was hiding from the world, it was rape, murder, and paedophilia. The photographs spoke for themselves, it was there in black and white, the proof. No matter how clean cut he might appear to those around him, his soul was blacker than night. He harboured the darkest of fantasies, and went to great lengths to make them reality, and Liezel was determined to make him pay for it in the most spectacular of fashions. He wouldn't just die, his reputation would die with him. She'd kill him, and then she would ensure that he would never receive a hero's funeral.

    She had approached Ada for more information earlier on, but the Hungarian was side-tracked by other, more important things. She sat absent-mindedly flicking through information on her palm top computer, scarcely paying attention to the fact that Liezel was in the room. The bitch could barely even muster up the contempt she usually held for Liezel, just kept repeating that she was busy, and that all she needed to know was in the file, her mind clearly elsewhere. So then Liezel went on the hunt for Ada's lapdog, Dietmann, finding him in his room, hanging from the light fitting by his own belt. His legs jerking violently. His calm smile. She watched the poor guy swinging there, her mind ripped in two. She could either let him finish the job he started, or save his life. The guy was always so mild, almost pathetic, Ada having beaten any kind of fight out of him with her cold hearted approach to their working, or even personal relationship. Dietmann had never fully confided in Liezel, simply did as he was told, didn't seem to be allowed an opinion. Her lapdog. Ada had clearly fucked him to get him back onside, but Liezel knew the kind of guy he was, he was almost childlike in his take on life, maybe some sort of tragedy had hit him in his previous life, maybe he was just a *doos* and over sensitive. She opted to save him. Scooping up his legs in her arms, she flipped each leg over her shoulders, almost inclined to drop the guy as a sickeningly warm, and then rapidly cool sensation came over her neck. He had pissed himself. Hoping that his dead weight would be light enough to take, she watched up to the light fitting and unhooked the belt from the metal construction, before throwing him onto his bed, much in the style of a professional wrestler. Getting her breath back she placed herself beside the bed, that bitter ammonia stench rising from his pants, catching in the back of her throat so much so that she could *taste* his piss. Holding back the urge to gag she unbuttoned his pants quickly, and ripped them off with his underwear, casting them into the corner, as far away from her throat as possible. Liezel couldn't help but take a sneaky peak at his cock as she peeled off his top and threw it onto the pile, it was actually a really nice size, Ada would have had some fun with it last night, that was for sure. It was likely that he wasn't even aware of what damage the thing could do, otherwise he may have been slightly more cocksure about himself, pun entirely intended, because most girls would go crazy for a go on it. Once he was disrobed she sat and intently watched his still body, listened to the light whistle in his nostrils, and waited for a flicker behind the eyelids but there was nothing. Ada's voice called a couple of times from downstairs asking for Dietmann. She wondered what she would say when she found out what the guy had done. Knowing her as she did, she would probably tut, sigh, roll her eyes and then gaze upon the poor soul with vile contempt, before wordlessly going about whatever business she was clearly keeping from them. It was at this point that a flash of inspiration hit her. Her bright blue eyes smiled malevolently. This could work very much in Liezel's favour if she played it just right.

Mutually Beneficial Projects

She would never admit it to anybody but her brain felt overloaded. There were only so many things that she could juggle in there, and it was close to bursting. She hadn't left the room since this morning, and the walls felt closer than ever. Liezel had been in pecking at her head about the Will Thunder file but when she told her that all she needed was in there, she was more than justified. The Afrikaaner did her huffing and puffing but ultimately she left her alone. It wasn't so much that Ada couldn't handle what she was doing, she could easily manage it, but what made it more difficult was that it all relied on the right things happening at the right time. She could do with bringing Dietmann in to help out, the weasel had not done a great deal other than satisfy her needs with his very nice cock, so it made sense to her that he should be given an opportunity to satisfy her needs in the professional sense also. She wandered to the bottom of the grand staircase and called out for him. Nothing. The useless piece of shit was more than likely weeping into yesterday's underpants. She called again. This was unusual. What *should* have been happening right now was that he should been bounding downstairs, eager to please, happy that she was giving him a sniff of attention, or responsibility. All present and correct and ready to be pointed in the direction of something to do in her name. She sighed, and returned to the study, sitting down and attempting to put all her ducks in a row. She would head to Marseille tonight, check into a hotel and ready herself for her various showdowns tomorrow. Things were in great danger of becoming very messy if she could not contain, and keep every issue separate to the others. Isaac Charles had offered to clean the situation up on her behalf, as he spoke very highly of one Rufus Traynor. He suggested that maybe it was only a misunderstanding between them, and that Rufus could quite easily be persuaded to finish the job for which Ada was supposed to pay him. She had spurned his offer with the greatest of respect, and kindly requested that he allow her to continue with she felt was justified, unhindered. Isaac Charles had reluctantly agreed to her request, and also confirmed that he would undertake the favour she had asked of him with the utmost of secrecy (she had not asked this of him, as it was widely accepted that Isaac Charles did nothing of this nature unless it

was with the utmost of secrecy). She had not known a man like him. He was a huge celebrity in his country, a host of clients that ranged from multi-millionaire national-treasure entertainers down to fly-by-night flavour-of-the-hour Z-list wannabes, he guided their careers to whichever outlet he felt would suit them the most. His high end earners would be groomed to succeed, and to deal with the media in the most professional of manners. His low end, bottom-feeding clients would give exclusive interviews in tabloids and ten-a-penny lifestyle magazines, for which he would command a great one off fee, before he cut them loose and let them try to carve their own paths in life. It was not something he had divulged to her personally, it was well documented. What was not well documented however, was that he was extremely well-connected in darker avenues, he had murderers and gangsters, of which Ada was both, in his phonebook, and had the ability to make anything happen.. He scratched her back, and she was more than happy to scratch his. They were mutually useful to one another, sometimes they could work together on what they termed *mutually beneficial projects,* working on the same thing, but with separate goals. Those were usually the most lucrative times.
Lifting the phone she dialled the hotel in order to secure a reservation for the night.
"Le Radisson Blu Marseille, you are speaking wiz Khadisha, 'ow may I 'elp you?" The nose on the end of the line said, at almost a *Punch & Judy* level of nasal.
"Yes, allo, I would like to make a reservation for a double room for tonight s'il vous plait."

The Very Definition Of The Term *Loser*

He was woken by the soothing voice, and the warm sensation of a hand stroking his forehead. His neck was sore, and his throat was dry.
"Ahh, Dietmann, welcome back to the world," the voice said, quiet and calm "it's a good job one of us cares enough for your life."
His eyes opened, the blurred figure of Liezel hovered in the corner of his vision, coming into focus, smiling sadly at his plight.
"Liezel? What? Why?" He croaked, the pain of the effort almost too much.
"You're more use to the world alive than dead you silly boy, what were you thinking?" She spoke frankly.
"I, Ada, she is..." He trailed off, hushed by Liezel, seeing the hurt in his face. She brought a glass of water from the bedside table to his face, his thin lips curling around the edge, slurping droplets into his throat, cooling the sore.
"You did this because of *her?* Dietmann, she is not worth the effort, you are better than that."
Was he though? He could not even kill himself properly, and now he was being pitied by Liezel, speaking to him in a way that she had never before, like he was a human. He felt like the very definition of the term *Loser.*
"No, Liezel, I love her, she hates me." He whimpered, unaware of the grimace that he drew from the Afrikaaner, but she was undeterred.
"She is unworthy of your love, Ada is a woman who will only ever look out for herself, she fucked you because you began to push back at her, she is a selfish wicked bitch and-"

"Do not say those things of her, she is a beautiful angel, she taught me what sex should be." He interrupted, in the high pitched whine of a child, but he did not care, Liezel was saying bad things about his beloved, he had to defend her. She rolled her eyes at him, and stood up beside the bed, her face taking on a stonier form, she was changing tack.

"Okay, I'm sorry to do this to you, but you need to be shown." She said, and left the room, the clomping of her heels against the heavy wooden flooring of the hallway quietening. Dietmann tried to pull himself up on his elbows to get a drink of water, but the effort was just too much at that moment, he dropped limply back onto the bed, close to tears. How could Liezel say those things? Ada had a lot on her mind, she had the responsibility of the organisation, he saw that now, she was not a bad person, she was beautiful and she was misunderstood. He lay, staring at the ceiling, until the sound of Liezel returning stirred him from his thoughts. The door swung open to reveal not only Liezel, but also Ada, his eyes lit up, she had come to see him.

"Dietmann, what have you done?" Asked Ada, a flicker of concern in her eyes.

"I, I, thought you did not care for me." He whispered, on the verge of tears, Ada said nothing, her stare burned into him, eating at his heart, his brain, his soul. Something was ticking over in that beautiful brain of hers. The silence was deafening, Liezel stood to one side, watching the exchange unfold. Dietmann faltered under the scrutinous stare of Ada, he could not help but think that she had definitely *not* come to return his love for her. The cogs visibly ticked in her face. She looked to Liezel briefly and wordlessly, and then back to Dietmann, striding firmly toward his bed, her face on the verge of saying something. His eyebrows raised involuntarily in anticipation. Ada perched her divine buttocks on the bedside table, and leant in to him.

"We fucked, that is all," she spat "you are being pathetic, grow a pair of balls for God's sake. It is embarrassing. I had a task for you but you have fucked up yet again, and now I shall be forced to do it myself, *again.* I am going to travel to Marseille for business. Maybe when I return tomorrow you will have finished the job. And you..." She turned to Liezel "I shall deal with you also when I return. Goodbye Dietmann."

She had broken his heart once, and when he had thought he was pain free, Liezel resurrected him so that Ada could break it all over again. What did these people want from him? Was it not enough that they treated him like scum? Evidently not.

As Ada slammed the door of the room upon her exit, Liezel turn her attention to Dietmann.

"I am sorry that I had to do that to you, but you must see what a selfish woman she is, open your eyes for God's sake, she's unworthy of your affection."

He didn't say a word, he just lay on his back, watching the ceiling behind the mounting blur of tears, and swallowing the urge to break down.

Chapter 15 - January

The Table-Turning Bastard

Foaming wet specks splashed back against his boots and jeans as the gushing vomit heaved from his mouth, the tangy stinging sensation of it coming through his nose, and dripping from the tip, onto the floor as he hunched over on the bed. The continental beer was definitely stronger than he was used to, and he hadn't done a great deal of drinking over the last couple of years, so it had hit him hard. What hit him harder was the appearance of this ghost. A guy he was supposed to have killed. A guy he thought he *had* killed. A guy he had told he Ada he had killed, but had quite evidently *not* killed, because he had been standing in front of him holding a gun with a scabby injured hand, directing him to take a seat on the bed. Rufus let out a barely concealed drunken snigger when the bloke called him *Silly Bollocks*, but followed his direction compliantly, and sat down, maybe a little too quickly because the room rocked from side to side, as if he were on some booze cruise ferry anchored in the middle of the North Sea. That was the point that the uncontrollable stream of vomit poured from his face, foaming up and soaking into the carpet, leaving a dry looking brown mush of half ingested lager froth to rest on the upholstery, the kind of folded-dough resembling froth found around the end of industrial shit pipes into some unsuspecting river. His captor, Tom, exclaimed a frustrated and disgusted "For fuck's sake!" And felt moved to rush forward to shove Rufus violently from the bed and onto his knees. His head hung heavy, rocking back and forth, strings of thick spittle joining his lip to the carpet, still he heaved the vomit onto the carpet, only now he was caked in it too. He was almost amused to note that he was struggling to care less, there wasn't a great deal he could do to help the situation, be it the sick all over his clothes, or the table-turning bastard pointing the gun in his direction. The bloke was talking to him, and the words seemed to enter his ears but the bouncer on the door of his eardrums were turning them away, maybe for wearing trainers. He chuckled to himself at the daft analogy, and raised his eyes unsteadily to meet those of his captor.

"You're supposed to be dead." He laughed, shaking his head in what he hoped was disbelief.

"Yeah, and you fucked it up pal, but what can you do eh?" Tom replied, moving to lean against the ledge of the window, and pull out a mobile phone, his guard dropped somewhat since his hostage had proved to be far less of a threat than he had anticipated. Rufus coughed up some foul tasting phlegm and sick from his throat, and spat it into the steadily diminishing froth by his knees. Tom spoke into his phone.

"Alright mate? Yeah, it's fine, he's pissed as fuck, nowt doing, yeah, four twelve, fetch your big nosed bird if you want," he waited for a response, and then laughed loudly into the phone "am just pulling your whistle mate, get yourself upstairs."

Tom grinned affectionately as he clicked the phone off, and turned back to Rufus, who had definitely felt better. He could smell the pungent shit around his knees, the air cooled the slime around his face and it began to feel uncomfortable, wiping it away with the sleeve of his coat he tried to pull himself back up onto the bed, drawing a cautious stance from Tom.

"Help me up?" He asked, between heavy groaning breaths, holding a hopeful hand out to his captor, who spurned the request with a look of revulsion.

Ryan Bracha   Tomorrow's Chip Paper

"Nah, you're alright pal." He said, moving warily toward the long table above Rufus' head, leaning over the vomit on the floor, and pulling the kettle from its perch.

"Baby?" He called out to what seemed to be nobody in particular, until the bathroom door creaked open slowly behind Rufus, his head turning labouredly to investigate the newcomer. The girl. His heart dropped, she had screwed him over. She might have known they were alive all this time. In Carcassonnes when he was calling Ada, was she phoning her back-up? Keeping them in the loop all long? He dropped his head in defeat, sobering thoughts firing into his brain like darts. They had done a number on him, and he may well have taken his last drink of too-strong continental lager, it seemed like a shame that he'd thrown it right back up. The girl, Jess, she didn't give an impression of being bolshy or cocky like her fella. She seemed sheepish, and scared, her fingers nervously stroking the front of her belly, caring for her unborn baby through the clothes, skin, and flesh. At least she hadn't made *that* up. That would be low. His features took on a sadder tone as he watched her step over the mess he'd made, and take the kettle from her fella, smiling at him with a look that Rufus could never even dream of eliciting from her.

"Fill us that up please baby." He said, returning her smile. She sauntered back into the bathroom to do as she was asked, all the while Rufus felt rough as hell, the out-of-body pissed dizziness still there but subsiding slightly with every chunk of reality that smacked him in the face. With a slow blink he acknowledged a heavy knock at the door, and dragged himself from the bed, it must have been room service. He didn't remember ordering anything, if he did then he wasn't hungry anymore anyway. He step-wobble-stepped only once, before he was pulled back by a force he had not expected, he was alone was he not? The ceiling spun as it looked down on him, the face of somebody forced its way into his vision. Tom. *Oh fuck* he remembered, he was definitely not alone. The door was opened by his captor, and into the room stepped the biggest man he had ever seen. Then he recalled who it was. The other failed attempt at murder. The guy was gazing upon him with loathing and anger. Drawing himself further onto the bed he balled up and stared up at the giant, terror-stricken.

"He's hammered mate," said Tom to his partner, "gonna fill him with coffee and see if we can't get any sense out of him."

Sunday Arse

This fella is fucked, man. He is defo *not* what I was expecting when I finally got to meet him. For sure, he's covered in sick and he fucking stinks, if this is who Ada sent to kill us then she was scraping the bottom of the mercenary barrel, at least that's what I'm reckoning based on first impressions. You never know, he might be an ice-cold cap-poppin' motherfuckin' *machine* in real life, but just now, well, he just seems to be an utter shambles. How he was planning to do Ada on behalf of Jess is anybody's guess. I've got big designs on finding out like. It was hilarious when Beefy came in and the fella absolutely shat it, curled up in a ball, whimpering like he thinks Beefy's gonna rip him apart. I'm looking at Cristiano, and you've got to give him his dues, he knows how to look mean when he wants to. It's not just his size, for sure, he does this silent killer stare, you'd think you were dead before you were actually dead if he gave it to you. I shake my head at him slightly, like, *not just now, pal,* and he gets my drift, and goes over to Jess, pulls her into his chest and his arms just swallow her up. He loves her almost as much as I do, no, that's not possible, but you get what I'm saying, he fucking loves her. Nobody will ever love her as much as I do.

    The kettle's boiled and I hand a coffee to this Rufus cat, saying to get it down him, we've got a lot to talk about and I need him sober. He's starting to catch on that we're not fucking about here, and does as I ask. I'm not being too much of a cunt with him like, I mean, he *has* kept Jess safe, and for sure, I appreciate that much, and that's why I'm prepared to give him a chance at redemption from trying to kill us all. Whether that comes in the form of information, or if he actually physically puts the bullet in Ada's face, that remains to be seen, but he definitely owes us at least one. He's clumsily blowing at the surface of the coffee, and taking baby sips, and we're all three of us watching him now, but he's still a bit pissed to be aware of it, like the only thing he can concentrate on is his coffee. My focus shifts to Jess, and she smiles at me. That smile I totally thought I was never gonna see again. I beckon her over and she comes and slides her arm behind my back, snuggling her head into me. My hand slides to her arse and gives it a squeeze, the best arse ever. I could eat my dinner straight off it, it's pristine. If it were an actual eating surface it would be that best china that you only get out for Christmas, or other special occasions, it's a Sunday Arse. I love it. Sunday Arse, that's what she's got. I digress. Rufus finishes his coffee, and I pour him another from the still hot kettle, noting that we only had four of those little sachets, I dunno if that's gonna be enough, especially when two of the fuckers are decaf. I finger the teabags, tallying them up, we've got four of those an' all, and I concede that it'll probably do, the poor cunt's bladder'll be bursting, and then we'll get nowt but piss out of him. Me, Jess and Cristiano are still all watching him and each other, nobody's saying a word, we're just waiting for him to come round. Jess is curled into me, Beefy's at the other side of the room, and Rufus is sitting on the bed, cutting a pretty pathetic figure, slurping away at the little white cup. The girl at the hotel back in Roda De Isabena had it pretty spot on, he's got a blonde shaggy indie-boy haircut that I reckon would usually look pretty cool but it's caked in sick and sweat just now. I'm happy with knowing I'm into women enough to say that yeah, he's not a bad looking bloke, apart from the scar, looks like he came a cropper at some point in his life, but now's not the time to be asking. There are more pressing issues than who else he might have annoyed at one time or another. The second cup of coffee goes down a bit quicker and I decide to test the water.

"So, Mr Killer, what's your story?" I ask him, figuring it's a broad enough question to get the ball rolling. He looks up at me with bloodshot eyes, and does a proper belly burp, it was a beast an' all, he'll be tasting that fucker for weeks. I stifle a laugh though cause we're playing serious, I'm not gonna let this cunt know that I proper love burps. He stays quiet though, all sullen and that, I reckon he's got a monk on, but I'm not about to start babying him up, he can man the fuck up.

"You listening to me or what?" I ask, bringing my face, and more importantly the gun, into his line of sight.

"Been following you pair for months, years even, Ada's been paying me to just follow you, I dunno why, I didn't ask." He says, and he's still a bit out of it but defo more intelligible.

"How did she find us?" I ask, I already know what he's gonna say.
"I dunno, I didn't ask." Surprise, surprise. I coulda won myself a fiver.
"So who are you then? How did you find yourself in our little conflict?" I can see we're getting nowhere on the Ada front, so I change direction.
"I kill people. For money." No shit, Sherlock.
"You a Manc? You sound like a Manc." I ask and he cracks out laughing, not the response I wanted.
"Yeah well, you sound like Billy fuckin' Casper." Cristiano laughs quietly through his nose, shaking his head with this incredulous look on his chops, Rufus glances toward him but his eyes divert back to me and the gun. I try to get proceeding back on track.
"Look, the only reason you're alive is 'cause you kept my girl safe, despite what the Cuntarian paid you to do, and that says to me we might all be able to get along if we clear some shit up, so you wanna behave yourself yeah?"
And I leave the ball in his court, he sighs, like the penny drops, and he looks at me.
"Okay, she's been paying me to watch you, follow you, y'know? I dunno how she found you, or why she had me chasing you round fuckin' Europe for so long, then suddenly, I dunno why, she says she wants you dead, I try to make you dead, didn't think it'd turn into this though did I? It's fucked up," then he looks off, all morose "I fucked up."
"Don't beat yourself up pal, bigger badder cunts than you have tried and failed." I laugh, I think I'd quite like the bloke, like, if we weren't living in this world where people try to kill people all the time, and we worked together at B & Q or summat, we'd probably get on. We don't though, we live in a world where he got paid to blow us up, so I need to keep it together.

"You told Jess you'd kill Ada for free, what's that all about?" I ask, and his answer will go a long way to helping me figure out exactly what we've got in our arsenal against the Cuntarian's. He shakes his head, this kind of frowning look, like he's irritated just thinking about it.
"She's a bitch mate, talks to me like shit, calls me up at all hours making demands, and it's fucking relentless, *all the time,* do this, do that, meet me at quarter past eleven," *Quarter past eleven?* "I've had enough of her, I just want to get my money, and fuck the bitch off for good." Bless him, all he wants is the money he's not owed, for not killing us.
"The thing is Rufus, she knows we're alive, we've spoken to her, and the only reason we're here is because she set the meeting up, I hate to burst your bubble, but I don't think she's got any intention of giving you your money, I *do* think she's got big plans to wipe you, me, Jess and Beefy off the face of the Earth, and I'm not gonna let that happen, so I suppose you've got a decision to make," and I try to say it as plain as I can, "you sober up and help us do it, or I can stick my Mr Bullet into your Mr Brain, and we can say no more about it."

Running On Fumes

I still feel like I'm in a dream. My Tom, *alive.* Nothing feels real. All of the stuff that's happened in the last day or so, my mind is struggling to keep up. I'm running on fumes, and I don't know if or when I'm going to get a chance to refuel. I have my Tom back, and I don't ever want anything to take him away again, but he's in that place, in his head, even if I try to talk him out of it he'll have some way of justifying it to me, and if he has any way of justifying it then he'll not stop. He'll see this through to the end and I'm so *scared* that I'll lose him again. I know there's Cristiano here helping, like before, and I think Rufus will keep up his end of the deal, so they kind of outnumber Ada. Like Tom says, if she had more firepower at her disposal then she wouldn't have hired Rufus in the first place. But still, it doesn't matter how much back-up, and strength in numbers that they have, soldiers die. It only takes one bullet. I can't lose him again. I hope I never ever have to feel like I have done this last day ever again. The restaurant in Barcelona feels like so long ago. It just seems like since then, the best day I've ever had, that life, nature, higher forces, whatever, has conspired to take everything away. How can I feel positive about what they're going to do? They're planning to walk into the mouth of Hell and then come out of the other side unscathed, and they're talking about it like they'll be taking candy from a baby. Tom and Cristiano *know* how dangerous Ada is. They know she'd just easily cut their throats as she could scowl at them, she could do that and not think twice. I just *wish* I could rest easily. Tom can sense my unease, and squeezes my shoulder, winking at me when I look up at him, and I just melt. That smile. It's so disarming. Rufus is talking now, and I don't know how to feel about him anymore. Tom is alive, the future that I thought was gone is back. Now technically Rufus has done nothing wrong, but I'm struggling to let him off the hook. I can't just become friends with a man who would take money to kill me. We've suddenly become the highest bidders in a tug of war on who gets killed, what if he's got Ada at his mercy, like he did me, and she makes an offer that's better than ours? I can't help but have these thoughts, I can't trust him. I know Tom is well aware of what he'll be capable of, and he'll watch Rufus like a hawk, but I'm just not as easy with this stuff as him. They're all talking and I'm listening.

"She says to meet her at," says Rufus, and then he swallows, like he's got real trouble saying "eleven fifteen, tomorrow, I'm supposed to wait for her call to find out where."

"That's it? That's all she's said?" Tom asks, getting everything clear.

"Yeah, fucking bitch, I asked if she'd make it half past but she said no just to fuck me off." Rufus seems really angry over the time, and I remember all the times he kept looking at the clock before we did anything, I think he's got issues.

"What is your problem with a quarter past eleven?" Cristiano asks, like he knows what we're all thinking. Rufus is frowning, still drunk, trying to find the words, and is frustrated that he can't.

"I, I like to do things at half past." He says, and Tom bursts out laughing, drawing a hurt look from Rufus. "You like to do things at half past?" He laughs, and Rufus must be wishing he hadn't said anything, his cheeks suddenly roll up like he's going to throw up again, and we all step back to get out of the potential splash back. Tom looks to me, and it's a face I know, it's his *apologising in advance* look, he's going to do something that he knows I won't like. It's never anything I can stop, he's already decided he's going to do it, but he wants me to forgive him in advance. Then it happens, he pulls out a bag of cocaine from his pocket, and we're looking at each other, having a conversation with our eyes. I'm asking him why, but he's just saying sorry. He looks at Rufus as he chops some of it out onto the table top.

"Having trouble getting sense outta you pal, get some of this up your whistle, should sort you right out." He says, a conspiring look on his face, Cristiano steps forward too, like he's expecting a go. Tom does enough for all three of them, and takes his go first, then he looks at me sheepishly, mouthing *sorry* as he heads my way and wraps his arms around me. He needs to stop doing it soon. We have a baby coming. But I can't say anything, we're in the middle of something nasty, and I thought he was dead, I can't find it in my heart to be angry, I'm too glad to have him back. Cristiano does his line, and then Rufus looks at all of us in surprise, edging closer to the drugs but at the same time he's unsure if it's some sort of joke. Tom picks up on this, and turns to him. "Fill your boots." He says, and Rufus moves toward Cristiano who's passing him a rolled up banknote, and he eagerly snorts the cocaine, his head juts to the ceiling, and he's holding his breath, his glazed eyes staring upward.

"That's the stuff." He says, finally, and his demeanour almost instantly takes on a new form. He seems slightly more with it. I've seen it in Tom before, when he's drunk he uses that stuff. He seems to speak with more clarity of mind, but I know once he does he'll think he can drink a lot more, and then he needs more drugs to clear his thoughts, and eventually they've both conspired to make him a jibbering mess. I hope he knows what he's doing. Rufus goes quiet, like he's thinking of something, and then his eyes dart between Cristiano, Tom, and I, not in any order, but it looks like he's talking to all of us.

"Okay, right, I have this thing, where I have to do everything at half past, or on the hour, it just helps me to plan, and remember stuff. I know it sounds stupid but it's my thing right? Not exactly OCD but it's kinda like the same thing, but it's not," then he pauses, and takes a breath "so you're saying she knows you're alive? That's pretty shitty, she's obviously planning to do somethin', but what? She never mentioned that she knew that when I spoke to her, when's she wanna meet you?" I don't know who he's asking the question to, but I'm saying nothing. I feel so uncomfortable with everything. Tom and Cristiano have obviously been doing drugs all day, and now they've got Rufus in on the act. I don't know how much longer I'm going to be able to contain myself. I'm torn between this relief, joy, and frustration. I wish they'd just all take a breath and decide to walk away. If Ada's coming for us we could cross that bridge when we got to it.

"She has not said when she wants to meet us, it makes no difference, I will rip her limb from limb any time that she wants." Growls Cristiano, and I know he's not joking.

"Like Beefy says, we don't know what's happening, she's got our number, and we're waiting for her call." Tom says, and Rufus absorbs the information.

"Lucky fuckers, she's never off the phone to me." It's as if Ada's ears are burning, because Rufus' phone bursts into life, and it's that song again. I'm so *sick* of that song by now. Okay, there's a bloody bad moon rising! Give it a rest! Rufus looks to his phone, and then the others, aware that we're all still far from friends, Tom gives him the go ahead, and we're waiting with baited breath.

"Ladyboss what can I do you for?" He says confidently into the phone, then listens, rolling his eyes. He's making stupid faces at her and Tom is close to pissing himself, I can tell he's itching to say or shout something but I'm praying that he doesn't. Rufus gives the verbal nods, some *uh-huh*, and *yep*, and *okay*, and then his face changes, some revelation is filtering into his fuzzy mind, his eyes bulge out almost to the point of popping out from his skull, and he starts waving his free arm around, his hand holding an invisible pen. I pull an eye brow pencil from my bag, and his overzealous hand rips it from my grasp, and he's up, in front of the mirror, scrawling something down. I want to see what he's writing but at the same time I'm thinking *That's my eyebrow pencil you're ruining there,* and I don't know when I might get a chance to buy another. Then he pulls away from the mirror to reveal his handiwork. Me, Tom, and Cristiano all lean in to see what he's written, and I do an involuntary gasp as it sinks in. *She's in this hotel.*

Chapter 16 - February

Deaf Ears

The echo of the knocking at the door rattled through the hallway and up the stairs, reverberating around the landing, finding itself stumped at her bedroom door, behind which she lay in bed for the eighth day in succession. She wasn't listening anyway. If she *were* listening she might have heard her sister Gail's voice, calling out with her pink lips poking through the letterbox.

"Claire? Are you in?" She called out to deaf ears. "It's not healthy, you in here all the time, you need to get out! Take your mind off it!" The empty rooms ate and swallowed her words before they reached the deaf ears. Even if they did reach them they wouldn't have paid attention. The words were useless. If they had arrived in the form of an e-mail, or text message, or letter through the door, they would have been just as ineffective. They would have been met with blind eyes.

"I'll take you shopping or something! We're worried about you! Mum's been in bits! Claire! Please!" They had been through the same pantomime for over a week, and every day had yielded the same results. Gail would call round to shout through the letter box, in whole-hearted attempts to draw her sister from her self-imposed exile from the world. Claire would continue to take solace in her bedroom, leaving only to feed herself on rapidly diminishing rations from the kitchen. The room smelled bad, and she smelled worse. Occasionally she heard the knocks at the door, but ignored them. Other times they went unnoticed and she remained in her own thoughts. Her mobile had died days ago, and she had no inclination to charge it up. It started last week, when the news people called her all the time, to get a quote, a sound bite to utilise as her opinion on the matter, to ask her why she had cast such aspersions over his character. People had spat at her in the street, called her a whore. She was the most used name on Twitter, and aside from a few token messages of support from charities and groups, she had been universally vilified for her accusations. What was the point? She didn't know anymore. She wanted him to pay for his crime but his team of lawyers cost more than hers, and they hung her out to dry. She didn't want to make a penny from this, her payment for being in the public domain would have been his incarceration. Giles Baker had told her, get into the magazines, the papers, on television, tell her side of the story. The money she might earn could pay for the mounting legal fees. But in the eyes of *his* adoring fans, she was using the whole thing as a platform to go on to bigger and greater things. It wasn't. Claire wasn't like that. She'd had a happy life before. She'd had a job that she actually enjoyed doing, it could almost have been viewed as a possible career, something to look forward to, that next step on the ladder. There was also James. Things were going great, no pressure, just enjoying each other's company. That was ruined too. To give him his dues he was man enough to do it face to face, but it wasn't a great consolation when he was sitting her down, telling her that he couldn't be involved with her anymore, not after *this*. It broke her heart. Was it that he didn't believe her either? Or was he simply taking himself out of her increasingly complicated equation? She didn't want him to end it. Claire had never felt as alone as she did when he did. "You don't need me on top of everything else." He had said. But she *did.* She wanted to grab him, the lapels of his jacket, and pull him to her and scream "I do! I do need you, I need your support, I need you to help me through this!" But she didn't. She just looked at her lap, and wept as he walked out of the café and her life. After that she came home, cried herself to sleep, and then never left the house. She had told Gail to leave her alone, to let her do this her own way, but Gail's tendency toward fulfilling sisterly requirements meant that this request would be ignored, she would appear daily, and her efforts would be spurned, as they had been today, and she turned sadly and walked back down the garden path, looking up to the bedroom window to look for signs of life. Nothing. Then she would climb back into her car and drove home, sobbing out of impotent frustration.

  Claire had cried herself dry by now, she had no more left to give, and as she lay in almost total darkness, aside from a thin sword of light that cut across her arms from the gap in the curtains, she felt inclined to sit up. Her mouth tasted like shit. She could smell the scum and gunk that had been building up between her legs, a tangy dirty stench. When she disturbed the bed sheets they threw up a light, sweaty, almost vinegar-like aroma that she was distressed to discover that she didn't find entirely unpleasant. She needed to piss. The bathroom seemed so far away, Claire had got used to going nowhere, doing nothing, speaking to nobody. A stronger person might have dealt with it better than she, but that was them, not her. She took her naked self to the toilet, her stubbled legs rubbing against one another as she sat, zombie-like, watching the door of the bathroom, letting the piss fall from her stinking vagina, turning to discover that she had used the last of the toilet tissue. It was the last straw. She needed to do something. She needed to clean herself up. She wasn't ready to face the world, not yet, but she had to do something. She had been festering in her own shit for too long, while *he* was out there, laughing it up, telling jokes at her expense. He thought it was over and that he had got away with it.

Claire returned to the bedroom, and reached for the television remote, crackling the set into life, that whistling sound that had irritated her before everything, the whistle that would persist unless she waggled the scart plug, she had no energy to mess around with it today. The whistle was the least of her worries. Because *he* was there. His fat fucking face. His lecherous grin. His awful Northern voice. It flooded back into her head. His foul breath, huffing the smell of Guinness onto her cheek as he pushed his thing into her, telling her how much she wanted it. She wouldn't be here if she didn't want it. She had only gone to get an autograph for James. She hadn't gone for *that.* But he wouldn't take no for an answer, and as he raped her he took her tears for something else, he thought her silence was as good as compliance. It wasn't. It was horrible. And now he was sitting onscreen, opposite Johnny Lightning for some reason, telling stupid offensive jokes to a cheering audience. This couldn't happen. The justice system had failed her, the media had failed her, James had failed her. She had failed herself. But where the horse had bolted on all other fronts, she could make amends for herself. She could make a stand and force him to pay. She didn't know *how,* but she could, and she would. The fat rapist would pay the piper, and Claire was determined that it would be she that made it happen.

The Super Duper Mr Cooper

"Are you sure there's nothing else you can give us?" Wayne Cooper asked into the telephone, a hint of desperation around his words. The show was in danger of petering out into nothing. There was only so much mileage they could get from Alex Green standing in front of the same crowds, the same house, the same flashing blue lights. The viewing figures were on the wane, as the audience had started to grow tired of Gareth Bennington-Lane's smug shit eating face and moved on to the other channels. Sky had enlisted the visual treat that was Penny Reece, her wholesome yet thoroughly fuckable beauty emanating with each return from the field to the studio. It was a coup for them, no doubt about that. He had worked with her a couple of years ago on the late night music channels, before he moved onto bigger and better things, and now Penny Reece's star was on the rise. She was likeable, unassuming, intelligent, humble, and above all, stunning. Wayne Cooper had wasted his fair share of spunk in her honour, but he would never tell her. If he thought she might respond in the way he would hope then maybe he'd have had a go, but he'd seen better men try and fail, and was resigned to keeping all relations between them in his own head, no matter how deliciously filthy they were up there.
The voice on the other end of the line sighed.
"Wayne, you know as much as I do, I promise you." It said, hopefully.
"In that case, you'll know that that's utter bollocks mate, you're holding out on me, I *know* you are." He exclaimed, but deep down he knew that this was as far as it was going, his posturing was just a last roll of the dice.

"I can't give you anything else, I'm sorry, you start broadcasting anything else I could tell you and it'll get Will Thunder killed, I can't have that." His contact said, hoping that Wayne would drop it. No such luck.
"That's what the public *want,* there's no bigger devil than a paedo, give them what they want."
"I can't do that. I didn't sign up for eye-for-an-eye bullshit, he needs to be dealt with properly, and me telling you sensitive information about the investigation won't help that to happen, go back to dredging up stories of kids he wronged at school yeah? Or maybe throw some more pie charts about what Facebook wants in there, I've got nothing else for you."
"Thanks Phil, no really, seriously, thanks a fucking bunch."
"Nice."
"Please, gimme something."
"No can do Wayne, I'll call you if there's anything else I can offer, but for now you're on your own."
As resignation beat its way into his body, he muttered his thanks and hung up the phone, threw it across the room and roared in frustration at the lack of help that his connection could offer. *Fuck Will Thunder* he thought, the prick was pretty much dead already, what difference did it make if the police leaked the whole thing to the media? None, no difference, that's what. Wayne collected the phone from the other side of the room with retrospective regret, swiping around under the low sofa for the missing battery. As much as he hated it, he needed the phone. He still had calls to make. On his knees, face pressed firm against the floor looking desperately for the tell-tale silhouette of the battery beneath the sofa he heard the door to his office opening with a light knock. Sophie, the intern,

clipboard in hand, a curious smile on her face. Wayne stood quickly, straightening his clothes.

"Sophie, what can I do for you?" He asked, somewhat breathlessly from the effort.

"There's a call for you, line three," she smiled, her eye suddenly caught by the floor by her feet, then pointed to it, "is that what you were looking for?"

The battery, it had skittered almost to the opposite side of the room, he grinned in a *silly me* grin, mock-rolling his eyes, and thanked her before stooping to collect the battery from her feet, taking in a deep smell of her perfume, his eyes only inches from every curve of her hot little body as he rose to become face to face with her, that shagger's glint back in her eye.

"I'd lose my head if it wasn't screwed on." He said, coolly, his free hand *so, so close* to gripping onto her hip, pulling her toward him and holding on to her arse as he planted his tongue into her mouth. A silence grew between them as he looked into her eyes, the conversation that seemed to simply be a mutual dare to make a move. Wayne's head slowly, and instinctively moved toward her, unblinking, he wanted her *so badly,* and he could sense that she wanted him.

"Not here," she smiled, ducking out of his eye line, and waltzing flirtatiously out of the room, that gorgeous arse wiggling in her suit skirt inciting the biggest erection he'd ever had, she turned her head as she walked away, "Remember you have a call on line three." She said, turning the corner and out of sight. He was *definitely* going to fuck that girl.

"Wayne Cooper." He spoke into the receiver, his mind still elsewhere, between the divine legs of Sophie the intern, his tongue lapping away at her cunt as she ground it into his mouth. Drinking from the furry cup.

Ryan Bracha   Tomorrow's Chip Paper

"Mr Wayne Cooper. The Super Duper Mr Cooper, just the man." A voice spoke, it was not a voice that was familiar to him. He frowned.
"And who's this?" He asked impatiently.
"Your mystery benefactor." What the hell was this? The voice on the end of the line had a slight echo, like it was being recorded, was it a wind up?
"Look, I don't have time to-" He started, only to be interrupted.
"You do, pal, you really do have time for what I've got for you, it's a proper revelation. Honestly, for sure, in ten years do you really wanna be the poor cunt that turned the Beatles down?"
For the next half an hour the voice spoke, and Wayne listened. The voice knew things. The voice had evidence to back it up. The voice would send an e-mail to him with physical proof. The voice had just given him the exclusive information he craved. The voice told him that he could expect more later, but for now he had enough to be going on with. Wayne could not agree more. This was explosive stuff. There was still that doubt that he was being stitched up, but that was expelled as quickly as it had arrived. The pop-up in the corner of his computer screen told him he had mail. It had come from mrrobertknocker@live.co.uk, with the subject that simply read *Don't Reject The Beatles.* It was from the voice, definitely. He scanned the text, opened the attachments, saw what the voice had told him in physical form. He shook quite violently out of excitement as he locked his PC, he needed air. This was massive. Wayne Cooper pounded open the fire exit onto the roof of the building, taking in an enormous gulp of oxygen, and then he threw his lunch up all over the pebbled floor.

A Stoner's Best Friend

He knew her name. *He* knew *her* name. Liezel. It was beautiful. It suited her. Of course it did, she was effortlessly cool, everything she did suited her. Her attitude suited her outfit which suited her body which suited her name. Liezel. He said it out loud but it was swallowed by the crowd. He called it again, louder this time, but again it was drowned in sound. His hands came to his mouth, creating a home-made loud speaker.

"LIEZEL! LIEZEL!" He yelled, but he couldn't even hear himself, how could *she* be expected to hear him? The crowd. He wished it would collectively fuck off back to where it had come from. A man beside him called out that Will Thunder could die in a pool of his own blood. Several people cheered and then echoed the sentiment in their own equally violent ways, their arms raised to jostle him, pushing against his cheeks. This was no place for a stoner. He was becoming more claustrophobic with every chant from the throng. Paranoia built in him that they were rifling through his bag, stealing his Prawn Skips, helping themselves to his spliffs. He had to get out of it. He wanted the serenity of Hyde Park again. He had found himself a great vantage point overnight, close to the front, when they all did as predicted and went home, only to return by morning, violently edge him out of his place at the front, and start again, calling for the head of Will Thunder. He didn't care about what happened to him anymore, he was no longer a factor in the grand scheme, he was the catalyst in bringing Liezel into Jake's cognizance, but he was surplus to requirements now. Jake needed to see her. He made the decision to get out of the crowd again until later, his lungs were filling with the stench of hypocrisy,

and he wanted to replace that stench with the wonderful taste of weed, and around here there were no places that he could shield himself from the ever present noses of the police. Hyde Park it was.
He placed his battered bag on the ground by the tree, and joined it, reaching into the back section and pulling out his rolling box. Noting that there were about fifteen left, he placed a spliff between his lips and crackled the end into life with his clipper lighter. *A stoner's best friend* he thought, they were useful, the flint stick was ever so useful for poking down the tobacco and weed, packing it in tight, and they were very reliable when it came to creating fire. He took a slow, calculated draw on the joint, pulling the delicious smoke into his lungs, holding it in until it burned, until his eyes and face felt hot, the same sensation as when he tried to squeeze a particularly big shit out. As he released the almost non-existent smoke from his lungs he thought about her again. Liezel. He almost shit a brick when they released that information. How did they know? Liezel Esterhuizen. Twenty four. From Pretoria in South Africa. Missing, presumed dead for over a year, now she had resurfaced into the most spectacular of fashions. They had shown a picture of her, smiling with her two brothers, at some South African family get together. There was no disputing that it was her. It was her eyes. Although the entire media network was now running the story with that same picture they'd revealed this exclusive information on *Politickle My Funny Bone,* citing the source as *an insider.* It became quickly evident that the "insider" was not police-based, as the detectives, and uniformed officers fannied around like headless chickens, pulling Alex Green off the telly away from the cameras, pointing at him, at the cameras, and at the house. One detective

was barking into his phone, clearly angry with somebody. Jake thought that maybe this wasn't just news to the public, it was news to the police too, and they weren't overly fond of it happening like it was. He didn't care though, he knew her name now. He spent hours trawling the news websites on his phone, desperately scratching about for fresh information about her, any more pictures than just that one they'd been showing. Missing, presumed dead. They didn't say where she'd been or why, just that she'd shown up to commit a heinous crime against a man who had committed even more heinous crimes. They speculated that she might be the wrapped up body that had been shown getting dragged out of Will Thunder's house by Stew Taylor, and that maybe she had got away and had come back for revenge. But then how would she have so much information about Will Thunder? Would she have not simply approached the police? Where would she get the huge dossier on Will Thunder? All questions that Jake's fuzzy brain struggled to consider, and eventually answers would come, they always did. After the revelation the crowd chanted her name, like she was a superhero in some Hollywood film. Jake imagined that when it was all done that she would open the front door to the house, stand at the top of the steps, the crowd would stand in open mouthed awe and silence, witnessing the mythical Liezel Esterhuizen in person. After a short time Jake would clap, slowly, a sole champion in the audience. The person next to him would join in, then the next, then the rest of them would start, and the cheers would be heard for miles around, and Liezel would see him there, a shining beacon of decency in the sea of rubbernecking jackal bastards, which would part to allow her to run to him, and snog his face off. He knew that probably none of his fantasies would come true, but if he wasn't here then how could he find out?

A pain suddenly shot through his hands as the spliff had been smoked down to the roach and burned his fingers, ripping him from his floaty fantasies, eliciting a gasp and curse from him. He cast the burnt out roach away into the grass, sucked his sore fingertips, and lit another spliff to ease the pain. Jake pulled his phone out again to check that he hadn't missed out on any new developments, and scrolled through the usual news sites, all devoted to the situation once again, after they had threatened to move on to a British child that had died in a foreign country. He hadn't missed any-

"That smells good pal." Said a pair of trainers, attached to a pair of legs, which evolved into a torso with arms and a smiling head. Jake instinctively pulled the joint behind his back, as if it made a difference. He didn't know what to say, he had been busted, he was either sharing it or losing it. He held the joint up in silence to the man standing over him, his eyes to the floor.

"You sure?" He said, genuine surprise in his tone.

"Yeah, go on, am pretty stoned." Said Jake, still unable to raise his head. The bloke sat down beside him, took a couple of tokes and passed the spliff back, looking at him with raised eyebrows.

"Where you from?" he asked.

"Uh, Donny, erm, Doncaster." He mumbled, this intruder encroaching massively on his quiet time.

"Donny eh? I used to know it well, you down for the fun?" Fun? No, not like the rest of the jackals, he was here for *her*, to show his support, to take her in his arms, lift her from the ground, and take into his bedroom. No, not *his* bedroom, it was a mess. A hotel.

Yeah, he would book a hotel room with the rest of his cash, and he would spent the night making sweet love to her, but this guy would never understand, he didn't know her like Jake did.

"Erm, yeah." He said, and passed the joint back, the guy wasn't going anywhere so Jake chose to ride it out, anything for an easy life. As the spliff was returned to him the guy began to stand. *Finally,* thought Jake, he wanted to be alone with his dreams of Liezel. Whoever this bloke was, he turned back to look down upon him.

"I'd probably get out of here if I were you, things are gonna start to get a bit explosive."

Chapter 17 - January

The Only One With Brain Cells

There are feelings within me that feel very, *foreign*. I'm sure that I remember it from my childhood, I think it is sadness. My stomach feels empty. Or knotted. These feelings tickle up my throat, causing me to swallow constantly. My thoughts do not seem to be allowed to focus. They continue to return to him. In bed. When they do I sigh. It is not a comfortable feeling. It is not a sensation I could or would ever enjoy, and I do not like it. I blame him for it, and upon my return to the house I will ensure that he pays for it. The sight of him, prone and pathetic on the bed, the injuries around his neck, his words. They are all burned into my memories forever. And this emotion I am feeling, the quivering lip, the uncontrollable sighing and swallowing. It is *his* fault. *He* will pay for making me so soft. I have no time for sadness, I have so many things to do. Fortunately, Isaac Charles is overseeing the game, attracting suitable players, ready for when Liezel begins. They are so stupid not to see what I have been doing, did they not think that I could do this? I said so many times, after South Africa, I *told* them that the game had to change, that there were ways and means of making it work, but they only frustrated me with their in-fighting and arguing. They had no way of seeing the bigger picture, with their petty squabbles. There was only ever going to be me that could take over the organisation, I am the only one with brain cells. I resurrected it as something far more inconspicuous, bubbling under the surface, reliant only upon a minimum amount of people. Mr Hoxton was a genius. He was the man who made us all. I know that we continue to owe him a debt of gratitude, despite his unfortunate death at the hands of Cristiano, and Thomas, and Jessica. I will ensure that I honour his name by destroying every one of them, and also the smart-ass Rufus. They all believe that they can outnumber, or *outgun* me, but they are wrong. I will watch the face of Thomas, as he lays his eyes upon those of his beloved *kurva,* for the first time since Rufus failed with the simple task which I have paid him so well, and then I will take so much joy from the change in his eyes as I plunge my knife into her neck, and rip her throat from her body. I am talking here about sending a professional to fulfil the jobs that an amateur could not. I am not wishing to say bad things about Isaac Charles, perhaps when Rufus worked with him he took his responsibilities so much more seriously, perhaps this is the reason that Isaac Charles gave him such great praise. But for me he has given nothing but petulance. Talking back to me with an attitude that was filled with nothing but disrespect. Does he not know what I am capable of? Evidently not, but he will. They all will. Not only Rufus, and Cristiano, and the others. *Everybody.* Liezel will know when she discovers the extent of my uses for her. Mr Hoxton started a great thing, I would not be here in Marseille were it not for he, but I have made it my own. There remains a great deal of, would the best word be mileage? In the human condition? Isaac Charles will find, and groom, possible contenders for the game. They will participate electronically, I will never meet any of them, but they will know that should they tell a single person about the game, then they will be in an unfortunate position where they may find themselves dead in their beds. Their husband, or wife, will be hanged from roof of their house, their innards ripped from them. Their children will be discovered headless, buried in the back garden. Believe me, they *will* know. Now is not the time to divulge details, do not hope to discover how the game is played *just yet.*

I am in my hotel room, and the television plays nothing, there are shows on, but I have no interest in them. It is merely a background noise to my thoughts, which always seem to come back to *him.* Dietmann. When they do return to him I end up in that same place where my stomach turns as it ties itself into a knot, and I close my eyes and sigh, I so wish that he was not such a pussy boy. His brain, the brain which helps within the operation, it is brilliant, his ideas and technical expertise are second to none. But his heart, it rules him, and it makes him a liability. It became so that I could not confide in him anymore, because his heart would take control of his brain. I tried, I really did try to make him stronger, to make him harder of heart. I hoped that by fucking him I could make him see that it is easy to remove the heart from the brain. It was about sexual enjoyment, *not* about love. But it seems that I only made it worse, and in another world I might apologise to him, and discuss things like the nobodies do. Like the people in soap operas do in the extreme. Like cinema tells us to do. This is what he wanted, I see it now, he wanted to love me like he has seen on television, heard in songs, read in poetry, but it is not a notion that truly exists. It is false, and it is created in order to sell a stupid paper card, with a heart upon the front. In real life, people, they only find ways to not be alone. The idea of love has been created. The reality is much different.

I need to take my mind from Dietmann, so I decide that I shall call Rufus, who never fails to anger me, and make the plans for tomorrow. He has not

answered his telephone in a while, this has become a source of constant frustration for me, I know that maybe he could once be using the toilet, or in a loud place that he cannot hear it, but when he does not answer his telephone in over two hours, this is disrespect of the highest order. I am surprised when he does answer it at this time, he sounds drunk.
"Ladyboss what can I do you for?" He says loudly, sighing at me, and I am sure that when I take the last breath from his body it will come out in the form of that very same sigh. It is so infuriating.
"Rufus, very good of you to finally answer your telephone, you do spoil me. I am in Marseille already, I have your money but I am tired." I say to him, and he does not sound so interested, but I continue regardless as I finger the curtain, and look out over the marina "I will meet you in the morning, eleven fifteen, at the junction of *Avenue Saint-John* and *Quai du Port*. You will see a large white building upon the dock, it has a red roof, and you will wait there for me. I am not far away, I am staying at Le Radisson Blu over at the other side of the marina." I feel regret at allowing him that information, I was not lying when I told him that I was tired, I cannot be bothered by him if he makes the decision to try to join me early, so I end the call with "Do not attempt to make any trouble for me, and if you behave yourself then you will be paid handsomely in the morning. Goodbye Rufus."

I Remember The Day

I can feel a headache coming on, the kind of headache that's only caused by booze. It's like I'm still pissed, and I could fight it off temporarily with more beer but that'll only get me into more shit. I was lucky this time. They could have ended me and done it without me, but, I dunno, there's something quite cool about this trio. I almost feel bad for trying to kill them. Almost. No, no room for total remorse in this business. Business being the operative word. I think they realise that, I think that's what kept me alive. They seem to see it as no harm no foul in the big picture. They're all alive, they know why I did what I did, and they're prepared to let it drop if I help them instead. The big bastard, Cristiano, or Beefy, as Tom calls him, he's been looking at me through suspicious eyes and I don't blame him. I'd do the same. He's the one they had stay in this room with me, told me in no uncertain terms that if I made a wrong move he wouldn't hesitate to annihilate me. He could too. His arms are almost as wide as my whole body. I don't know that things would have been any different if I'd been sober last night. They outnumbered me three to one, but I think they would have still given me a chance to make amends, Tom said almost as much himself, I showed Jess some mercy. I kept his girl alive, he owed it to me to say my piece. I vaguely remember being a bit of a twat, but then they put a line of coke under my nose and we were suddenly bosom buddies. Amazing what that kind of thing can do for potential enemies. After I spoke with Ada we tried to put the plan into place, there's no way she can get as far as *Quai du Port.*

    Cristiano's feet twitch by my face, his knees jerk up into my midriff, knocking the wind out of me as he lets out a loud snort slash snore, his clogged nostrils obviously struggling to allow any air through his nose, and his tongue slaps sloppily from the roof of his mouth to the bottom teeth. I'm not anywhere near tempted to get out of bed and the room, if Ada actually does know what we know she knows then I'll have a job on to get anywhere near her on my own, and I don't care if my three targets are alive or not, she *owes* me that money. She's taken too much of my life to not pay me. A thought hits me, and it's Charley, I wonder how she is, but the affection with which I think about her is subsiding even more. It pains me to say it but if this all goes okay and I'm on a plane back to Manchester by nightfall, I don't know that I'll want to go back to the life I had. I've forgotten her smell, her taste. I look at my phone and scroll through the pictures in the photo album. Me and her, a couple of years ago, when we were closer. There's a bunch of pictures from when we drove to Morecambe, and she was doing that daft pose next to the statue of Eric Morecambe. I remember the day. The weather was shit, but I'd promised her that we could go and see the statue, so we went. We ate chips in a bus stop, talked about the future. Talked about how we'd go back when we were old, do the same things. It was a good day. I smile with a degree of sorrow, she's a lovely girl, and she deserves better than anything I could offer her. She needs a man who's not eventually gonna wind up dead, or nicked. She knows what I do. She knows what I am. She could end me if she wanted. I need to speak with her.

    In the hall outside the room I wait for eight thirty, then dial her number and wait for her to pick up. She answers in a sleepy voice, and it kind of all floods back into my heart but I know why I'm doing this, I can't lose sight of that. Her voice picks up slightly when she realises it's me, but there's this doubt seeping through at the same time. I think we both know what I'm going to say, and I think we both know it's for the best.

"Hey, Roofy, where've you been?" She asks, Roofy, I always thought that Rufus was always a daft name for a kid in Manchester, but she loved it.

"Uh, a bit busy to be honest girl, it's been crazy." I say, struggling to keep the affection out of my voice, I have something to say and it needs saying before I get dragged back into small talk, or, worse, filthy talk. She loves to talk dirty.
"Where are you?"
"Marseille."
"France?"
"Yeah France."
"Why are you in France?"
"Trying to collect some money, but it's going a bit weird, I just wanted to speak with you before it happens."
"Before what happens? Rufus are you in trouble?"
"No, well, yeah but I'll be fine, I need to talk to you about something."
I can hear her rustling about and sitting up in bed, readying herself for the inevitable.
"Oh dear, that sounds ominous."
"I think you know what I'm going to say, I can't do this anymore Charley, you deserve better."
The door to the room rips open hard, loud, and heavy, and Cristiano looks at me, he obviously thought I'd done a runner, like Charley knows I'm doing now. I wave him away, a plea in my eyes. He gets the message and retreats back to the bedroom. Charley hasn't said anything. I sigh and there's this lump in my throat, I hate myself.
"Sorry." I whisper, and I hang up the phone. This heavy feeling weighing in my chest. I could have done it months ago, saved her a life of waiting for a man who wasn't gonna come home, instead of taking advantage of her sexy side, sitting in hotels miles away and wanking myself into a frenzy whilst she fucked herself with a dildo on webcam. Yeah she enjoyed it too, but was it because I was supposed to

be her man, the one she had plans on growing old with. I'm such a prick. I swallow down the urge to break down. I'm harder than that. The phone buzzes lightly in my hand. It's a text. It's from her, I know it's from her. I take a deep breath and open the message.

It's okay. Be careful Rufus x

It breaks my heart there and then. She's a gem. She'll make some lucky twat a very happy man one of these days. I delete the message regretfully and put the phone back into my pocket, before I knock on the bedroom door, getting Cristiano to let me back in. He pulls the door open as heavily as before and stares at me with a degree of anger in his eyes.
"I thought that you had run away." He says with relief.
"No such luck mate, just had something to do before we kick it off." And thankfully he doesn't ask any more questions, like he can tell I'm not in the mood.
"Okay, let us go and wake the others, we don't have a lot of time."

A Seasoned Side-Switching Professional

There's a knock at the door that wakes me up. It's Mr Beefy, I can tell, he can't do anything gently that cunt. My face is squashed against the pillow and my nose touches the corner of the hard wooden bedside table, it smells old. For sure, I would have put some nice leather looking ones in this room, ones that match the headboard like. One eye is still closed as it's pressed against the linen pillow case, the other is open, looking around at anything in its line. I can see the edge of the curtain, my crumpled up clothes at the side of the bed, my phone on the bedside, and the

bottom of a lamp that seems to be growing out of the wall. My left arm reaches away from me, looking for Jess. The fingers find the waistband of her pyjama bottoms, and snake inside to get some of that lovely lovely contact with her arse. Her Sunday Arse. I roll over and allow both of my eyes a go at seeing what's going on. Not much. Beefy knocks at the door again, and I can hear his lips pressed right at the crack where the hinges would be.
"Tommy man, wake up, we got shit to do."
Jess stirs, and turns to face me, her eyes open.
"Hey you." I say, smiling, my hand moving the messy hair from her gorgeous face. She smiles at me.
"How'd you sleep?" I ask her, and she does a proper yawn, like her head could fold over on itself, like that old toothpaste advert from when I was a kid, and tells me that she'd slept better. I can't believe how long it feels since we last slept together. It was last night, that's all, but I was in such a state that I don't remember it, and then since then, well, you know the story.

As Beefy does another knock, this time a bit more impatiently, I swing the door open, stealing some of his knocks as his fist almost snots me one. His eyebrows go up 'cause I surprised him.
"Tommy, it is almost nine o'clock, we need to move soon, get ready and we will finalise the plan." Then he heads back to the room. There was no way that I was gonna ask Jess to sleep in the room that Rufus had thrown his rocks up all over, so me and her took his room. Cristiano begrudgingly accepted that he would top and tail with Rufus, partly 'cause there was no chance of him getting in with me and Jess, and partly 'cause we're still not one hundred per cent on trusting the failed hit man. Yeah he seems to have switched sides with all the aplomb of a seasoned

side-switching professional, but that's why it's so unsettling. Put it into perspective yeah? A married man cheats on his wife with a woman who's thinking *yeah, I got me a man* but then after a while, can she trust that man not to fuck off with another slag later in life? You know? That's how I'm seeing it. If he wants to cheat on our arses, then we just have to make sure we cut his dick off and stick it up his own arse, figuratively speaking. For now though, we all kind of have to trust each other to a degree, just to get through this, I mean, for sure, we all have a mutual enemy, no point burning our bridges just yet.

    We kind of muddled through a plan last night between us, but it was filled with that confidence that only coke'll do for you, where we were gonna all sit and wait, sunglasses on, maybe some Panama hats, guns under a rolled up copy of *Le Monde.* We'd be sitting in a busy seafront café terrace, maybe Jess to one side at a phone booth, head wrapped all Audrey Hepburn style, watching, ready to make the call. In our heads it was gonna be the ultimate in movie clichés. It never happens like that though, and once the effects of the drugs began to dissipate, the plan got slightly more realistic. We either can't allow her all the way to the marina, or we make sure she makes it *all* the way, I know, your guess is as good as mine. Me and Jess took the car over the way to check out the area, see what kind of vantage points there were, and there were fucking tons. It was agreed that Ada would probably have some sort of back-up. Rufus couldn't offer any potential names, he said he had only ever spoken with her, nobody else ever got involved. Now this says to me that either the organisation has got a shitload less organised since we left it, or there actually *is* no organisation anymore. Rufus says they met through a mutual acquaintance but wouldn't say who that was, he said that this acquaintance would defo not be involved, he said it wasn't their style and we could get that suspicion out of our heads, which was fair enough, so we moved on. When me and Jess got back from our little trip we figured the basics of the plan out, and I reckon the rest of it we play by ear, why not really? We can't predict what the fuck's gonna happen to be fair, she might have an army, but probably doesn't. She might just sniper our heads off from the hotel, but probably won't.

While Jess is in the shower I sit on the edge of the bed, staring at myself in the mirror, I look dog rough. I'm thinking I can't have her involved, not with my baby in her belly, but she's like she was when we first met, she's not going anywhere without me, she won't stay here and wait. I concede that she's coming with us, with a heavy heart, but I don't want to be putting her anywhere in Ada's line of fire. The phone rings, the second phone, the one that Ada has the number for, she's the only one who has the number so it's no surprise when she's on the other end of the line.

"Hello?" I say

"Thoma-" She starts, but I'm feeling like winding her up, so I interrupt her.

"Thank you for calling The Society of Vengeful Pricks, your call is important to us, please hold," and she goes silent, a bit confused maybe. I'm funny.

"Nah, I'm just fucking about with ya, what do you want?"

"You are a prick."

"Coming from you that's a real compliment. Thank you."

"Fuck yourself. Eleven fifteen, *Avenue Saint-John* and *Quai du Port*. You will have a front row seat to me cutting your bitch's throat. Do not be late."

And that's that, she drops a giant piece into the jigsaw. She wants us all in the same place, and it's given me a little idea. Risky but it might just work. I dunno exactly what she's got planned, I'm just looking forward to fucking it up!

Uncle Cristiano!

I do not feel like I had any of the sleep last night, but the man Rufus told me that I was snoring, he said it was so loud that the door to the room was vibrating in the hole. Snoring? Me? I do not snore! I have never snored! I feel so so tired, but I also feel very ready to tear Ada apart, oh man, I will rip her into tiny pieces like she was a paper receipt, then I will scatter those tiny pieces all over the marina of Marseille. I should have done it all of those years ago, when I destroyed the old fool Hoxton, I should have waited until she returned from her business trip, and then smashed her weak body into a thick paste with his broken skull. My friends, Tommy and Jessie, they would not be in so much trouble now if I had done that to her all those years ago. I did not do it then, but I have the chance to help them forever, and their tiny baby. I can make the future a safe one for their tiny baby, and then who knows? Maybe they will call the baby after his uncle Cristiano? That would be the greatest honour that they could ever bestow upon me. Cristiano and his uncle Cristiano! I tell you, he's going to be one pretty baby! A heartbreaker, just like his uncle Cristiano! So I must do this, I must tear Ada to pieces in the name of the unborn child of my friends, as I should have done in the past.

Tommy came to the room with excitement in his voice, telling us that she bitch has demanded that we meet her at the same time that she thinks she will meet the man Rufus, and Jessie. She is so deluded. She thinks that she gonna get us all at the same time. She thinks wrong! Little Jessie is still in her room, making herself ready for action, but I am thinking the same as Tommy, she must not be seen, she must keep that tiny baby in her belly safe from harm. We have decided that she will stay in a café, still where we can see her but in a place where there are many people, so that Ada does not try anything too dangerous or else she might come into more danger herself, but Jessie, she's stronger than you think, she's asking about what if Ada sees her, how do we go about our plan then? Rufus has been a little bit quiet since he was using the telephone, I do not trust his face, his eyes are very suspicious, he cannot make them meet mine, and I believe that if a man cannot meet your eyes with his then he is a born liar! I shall watch him like I am a hawk. Did you know that a hawk can see about eight times better than you can? True fact, you know that every day is a school day right? Now I taught you something, you go and store that nugget of information in your pocket for another day! You tell your friends that Cristiano told you! No, I do not trust the man Rufus, but I am happy for him to prove me wrong and do his part of the plan. Tommy seems to think he is an okay guy because he let little Jessie live, but I would make a bet that the man Rufus has not once met her eyes with his, he is sneaky, like a snake. The word snake is *in* the word sneaky, it is so fitting for the man Rufus.

When we are on the *Quai du Port,* when we see Ada there, waiting, I so want to simply walk to her and punch her right in the face, and to hell with the consequences. But the thing is that we do not know if she has brought her puppy dog Dietmann with her, or the Laughing Brothers, Lukas and

Yannick. Laughing Brothers? This does not sound correct. The children's comedy people of England, Tommy gave them the name. Laughing Brothers. I ask Tommy what the name was.
"Chuckle Brothers?" He says, Chuckle Brothers! Of course! Yes, the Chuckle Brothers. Lukas and Yannick. I am sure that they are pansy boys, they are never seen apart, maybe they have deep manly love for one another.
"Yes, the Chuckle Brothers, do you think that there is the possibility of them being there?" I ask, Rufus makes a confused face that Tommy sees.
"Lukas and Yannick, Ada's go-to guys for corpse disposal, this goes tits up and it'll be those boys chopping you up and burying you." He explains, and Rufus then makes a face which is concerned.
"Really? Fuck me." Says the sneaky Rufus.
"Not unless you're really nice to me or pay me really well," laughs Tommy, he is too quick for me sometimes, and then he goes on "honestly, they're both a bag of wank, no danger to you unless you're already dead, so just work on staying alive and you'll be fine."

Three Boys And A Little Lady

I run the big padded brush through my hair, it feels nice. The shower, I loved it. Maybe it's just something like *small things pleasing small minds* but the colour changing glow of the shower head was mesmerising as the water whooshed against my breasts and tummy, teasing my small nipples from their slumber. Tom would go mad for it. Then the feel of the jets of water massaging my tired face, washing the sleep from my being. There's just something so satisfying about a good shower, it was always even better when

Tom and I would shower together, but we enjoyed them for very different reasons. I love the intimacy of being naked together, scrubbing each other down, it's just so *primal,* and it feels so nice when it's with somebody that you truly love. Tom, well he enjoyed it for very different reasons, his erection constantly pressed against my leg, him trying to kiss me all over, squeezing at my breasts, it was nice, but it was just *relentless!*

I'm dressed before long, and enter the other room to witness the boys perform the ritual of making plans once more. Last night was surreal but the shower washed all that away too, reality is setting in. Tom intersperses the plans with stories of when we were all in the organisation, and Rufus looks ever more like a fish out of water. I'm under no illusions that he's not a dangerous man, but he always worked alone *for* people like the organisation. He's used to asking no questions and telling no lies. Cristiano nods along and puts his own spin on the same kind of stuff. They're reminding me more and more of Tom Selleck, Ted Danson and Steve Guttenberg. Three Boys and a Little Lady. That's what we are. Or when we finally get down there onto the marina, they'll start swinging planks on their shoulders, ducking down to pick a can of paint up just as the plank whooshes over their head. It feels that much of a farce. Maybe I'm being unfair, but the fact of the matter is that even with me out of the equation, even if I *do* go and sit and watch the whole thing play out from behind a menu and a cappuccino, they're extremely out of practice. Tom and I have spent every day up until the last forty eight hours on a millionaire's road trip, yeah we've had to keep looking over our shoulders, but we haven't exactly been dodging bullets and killing bad guys. Tom's thinking it's gonna be a walk in the park, but is it? Cristiano is bigger, smarter, and stronger than I remember him being, but again, all he's had to contend with was logs and prostitutes, living the life of luxury in the mountains. And Rufus? We can only take him on his word, because our experience of him is a failed attempt to blow us up, and him throwing his guts up all over himself. It doesn't exactly set the heart pumping with confidence.

I sit myself down beside Tom and he turns with a smile, and kisses my neck, whispering *hey baby* into my ear, and it tickles in a very nice way.

"So what are we doing?" I ask, because it's just three boys talking like they were playing games but Tom looks to Rufus who goes under the bed and pulls out the big bag he carried into the hotel with him, and pulls out a series of weapons, one after the other. Knives, pistols, machine guns, and other stuff. I don't know the names of any of them, they're all the same to me and they scare the living daylights out of me. I can feel my skin crawling just at the thought of touching any of them.

"Our boy Rufus here has been sitting on a small arsenal baby, and very useful it will be indeed!" He says, but he knows me, and he knows by my face what my concern is, and he knows what question I'm going to ask, so he pre-empts me "We can't just walk in there all guns blazing though baby, we need to be smart. So here's the plan"

Romantic Melancholia

It's eleven, I'm standing on the marina. I don't care if she wants to meet at quarter past. I had to be here for now. The more I know about Ada and what she's all about the less easy I feel about this, she seems a dangerous bitch. No wonder she was acting like the

Big I Am on the phone, it doesn't sound like she's used to dicks like me acting like dicks around her. But still, we have strength in numbers. We have people who know her and what she's capable of, we have the weapons, we have the muscle. All we need now is a bit of luck in the timing.

I'm feeling very exposed here, wandering up and down, here in my aviators and my favourite brown leather jacket, the one that Charley used to take the piss out of. Her thing was telling me that a dead world war one fighter pilot had been on the phone from beyond the grave and he wanted his coat back. I'd always retort that the eighties had been on the phone and wanted their jokes back. She was always funny though, really funny, I dug her humour. And she was fit. I'm regretting what I did already, but it's for the best. She's better off without me. The low winter sun is beaming at me across the harbour, it's warmer than it should be at this time of year, and the coat is feeling surplus to requirements but it's more about concealing things than anything else. I'll have to take the sweating for now. These fifteen minutes are gonna just drag, I know it. If she's got anybody watching me then they'll not have a lot to see.

There are a few people dotted around the area but they're all doing their thing, nobody seems suspicious. One old guy is on the deck of his humble boat, he's on his knees, both hands working the scrubbing brush against the already bright white surface. He's obviously not got much on, that little boat's his pride and joy and he'll spend his life keeping it in tip-top condition, something to keep him occupied. I'm making up a life for him to keep my mind busy. His name's something clichéd like Francois, or Pierre, a widower from Northern France, who'd spent his life working his fingers to the bone to make a good life for him and his wife. They'd always wanted kids but she couldn't have any, so they looked after the youngsters in the village. Nothing seedy. They just loved the laughter of kids, and he'd use his spare time to fix up and hand out old bikes. The kids would fetch their broken down ones for him to fix up and he'd do it without question. His wife passed away and, heartbroken, he decided he wanted a fresh start, so he travelled south to Marseille, and bought a boat. He called it *Marie* after his dead wife, and spent every waking hour keeping her pristine. It's not like he ever actually sails it, he just wants this reminder of her with him. It's like he's keeping her memory alive. I feel sad for Pierre now, and I want to go over and help him out. I'm probably a million miles wrong, but in my head that's his life, and that's how it's staying. It's probably this whole Charley thing. I'm feeling this romantic melancholia riding on my back, and really Ada is the last thing I need.

I check my watch, seven minutes past eleven, still nothing doing, and I have this underlying suspicion that she's gonna show up at half past just to piss me off.

Yeah, But Jess' Is Better

He's not doing much, just walking up and down, looking at his watch, staring at some old boy cleaning his shitty little boat. For sure, there's hundreds of yachts in this harbour, and he looks to have the absolute smallest. It's basically a rowing boat with a sail and a downstairs bit. Maybe a bit bigger. It's defo clean enough by now, but he's scrubbing it down to the bone. Beefy's in the driver's seat and his attention's been caught by a pair of long legs striding by, at the top of those legs there's a Sunday Arse

which melts into this slim piece of meat that just *knows* that it's being watched everywhere it goes. Yeah, it's good to look at but so's Jess, and she's a lot more humble about it. That's when you know you're loved up, it doesn't matter how good looking the woman, your mind will always end up back on *your* woman. Like, I'm watching the Sunday Arse, and I'm thinking *Yeah, but Jess' is better.* Cristiano spots me looking as well and this sleazy grin appears.
"Is that not a beautiful ass?" He says, his eyebrows raising.
"Yeah, but Jess' is better." I respond, shrugging. Beefy laughs so much the car shakes, like, to an observer from a distance you could swear we were making sweet man love in here, the car's rocking that much.
"Tommy man, she is not here, you do not have to be so pussy whipped." He laughs, slapping my back, almost giving me whiplash in the process.
"Nah mate, when you get a woman you'll understand." I say to him, the Sunday Arse already out of sight. The clock's reading eleven past eleven, as far as Ada's concerned we've got four minutes to get there, but as far as we're concerned we're waiting as long as we have to. We do not get out of this car until she's showed up.

These People Are So Stupid

They think that they are smart. They think that they can pull the wool over my eyes and I will allow them to do so without a fight. They are dead wrong. I can see that Thomas and the buffoon Cristiano are watching the lying snake Rufus, they are looking directly at him. They know something. I know that they know something. The lying snake continues to look at the car that they sit in, he cannot help himself.

He is so predictable. I can see what he is doing. First, he looks at his watch, and then he searches for me, I can see the frustration in his eyes, I am late, of course I am. Then, he will look at the car, only briefly, very briefly, but he looks at the car, and it is the *way* that he looks at the car which makes me think. He looks like he is asking questions to the car. He is asking them what he should do. They are silent but they are telling him to continue to wait. She sits, watching from the café, like that is a safe place. Like I would not walk into the area and put my bullet into her head. Like I would not put a bullet into the heads of every person in there. They are nothing. This is the key to success in my business. Put everybody in their place. Like chess, think out every single move before you play it. Thomas and Cristiano, they think that they can take their eyes from Jessica, the slut, they think that she is safe so they keep their eyes only on where they believe I will be. They are wrong. They do not see me as I walk straight past their car, they are so side-tracked, I cross the road without stopping. Everybody is watching somebody else watch somebody else. Jessica, she will not see me, because she watches Thomas, he will not see me because he watches Rufus, the lying snake. These people are so stupid.

    I am only a few metres from Jessica, and still she has not seen me approach her. She is concerned only with the car that Thomas is in. She has not changed, she is maybe slightly more tanned than I remember her but she is still the same girl. Still infuriatingly beautiful. I shall wipe the smug beauty from her head, and I shall ensure that Thomas sees me do it. Once I have dealt with these imbeciles I can then go back to my real business, I can forget petty issues with ghosts from the past, and lying snakes. I can deal with Dietmann and his sensitive bullshit later, I have not forgotten about him. My only hope is that he has not packed up his suitcase and gone to cry elsewhere. No, he would never dare.

"Jessica, it has been too long." I say, and I delight in the shock on her face, which quickly becomes fear. She looks to her stupid boyfriend who is too engrossed in the lying snake. I do not have to turn to see him to know that. I take my place across from her at the table, and pull her glass of lemonade to my lips. The ice has melted too much in the drink and it tastes too watery, but I did not drink it for enjoyment, I did it just because I can. The slut does not say a word, she cannot, she dare not.

He's Screwed Us Over

She's colder than before. This is not the woman I remember sparing our lives all those years ago. The one who took us in. I can sense it in her demeanour. She's like a robot. Not a warm hearted film robot, who fulfils household jobs for a wholesome all American family, one that endears itself to that family and the audience. She's dead behind the eyes. I can't speak, I can't move. There's the flash of the gun for one, the dark grey handle in her impossibly slim waistband. She knows I've seen it, she's made sure that I've seen it.

"So how have you been?" She asks, like she cares. I don't say anything, and I'm willing Tom to see us. To save me, again. I don't know how it is that I keep finding myself in these situations. I want that life, the life that some people seem so disdainful toward. The life that people work so hard to get away from. There's something to be said for that life where the only worries are bills and money. I would give anything to trade places with anybody who has two cars that they can't afford, red-headed letters threatening court action if the outstanding balance is not cleared within seven working days. I would be alive, and my only fear of death would come because of an unidentified lump. That's the life I want more than anything. Not this one, with a Hungarian woman hell-bent on revenge. *Please Tom* I'm thinking, *please look, I need you.*

"You look well, I suppose that is what happens when you have fifteen million Euros to keep you well. I see that you are reunited with your Thomas." And she turns away, her head tilted toward over her shoulder. "Rufus is a fucking imbecile." I still don't respond, I will not give her the satisfaction. She takes another sip of my drink. She can have it, it's diluted too much in the sun. A waiter appears beside us, noting the new arrival.

"Bonjour mademoiselle," he says to Ada, "would you like to order a drink at all?" His pen poised to write down her order.

"No." She says without addressing him directly, he looks at me in confusion, but I can't do or say anything, what is there to say? He mutters something, and walks away, shaking his head. From the corner of my eye I can see him relaying the story to the girl at the bar, but I keep my focus on Ada. I have to keep her busy. She kind of half sighs, and half laughs at me.

"You think that your Thomas will save you now? Yes? He will not. He will stand by helplessly as I cut your throat, now, get up, let us finish this." Her head jerks to beckon me to stand up, and I comply, my baby is my only concern.

"Go to Thomas," she tells me, "and if you decide to make any stupid moves just remember that I will end your life without a second thought." And I believe her, so I walk, checking for traffic on the road, toward the car.

It's at this point that Tom finally spots us, and he's out of the car before I can even blink, his hands in the air in an act of, surrender I suppose. Cristiano is out of the other side, and he looks furious. Rufus is nowhere to be seen, but I know he's there. This is where it's supposed to happen, but it's not, Tom is looking toward the harbour, and then back at us, he's trying to be cool but I know he's panicking. She should be dead by now. Ada calls to Tom as we edge our way toward them.

"Thomas, Cristiano, move to the marina, slowly, or I will shoot her where she stands. Go to Rufus." They follow her instruction, slowly backing away from us, and Tom hasn't blinked, he's thinking the same thing as the rest of us. *What the hell is holding Rufus up?* This is not how it should be happening. There's this sinking feeling that seems to be spreading between us. He's screwed us over.

Lying Prick

He's fucked us, each and every one of us. In the arse. I *knew* he would. Why the fuck did I think it was a good idea to get him involved? My fucking gut, that's why. He seemed like a genuinely alright bloke. Fucking Manc cunt. A Yorkshireman should never trust a Manc. It's plain fact. So where Beefy wanted to smash him up, I said no, trust him I said, see what he can do for us, I thought. Well, you know what thought did. Thought it were a fart 'til it shat itself. I just *know* that he's waiting round there for us, he's probably been on the blower to Ada all along. Some fucked up pride in his work where he needed to finish the job. That's what he's done. I'll get to him before we're all dead, fuck Ada now, if they want to wipe us out then I'll make sure I take him with me. Lying prick. Why not just kill us in the hotel room though? He had the chance when we didn't know about the bag of guns, he could easily have taken at least some of us out. Something's just plain wrong right now.

"Rufus, you prick!" I'm shouting to nobody, because he's still out of sight. Then I'm getting a weird feeling that he's just done a runner. The only side he's been on is his own. Oh, I don't know anymore. All I'm sure of is that whilst we've been making this plan, he's just been thinking of himself. Waiting for his exit. His out. His escape. The cunt! Why is nothing ever simple? Tell me that!

"He is a lying snake," says Ada, past Jess, to me, "his word is worthless."

"Ah-ha!" Cristiano exclaims. "I thought the same thing, a *sneaky snake!*"

"You shut your mouth Cristiano, unless I speak to you!" She shouts at him, and we're almost at the main strip that runs alongside the water. Still Rufus is nowhere. Where the fuck is he? The road is proper quiet and it's just us four. There's me and Beefy, we're still edging back onto the marina, and between us and Ada there's my girl. It wasn't supposed to happen like this, I've put my girl in danger, a-*fucking*-gain. Yeah, she was supposed to get seen, I know how Ada works, she was always gonna try for Jess first, she said as much on the phone. We were supposed to act all gormless, so she could fetch her over, and then Rufus was supposed to pop her while she was concentrating on summat else. Only he didn't. He let us down.

Forty Eight Seconds From Dead

It's eleven twenty eight and fifty three seconds, fifty four seconds, fifty five. I'm willing the hands round. They're all almost in view and I'm in danger of fucking this all up. *Please, hurry up* I'm thinking. Tom already thinks I've set him up, I can tell from his voice. I would have appreciated a little bit more faith than *that*, I've been nothing but straight with him since last night. He knows I need to wait until half past. I told him. They *all* know. Eleven twenty nine and twelve seconds. I've got Ada in my sights, and she's forty eight seconds from dead. I want to shout to Tom to tell him to calm down, I have it under control, just slow down, keep her contained for a tiny while longer. Eleven twenty nine and twenty nine seconds. I have to keep it together, they'll be fine, Ada's not gonna do it there, however much she threatens. There's too many people about. Just keep it together. Come on. Breathe. She's still in the open. Eleven twenty nine and forty eight seconds, forty nine. She's eleven seconds from dead. Eight seconds. Five. Four. My finger is on the trigger, her miserable looking face is directly in my sights. Three. Just be patient Tom, she's two seconds from-
Fuck!
Her head explodes, like a melon that's been hit with a sledge hammer. Her body crumples to the floor, pouring blood and lumps of brain all over the road. An oncoming car screeches to a halt, its driver climbs from the car, goes to the body and turns, throws up through her hands. Jess runs to Tom, who pulls her close to him, squeezes her tight. Cristiano walks to the body and checks she's dead. There's no coming back from the shot she's just taken. She's pretty much got no head, she's not a chicken, she's people. *Was*

people. I didn't get paid. I step down from my perch, putting the gun away quickly. Pierre has stopped scrubbing his boat, he's up on his knees, one hand shielding his eyes from the sun, witnessing the carnage. People are running from the cafés to see what's played out. I'm walking quickly toward Tom, and Jess, who turn to see me and head my way. Cristiano's heading back from the corpse, and the guys are looking pretty pissed off.
"You took your fucking time dickhead!" He says angrily, slamming the palms of his hands into my chest, courting a response from me.
"It wasn't me," I say, "I was waiting for half past."

Undignified Mess

The gun hung heavy by his side. His feet would not move. Even if he wanted to run he couldn't. His tormentor was gone. She lay in a crumpled heap on the road, her head opened up for the world to see the inside of. No matter what went on inside her head, the actual physical side of what was in there was the same as everybody else when it came to it. Like the Milchreis, rice pudding they called it in England, that he would spoon generous portions of strawberry jam into when he was only a child, and mix it around to create a lumpy pink and red concoction, that's what the cracked and sharp bowl of her head looked like it contained. When she was only dead meat. No more, no less than anything else. This woman, who acted so superior to everybody, reduced to an undignified mess on a road in Marseille. He should have felt relief, like a weight had been ripped from his shoulders, this should have brought an instant open door to a brighter future, so why did he feel no different? He had lost her once, lost her twice, and now through his own actions had made sure that he had lost her for a third, and very final time. There was no return to be made. Staring at her corpse, the snaking stream of blood that ran from the road to the edge of the pedestrian paving, the causeway, upon which stood- His mind blanked. He was seeing something, some*body,* but it could not be. How could it be possible? Tom, and Cristiano, and Jessica. Another man was with them but he did not recognise his face. Ada was here to meet them? Was that correct? It could not be, she was always so loyal to Hoxton, so dedicated to the organisation, and what it stood for. How could she be in league with these traitors? He could not speak, or blink, or think. Simply stood, open-mouthed at what his eyes refused to believe was real. A tug at his arm snapped him into reality. Liezel.

"You did as you had to Dietmann." She said, but he could still not comprehend the situation. Ada, in contact, be it in league with, or otherwise, with the traitors. They had not seen him yet, still they were in their own version of incomprehension. The four of them looking at Dietmann's handiwork. He could not tell if they appeared happy with Ada's death, or upset, like she was their friend, Tom was pulling Jess to him and placing his arm around her body, which would suggest that Ada's demise was perhaps a relief to them. Cristiano did nothing, only stood as he always did, the great hulk of stupidity. He had always resided at the bottom of the ladder in the organisation when he was there, only useful for muscle, derided even by Dietmann, the youngest. Liezel was pulling again at his sleeve, telling him to come on, before the police came, but he was not going to move. He needed answers. He ripped his arm from her grasp and began forward, first to the four of them, but drawn instinctively to Ada's prone mess of a corpse. He had killed her. He had taken the love of his life, and he had ensured that nobody else could have her. Yes, he had gone on with Liezel's half-baked ideas of finding her, speaking with her, telling her that he was worth more to her than she would ever realise. He had allowed her to put him in the car, and drive for over two hours from Monte Carlo, speaking incessantly about what a bitch Ada was, but at the same time telling him that he should speak with her. He could see now what she was doing, she *wanted* this to happen. She filled his brain with so much bullshit, all the seeds of doubt, of hatred. She would not allow him to speak, that was how she did it, she talked and talked and talked and *talked.* So much. She had manipulated his mind. Police sirens were sounding in the distance, but still he was going nowhere. The crowds that had appeared dispersed quickly around him with sounds of screeches of terror as one by one the people saw the gun in his hand, like he was waving a giant, slimy turd in each of their directions. Sluggishly he approached her body. Liezel's voice a mere irritation to his ears, that same song, she should learn to change the record. His eyes rose from the glistening open wound in the face of his lover, his love, his superior in every fucking way, to the traitors. He had taken her from the planet. Taken the breath from her lungs. The thoughts from her head. *He* was responsible. Nobody else. Not Tom, or Jess, or Cristiano, or the unknown man. Liezel had manipulated him, but he had *allowed* her to. Tom's face creased in recognition at Dietmann, his slack jawed features twisting as they realised who he was. His mouth would not work, he could only look to the others, who performed the same ritual. All except the stranger. The stranger appeared to be encouraging them to leave, or do something. Dietmann could not hear his words but he could see from his demeanour. Liezel followed his line of vision to the four of them, but she did not know them, she was doing the same as the stranger. Still she tried to pull at his sleeve but it had become enough. He raised his gun to her face, held the now cold nose of it to her forehead.

"Are you in league with *them?*" He asked her, his gun waving toward the others. She turned to them but there was no recognition.

"Are you crazy? Who are they?" She yelled, incredulously, her arms flailing around. She could not have foreseen the predicament that she was in. About to join Ada in Hell.

"YOU!" Dietmann shouted to the four. "You treacherous pigs!" His gun now pointed in their direction. The sirens grew ever closer. Tom pulled Jess behind him in some misguided effort of chivalry. Once he had shot through Tom he could just as easily kill Jess. They each stood, still open-mouthed. No words. The crowd of people had all but disappeared, people hovering behind walls, pillars, doors, anything that they thought could protect them from this gun-waving madman. Only the still bleeding body of Ada, the treacherous pigs, and Liezel remained upon the road with Dietmann. The echo of the siren roared from the tunnel that ran under the marina. The police were almost here. Dietmann took the line of the gun from his targets, dropped to his knees and grasped the still-warm hand of Ada, squeezing it tightly, willing her to return to life. She did not.

"You can all go to Hell." He whispered, directly before placing the barrel of the gun between his teeth and blowing his own brains out.

Chapter 18 - February

A Chinese Manchester United Fan

This had to end soon, she, Liezel, couldn't milk it much more than she had. Four days. Even his own brain was beginning to tire of the situation and he was the one who was able to go home and get sleep. The girl in the house was doing this alone, she couldn't go on for a great deal longer. He even fancied that they could simply ride this out, let her do her thing to William Walters, if she was going to actually kill him then surely he would be dead by now, and then eventually she couldn't go on before she just passed out from exhaustion. Not exactly what them upstairs wanted to hear, nor were the guys that were dotted around the rooftops with itchy triggers fingers exactly enamoured to have been instructed either, but this was *his* scene, not theirs. Until he was told otherwise then that's what the plan was. Anyway, he was still pissed off with Cooper, the selfish prick had run the name-revelation story without so much as a glimmer of a look in his direction. It was probably some ill-advised effort at showing him up for the lack of information offered when they spoke. He just plundered ahead, revelling in his ability to bring something new to the public. Liezel Esterhuizen. Even Mr and Mrs TV Dinner had got the jump on him. This was not how it should be. Ever. Philip had absolutely no idea how he came about such information, but once this was over he would make damn sure that he'd find out. It had threatened to derail everything, the police had already been vilified by some circles for their perceived inaction, accused of standing idly by and allowing the perpetrator to continue unhindered. The very same circles, fucking

Daisy Beckford, would no doubt be up in arms if they had gone in, all guns blazing, and killed the pair of them. On the flip side there was the general public, screeching in solidarity against the celebrity sex offender. The unified lump of hatred had threatened on several occasions to pour forward and do the job for him, if he didn't make the order to end the life of William Walters, Will Thunder, whatever the hell he wanted to call himself. Put simply, he was fucked if he did and fucked if he didn't. Wayne fucking Cooper had opened up the proverbial can of worms for him, for the sake of an *exclusive.* The prick. He was on his own now, if he wanted to play the sneaky shit, then he could play it, but the guy was playing on his own. Like some cunt of a kid that had spurned all of his friends because they scored a goal against him with his own ball, then in a huff disappeared, ball under arm, back to his mummy. When he calmed down, he'd return to the field of play, his friends having discovered a ball of their own, and telling him to piss off and play alone. That's how Wayne Cooper would find himself soon enough, alone, and regretful at his spur of the moment decision, with steadily decreasing viewing figures. The fickle dinner-on-the-knee in front of the television population, a fat dog at their feet, sticky faced kids putting finger prints all over the stolen flat screen as they screeched for *In The Night Garden,* would shift allegiances quicker than a Chinese Manchester United fan when Manchester City won the league when it came to their supplier of *info-tainment.* The media vultures would steam roller any protocol that Phil needed to follow to ensure justice was served, and it frustrated him to his core. When he was a younger officer, fresh on the Met, in the early nineties, the police held all of the cards, there were four channels, and only two, maybe three of them had any kind of news bulletin, and they got what they were given. The rapidly growing army of red-tops were in their ascendancy, and the ill-fated media magnate Terence Wilcox was leading the charge. It was such a shame when he perished in the fire on his luxury yacht off the coast of Portugal, he had thought at the time, albeit somewhat sarcastically. The news became no longer about information, it became about money, and it made his job a hell of a lot harder to do. This was the worst it had ever been, though, and this situation was beginning to test his patience. He'd already reprimanded Alex Green for his earlier stunt, releasing the name of Liezel Esterhuizen without discourse with the authorities, and more specifically, Detective Inspector Philip Benson. He had also informed him that if he had any further information he should be under no illusion that he wouldn't be removed from the area, and his balls removed from his body. It came as a huge shock then, when the crowds began to circulate around the field reporter once again, and quietened to hear his newest revelation. It was as if he were Jesus, about to feed the five thousand. The silence as he spoke may as well have been an all-night rave, compared to the stunned laconism when he'd finished.

Keep Two Chevrons Apart

He had no idea what he was doing here. Just followed the bloke on a whim. Something about the ominous nature of his last sentence before he had laughed, thanking Jake for the portion of his spliff, and wandered off, set him on edge. *Things are gonna start to get a bit explosive.* Why would he even say it? What did he know? Was he going to hurt Liezel? The paranoia set in once again and Jake was determined not to allow him the chance to hurt her. The fantasies flooded his imagination once again, this time he was disarming a bomb whilst Liezel looked on, her face filled with fear, and awe as her intrepid hero saved her life. With sweat in his eyes his trembling fingers would disable the wires one at a time, each one bringing him closer and closer to the zero hour, and their imminent deaths. Of course there would be music, sharp thumping beats pounding heavily over screeching violins and matching bass line, Liezel would be holding her breath, her hands gripped around the ends of her sleeves, and as the clock ticked down past ten seconds his eyes would tighten, focussed entirely on the job at hand, one wire left to pull, and as it reached two seconds he would save her life. She would run to him, he would swing her around in his arms, and she would kiss him hard on the mouth, before pulling away, smiling, and declaring him her hero. He couldn't allow her to come to any danger, and his spidey sense was tingling hard. This weed-thief hadn't just sat down, uninvited and taken the delicious herb from his own lungs, like taking the food from a baby's mouth, he was about to cause grave danger to the only reason he was in this stinking city. This was not something he could abide.

    The bloke had walked toward the Kensington area, the area that Jake had come from, and chose to do it in the shadows. Jake followed from a good five tree distance, like at times when he'd been on the motorway in his mum's Fiesta, as a passenger of course, he doubted that he'd ever be able to afford to run a car, let alone pay for lessons. On the motorway, as a safety precaution drivers were instructed to *Keep Two Chevrons Apart.* Chevrons. He sniggered every time he saw the word, keeping his mum well abreast of the chevron count between her and the car in front. That's what this tree count between he and the weed-thief reminded him of. Chevrons. He was five chevrons away, and was determined to keep it that way.

From the safety of the shadows he watched the silhouette of the weed-thief approach another silhouette, of similar build, but he couldn't make out any other physical features in the diminishing light of dusk. The silhouettes were in muffled conversation about something, but he couldn't make any actual words out. There didn't seem to be any kind of confrontation, no, they were definitely in cahoots with one another. Jake hugged the tree from which he leant, craning his neck out as much as he could, as if the extra two or three inches made any difference to his aural vantage point. It didn't. The pair spoke in tones which were far too hushed. They became one for a brief second as the silhouettes touched knuckles, and were about to part ways until the loudest noise Jake had ever heard in his entire existence sounded out, and rocked the silence. His phone. Making the dying swan screeching bleep advising him that it was down to blah per cent battery. The silhouettes hadn't even looked his way before they rushed him, destroying the chevron count in seconds. Jake's stoned self hadn't had a chance to begin to know what was happening, he was tackled to the ground by one of the silhouettes, whether it was the weed thief or his friend he couldn't tell. He was rolled to the ground and felt a piercing whistle in his head as his attacker smashed his fist into Jake's cheek, and then drop a knee onto his neck. He crushed his throat as he rummaged around above him, forcing an unintentional gargle-cum-squeal of pain from Jake. With his neck still

squeezed from the bony force of his attacker's shin, his pained squeal evolved into the terrified squawk of a six foot guinea pig in fear of a vet as the sound of a bullet entered a metallic chamber beside his ear. This was the end of his own pointless life. A self-proclaimed king of cool reduced to meat. He had a life line though, when his imminent death was halted only by the weed-thief calling out to his mate.
"No Rufus! We promised!"

Thanks For Everything

The hard jets blasted the base of her neck, massaging her spine with a heat that seemed to travel around her bloodstream, warming her to the fingertips. Dark grey scummy water circulated the plughole, struggling to infiltrate the pale matted clump of hair that had webbed over it, from over a week of reclusion being scrubbed from her weak body. She poured generous gloops of dark green pure mint shower cream over the loofah sponge and rubbed it against her reddening skin abrasively, the mint creating a tingling sensation over the sensitive dermis. The loofah found its way to her crotch and scrubbed equally hard. Usually, before it happened, this would have been an opportunity to slide her fingers delightfully into herself, indulge in a little of the old self abuse. But that was then, the new Claire couldn't bring herself to, well, bring herself off. He'd been in there, he'd spoiled even the smallest of joys for her.

After it had happened she had gone back to her car, and sat in silence, numbed by the prior hour's events. She just couldn't comprehend it. A man of his stature, did he think he wouldn't get found out? That she'd be so star-struck that she'd be thankful of

his buried acorn thrust uninvited into her? As she rolled out of the studio car park the unopened and still wrapped case of the *Taste Mike Rotch Tour* DVD lay cracked on the floor, the words *Thanks for everything,* with a winking smiling emoticon that formed the head of a crudely drawn penis and balls, and his signature, scrawled over its cover. She had arrived at home, and cried. She cried so much her throat stung from swallowing and the bright red rims of her eyes burned. She'd heard so much about situations like this. Situations where girls had gone home and showered themselves to within an inch of their lives, scrubbing away all evidence of DNA, of the rapist, so she was determined to resist the temptation. She liked to think of herself as strong willed, and independent, able to do anything. She liked to think of herself like that, once. She couldn't do it. She washed away every last inch of him, every drip of his dirty spunk, every salty drop of his stinking onion sweat and spit. She then called the police, Gail, and James. In that order.
Gail had arrived literally minutes later, smothering her with kisses, and hugs, tears, tea and sympathy. Claire replayed the whole thing to her, leaving nothing out, enduring a gripped love around her at every twisted sordid detail.

The police arrived three hours later, smothering her with neutrality, questions, and doubt. Claire replayed the whole thing once again to them, leaving nothing out, enduring *are you sure?* at every twisted sordid detail. They cast aspersions over her character, her reasons for being there in the first place, and her ability to resist such a famous and powerful man's allure. She found herself becoming angry with their cold approach, like they'd seen her type before, that was how it felt. The irritation in the policeman's eyes when she divulged the information that she'd taken a shower, scrubbed him from her. Gail had become angry on her behalf, wailing like a banshee, telling them to get out there and arrest the fat prick. Fat prick. It *wasn't* that fat. It was small, an uninspiring, and exactly the kind of cock she would expect him to own. Eventually they left, and she had to almost forcibly remove Gail from the house so that she could spend some time alone before James arrived. He never arrived.

The rolling news reports had broken the story so, so early, the bright yellow bar scrolling declaring allegations of rape by an unknown woman against comedy legend Mike Rotch. They had even put that, *comedy legend.* Unknown Woman Vs. Comedy Legend. She felt defeated before it had even started. Claire didn't know how she tracked her down, but some woman from Giles Baker PR was on the phone before sundown, and then the whole circus began. Over the course of the next month she was dragged from police interview to court appearance to magazine interview to more court appearances. In her own mind she had remained dignified, had never thrown dirt unnecessarily, explained anything out of context, or told lies. She'd faced him down, been dumped by James, been pulled through the wringer, and ultimately it was all for nothing. Her reputation was sullied, her life felt essentially over. She would forever be the woman who accused the *comedy legend,* of raping her. Then the harassment started and she fell to pieces.

She stepped from the shower after about an hour of water-blasting and scrubbing, feeling almost a stone lighter from the scum and grime that it had removed, her hair squeaked from cleanliness rather than greasiness for the first time in ages, bringing to her mind those adverts from when she was younger, where a smiling perfect mum ran her finger over a clean plate. Oh, for life to be that simple. Pulling on her tights she began to feel almost human again, not exactly ready for anything, but as close to it as she could at that point. Her dress, a to-the-knees number, sort of floral but more a dark, dark blue floral, like flowers might look if they were viewed at night, how almost anything would look at night, she thought. The evening, or late afternoon at this time of year, had this uncanny knack of stealing the colour from everything. It was probably a case of simple science, but she was damned if she was looking it up. She had other, more pressing matters to deal with, the case of the living, breathing, *raping* fat fuck that was Mike fucking Rotch, to be precise.

Chapter 19 - January

You First

"Is that good or bad?" The guy asked her, pointing toward the corpse of Ada. She didn't really know what to say,
"Good?" She went with, not entirely sure what was happening.
"Okay, well I don't know who the fuck you are, but you might as well get in the car." The guy that Dietmann had been so shocked to see, and had reacted to like they had were *Unclean!* had said to her as the rest of them clambered into their vehicle. Dietmann's corpse had fallen dramatically onto that of Ada, his hand still clasped around hers. Two fucked up humans together forever, *how romantic,* she thought, before accepting the offer from the stranger. Without a second thought she rifled through Ada's pocket, pulling keys and a mobile from her jacket, and rushed toward the car urgently. She found herself seated herself beside the man mountain in the back seat, crushing the blond scar-faced man against the other side. The man mountain shuffled further away from her almost apologetically, in a gesture of chivalry, and compounded the discomfort for his friend. The driver, the man who had offered the ride, sped away from the scene, leaving Dietmann and Ada to rot, with the red-haired girl in the front passenger seat. Liezel noted that between shifting gears his hand remained firmly upon her thigh, squeezing it, as if to ensure that she was still there. Nobody had said a word until the car approached more road works, grinding to a halt around the back end of the marina, she couldn't tell if more sirens were headed their way, but she wasn't going to take any chances by

looking back, behind them. The driver was the first to speak, his eyes directed through the mirror at the blond man at the other side of the hulking monster. "Do you wanna tell me what the fuck that was about?" He said, calmly but more than just a hint of irritation seeping through his words. Liezel chose to remain quiet, try to figure them out before their attentions turned to her.
"I had it under control, but I told you, I have this thing-" The guy in the back said, as if he were going to continue.
"Yeah, yeah, half past, I know, but mate, there's a time and a place, and when my baby's at stake, both of em, waiting for half past is not the fucking time!" The driver interrupted him, slamming his hand on the wheel as if to emphasise the point, inadvertently honking the horn. As if somehow awoken from their slumber the drivers of the other cars in the queue began to honk theirs too, like it was going to instantly create a thoroughfare for them all to float through. No, it only polluted the ears of the world, like the road-works that they were waiting in polluted the view. She'd heard of Marseille becoming the City of Culture next year, and hoped that these very same drivers would appreciate it eventually.

The blond guy in the back couldn't bring himself to retort, the driver had played his ace card early, and it had stumped him. Beneath the sound of the constant horn-honking the silence remained. They had their own issues to resolve before they got to her, everybody seemed to be mad at the scar-faced guy.
"So, who are you people?" She spoke out, chancing her arm, they were obviously enemies of Ada, which by some extension made them pretty okay in Liezel's eyes. Suddenly there were four faces looking at her,

as if they'd forgotten she was even in the car. Their turn to move forward came, and the driver spoke as he shifted it into gear.

"I'm Tom," he said, his eyes flickering at her in the rear-view, "this is Jess, the beefy bloke next to you is Beefy, erm, Cristiano, and the half-past fan next to him is Rufus," Liezel could tell that he was still pissed off at Rufus by the way he said his name, but it would probably be forgotten before long, "What about you?" He asked, introductions considered done.

"Liezel." She said, they'd only offered names. Tom looked at her expectantly, but she said nothing more. He laughed a little.

"Fair enough, so what's your story?" He continued, mirth still evident in his voice.

"You first." Said Liezel, the ball was in their court. Tom shook his head with a grin, and rolled his eyes.

"That's how you're gonna play it eh? Okay, short version, Me, Jess, and Mr Beefy used to work with Ada and Dietmann in some fucked up organisation. We kind of robbed and killed our boss. Ada sent Johnny Half-Past to kill us, he messed it up but now we're all pals." He spat out as the car circled the edge of the marina. As the information sunk in it rattled Liezel, she was in a car with *them*. The people Dietmann had told her so much about. The way he spoke of them was as much with reverence, like they were German folk heroes, as it was with vitriol. Sometimes she'd suspected that he wished that he'd done it first, but the more she got to know him it was just a case of he was in awe of the balls they'd displayed in doing anything at all.

"Your turn." Tom said, clearly the most vocal of his posse. Liezel wasn't sure that there *was* a short version of her story, so she told them everything. From the advertisement in the newspaper, to her game, which Cristiano seemed to appreciate more than the others, interjecting every so often to input his own experience of it. The more she spoke the more they seemed to warm to her, especially Cristiano, who crushed the ever quiet Rufus further still into the side of the car, so much so that he threatened to become a part of the plastic interior, a blond, scar-faced, limited edition interior, one of a kind.

She'd got as far as the missions that Ada had been sending her on when they pulled up outside the Radisson Blu, Tom giving her the signal that they could continue upstairs. For some reason Liezel felt no fear, no wariness with these people, they seemed easy going. She could almost admit to feeling an affinity toward them, which was unheard of in recent years, considering that the frosty atmospheres in Monte Carlo of Ada's constructing were all she had known. The filthy stinking paedophiles and rapists that she'd encountered were the furthest thing from a release from it. It was like she'd forgotten what friendly faces looked like. The way that Tom was affectionate toward Jess, Cristiano's beaming big face, even Rufus, although he still seemed in their bad books, had an aura about him. There was definitely something about them that didn't just say they'd maybe help her, it said they would probably love to.

Who's Got A Sweaty Fanny?

It never rains, I'm telling you. You wait years for one adventure, and then nine come at once. It's like adventure fucking dominos. Pick your cliché. Honestly, it's like we wrap something up, then it opens up a whole other can of worms.

Liezel finishes telling us her story, and for the first time in forever I'm speechless. I mean, what the fuck kind of circus has Ada been running? I find it hard to believe that she's not been continuing the good work of one Mr Philip Hoxton, or whatever he chooses to call himself in the afterlife, Deadward Scissorhands? Fuck knows, but yeah, she organised and ran the game in South Africa, and then sends new recruit Liezel off all over the world to research paedos, knowing full well that she'll hack them up. Okay, so that's not strictly true, Liezel says the first time she did it Ada went mental, telling her she'd fucked it up, but then after it that it all got a bit shady. She stopped getting pissed off, and carried on giving her carbon copy tasks, spent a lot more time on the phone or at her computer. Liezel says she's done these jobs at least seven times. What the fuck was Ada up to?

    The thing is, I agree with Jess, this is not our problem. Ada's dead, that's all we wanted, but something *still* sits uneasy with me. What if it's *The queen is dead, long live the queen*? What if whoever she's been on the phone to all the time is ready to step up and carry on until we're all finally dead? I can't have that. So the idea is that we head to the house with Liezel, rip it apart looking for evidence of any co-conspirators, and if we don't find any then it's happy days. Me and Jess can go back to the excitement of being future parents, future husband and wife, future everything.

    Rufus has decided he's coming to help tear the house up because he wants his money, even though the incompetent nobhead hasn't killed a single person, he thinks he's owed at least *something.* It's up to him, it's his life, he's welcome to join the party. I'm still a bit annoyed at him for not finishing the job with Ada, but in the grand scheme we're all alive and she's dead, so it'll pass. Beefy's obviously fawning over Liezel, I reckon she could have asked him to drive to Monte Carlo to eat her shit, straight from the whippy machine, and he'd have been up for it. Bless him, he's been an absolute superstar, I've got a lot of time for that bloke, *a lot* of time.

So here we are, in a convoy, The Society of Vengeful Pricks. In the rear-view I can see Rufus patting away to some tunes on the steering wheel of his Renault, which reminds me I need to have a good old chat with him about CCR, from what Jess told me he's a pretty massive fan, he even checked her into the hotel as Susie Q, the daft bastard. Up ahead there's Liezel powering on, leading the way, but I still remember the directions from back in the day. Beefy's sitting next to me and we've kinda run out of conversation for the time being, you know those moments where you talk for ages in a car, and then suddenly it goes silent and you can drive for miles before you start up again? Well, we're in one of those lulls. In the corner of my eye I can see him playing a game on the shit phone we got from Barcelona, one of those games where he has to keep a ball from dropping into the depths of wherever, little groans emanating from him whenever he loses. I look in the back seat to Jess, still asleep, and the signs for Cannes start rolling by the windows, not far to go now.

I can't believe that Ada's still using the house that Hoxton had, personally I'd feel a bit weird about it all, you know? Where your boss has had his face smashed in and been peppered with bullets? I wonder briefly if the ghost of Hoxton still stalks the place, but the notion passes. No such thing as ghosts. Liezel says the skulls are all still there an' all, except a bit more decorative, but she never asked about them. I half fancy that Ada's had him stuffed and put in her room, like a statue in his honour, maybe with his cock out and she locks herself onto it for a bit of a rogering now and then, thumping her sweaty fanny against his wrinkled old lubed up taxidermised todger, his wiry man-made pubes scratched the ring of her hoop. This thought makes me chuckle a bit to myself, so I interrupt Cristiano and tell him my thought. He absolutely cracks up, his bin lid of a hand slaps the dashboard.

"Sweaty fanny! That is a classic!" He roars, and suddenly Jess chirps up from the back, in that sweet voice she's got when she's just woken up, you know the one that girls do? When she rubs her eyes at the same time and it evolves into this cute as hell stretch, and she squeaks while she does it, then for about five minutes she talks in the high pitched half-dazed voice.

"Who's got a sweaty fanny?" She asks absent-mindedly, and Beefy's about to tell her but I shake my head, no, not the time.

"Nobody baby, get back to sleep, you've got an hour before we get there."

Some Sort Of Olden Day French Banksy

He'd put too much time and effort into this *not* to get paid. A deal was a deal. The two glaring facts that he'd not managed to kill anybody yet, and that the person he had made the deal with was dead, were irrelevant. He now had access to her home, her office, and potentially, her safe, and he was getting something out of this trip, whether it was cash or something he could sell on.

The sun had had his hat on all day, but by the time the cars were crunching up the gravel driveway of the house that Ada had left to them in her non-existent will, the sun was being called in by his mum for tea, just before he was about ready for putting his pyjamas and slippers on, and settling down with a drink of pop and Blue Peter on the telly. It shone through the overhanging evergreen trees which tickled the roof of the cars as they slithered up the path, opening up eventually to reveal a huge courtyard and sandstone looking mansion house. The house looked an impressive as it did expensive, the six bay windows at ground floor level were as least as tall as Rufus, as were the upstairs ones. A four door garage stood to the right of the building, no doubt housing a variety of pricey cars, but the closed doors stood to withhold such information for the time being.

Rufus pulled himself out of the Megane and whistled his appreciation of the size of the house to Tom, who gave him a nod of agreement.

"It's awesome pal, honestly." He said, evidently warming back up to Rufus, Jess joined them from the back of their car, and grabbed hold of one of Tom's bruised hands, pulling it to her face and kissing it gently. He smiled at his girlfriend with affection, and reciprocated with a peck on the side of her head. Charley came to his mind once again, and danced with his guilt. Still he thought it was for the best, but watching the pair of them he couldn't help but regret the conversation that morning. He'd left it on something of an ominous air, as if he were a soldier, making one last call to his wife back home before he went behind enemy lines, like it was the last time they'd ever speak because he could be dead. He owed her at least a phone call to let her know he was okay. He owed her *that* much. Liezel had let the others into the house, but Rufus endeavoured to hang back, pulling out his mobile. He looked back at his recent calls, she was there, last called made. Charley. That picture that he'd assigned as her contact image, from Morecambe. His finger hovered over the green telephone image, the one that would call her, it seemed to hang there for minutes. Rufus sighed, yeah she deserved to know he was okay but he couldn't bring himself to do it, *why* was he calling her? If push came to shove and she started asking questions about *them* then what could he say? *Oh, I'm sorry, I saw two people being affectionate and wanted to call you, but when I think about it with a clearer head I'll only break your heart again*? As the clock on the phone clicked to five thirty one he locked his phone with regret and put it back into his pocket, she could wait. When all of this was done with he'd go and see her face to face, explain what he was trying to do. He needed to put her out of his mind, because he was standing in front of a mansion with the keys to the cookie jar. The others might have other motives for being there but his were plain and simple. Loot the place.

    The mouth of the house swallowed him whole, leading to a throat of pure luxury, a grand staircase rolling round the edge of its interior to an upper level that he'd have a good look around later, he was simply following the voices of the others through the building, deep into its stomach. The stomach itself was a colossal open-plan cavern of yet more luxury, doors dotted all around the perimeter to rooms that would no doubt store more extravagance. At the far end of the floor stood a kitchen that he was surprised to see was made of mostly slate and chrome, rather than gold and platinum. He had lived a pretty decent life on the money he brought in, but this was a glimpse of something altogether different. His modest flat would easily fit into this one room, he considered that it would probably fit in the kitchen, but kept his mouth shut, just cased the place silently as he approached the others. Liezel was pouring drinks into glasses for everybody, it was also her that was doing the talking. "Ada always kept her room locked, I don't know what's in there, I've never seen it, never needed to." She said, her tone hinting that she was responding to a question. As the discussion continued Rufus took his glass of juice for a walk, scrutinising the works of art upon the walls, some by people he'd heard of, most by people he had not. The paintings may as well have just been six feet canvasses with the words *You Are One Uncultured Cunt* daubed on in shit, such was his lack of knowledge on the matter. As he stood before one, it was massive, taking up most of one of the walls, and looked essentially like a bunch of nudies dying on a raft, all cocks, tits and beards, he was aware he had company.

"The Raft Of The Medusa," a voice said, Jess, he glanced at her and then back at the painting, it looked a bit dramatic, he couldn't imagine ever having the patience to paint something like that, Jess continued, "it's a French painting, by the Romantic painter Theodore Gericault, a masterpiece. It caused outrage in the Seventeenth century, especially with their versions of The Daily Mirror, at the time all of the painters were blowing smoke up the government's arse, Gericault was outlining its inadequacies. It's subtle but powerful, it shows the survivors of a French ship that had run aground, on a crudely made raft, because of a lack of lifeboats. He could have been beheaded or something if he'd just come out and painted the sinking ship, so it's very brave. I think it's beautiful. Only fifteen people survived out of almost a hundred and fifty." The girl some brains in her head, that was for damn sure.

"Yeah? Is he some sort of olden day French Banksy?" Asked Rufus, attempting to place some sort of present day context to her story. She smiled and rolled her eyes.
"Not exactly." She said, but with not even a hint on contempt for his observation. *Idiot,* he thought, but he didn't *ask* for the story of the painting.
"Is it worth anything?" He asked, a far more important piece of information is his opinion. She shook her head.
"No, this is a fake, the original is in *Le Louvre,* and it's basically priceless."

Flecks Of Disappointed Limescale

Jess is over talking to Rufus in front of some whack off great big painting, she knows shit loads about art, loves it she does. When we went to the Louvre I didn't need the little headphones tour that you get. No, she spent ages in front of all of this stuff, getting right passionate about it all, all the little details of the stories behind the pictures, what the artists were supposedly going through or why they did what they did. Most of it went over my head but when you see her in full swing, honestly, it melts your heart. She looks my way and I give her a little smile, before turning back to Liezel.
"So I reckon now's as good a time as any yeah?" I say, no point wasting time gassing about nowt when there's answers to be got. Beefy's watching Liezel, and he's spotted an opportunity to impress.
"I can break down the door if you wish?" He's still just trying to stare deep into her eyes, his biceps twitching, I dunno if he even knows doing it sometimes. It's hilarious. Liezel rolls her eyes and shakes both her head, and the keys that she'd

extracted from the twitching corpse of the Cuntarian, much to Mr Beefy's disappointment, honestly. You can actually see him exude disappointment, like his enormous brown head is a steam iron and somebody's pressed that button you get on the top to make the mist whoosh out, that's what he is, a steam iron, spitting flecks of disappointed limescale all over our clothes. Hated it when I used to have to iron my clothes and got them bits all over them. I digress. "That will not be necessary." Says Liezel, and looks my way as if to beckon me to follow. While we walk I'm wondering if Ada's not only jumped into the old man's grave, I'm wondering if she's jumped into his bed an' all. Not while he's in it, of course. I say that, but then really I wouldn't be surprised. What I mean is, she's using his study, has she taken his bedroom too now he's gone? I'm sure we'll find out.

     We stalk the wide corridor, easily enough for five or six wide, but we're walking single file, me, Liezel, and Cristiano. Jess seems to want to stay in the lounge, which is fine by me. I know she didn't really want to come here, but she knows I won't be able to settle if there's the chance that somebody else is gonna come looking for us. The walls are still covered in the same old shit copies of paintings as we walk the length of the hallway, she's not had the decorators in since we left. Not like *that.* Get your head out of the gutter, but since we're on it, the way Ada was, it was like she *always* had the decorators in. Perennially pissed off. You know?
Anyway, Liezel stops at a door, it's defo Hoxton's old study, surprise surprise. Shuffling through the keys she stops at one and starts to fuck the keyhole with it like the cock of a fifteen year old virgin poking at his schoolgirl sweetheart's fanny. It's not happening. She tries a few others, and I can see Cristiano visibly

itching to just power through it, but eventually the fifteen year old virgin comes of age and becomes a superstar fanny fucking lothario, and the portal swings open. Jackpot.

The room takes my breath away. It's basically the same as before. The old boy's desk, the filing cabinets, the door to the vault, and most disconcertingly of all, those same fucking skulls, but what Ada's done is plant them all over the room, like they're looking down from all angles. From their eyes there's light bulbs, like, spotlights all over. The mad bitch has gone right to town. Looks to me like she *has* had the decorators in. Well, an electrician at least. Speaking of going to town, Liezel's already in the drawers, pulling out papers and books. I move to the other side of the desk and she's handing me bits to go through as well. There's not a great deal of information in there though, some numbers, they look like IP addresses, there's also some random words, and some decimalised numbers, but no actual names, and it's names I'm after.

"That's a lot of IPs." She says, her brow furrowing, and she pulls the sheets of paper from me, scanning the info, then she drops them and gets up to leave the room.

"Carry on if you wish, I need to get my laptop."

A Thousand Times Over

I always liked the prints in this house, none of them ever genuine paintings, but they're still very lovely to look at. I always loved art. I can't paint for the life of me, but I love to look at the work of people who can. I'm in awe of their talent. I don't think Rufus is interested in the stuff I'm telling him but I'm enjoying myself, the passion just comes up from within me and

I can't help but smile when I talk about their stories, like I can't believe that nobody else is feeling the pleasure that I'm taking from them.

Every time, after making a forced effort to ask a question about what I'm telling him, Rufus inquires about their worth, so after the fourth print, Van Gogh's *The Starry Night* I just tell him that none of them are worth anything. That they are for show. He seems unimpressed.

"Is anything in this place worth anything?" He asks, picking up a vase that could be worth hundreds of thousands but he's disheartened by my revelation, and he's throwing it a short distance from hand to hand as if he were an American baseball player, throwing a ball into a glove.

"I don't know, it's been so long since we were here last." I answer, taking the vase from his grasp and placing it back on the small round table that he took it from. He seems slightly put out by my action, and he's about to continue on his wander but turns to me and frowns, like something's just occurred to him.

"What are you lot going to do if you do find anything?" He asks.

"What do you mean?"

"I mean, the old bloke you screwed over, he's gone, the bitch Ada is dead, so's her mate, whatever his name was."

"Dietmann."

"Yeah, him. What if you find out somebody else is involved?" He asks, and I have to admit to myself that I don't know the answer. Tom is so single minded sometimes, that I find myself going along with it just because he always puts such a compelling argument forward. But we're still alive, we've come through everything and it's down to him. I owe him my life a thousand times over.

"Tom knows what he's doing." I say, turning away from him as if to draw a line under the conversation. I'm not getting into it with him. His phone starts up, a different song to before, but it sounds like it could be the same musicians as the other ringtone, all drums and twanging guitars, as the singer starts up with lyrics that sound like *Some folks are born, made to wave the flag, ooh, they're red, white and blue.* It's definitely the same band that he's been banging on about since I've known him, and he holds a finger as if to excuse himself, turning his back and talking quietly into the phone whilst he slowly moves further away from me. The hushed tone he's using seems very reverent, and level. I'm slightly intrigued as to what the person on the other end of the line has done to deserve such respect, but it's really none of my business so I decide to go and find Tom.

Recalcitrant And Aggressive

"Rufus, darling, please tell me I'm not seeing what I'm seeing, please! Tell me that my eyes deceive me!" No *Hello,* no *How are you?* The bloke was clearly distressed, but Rufus felt inclined to drag it out, not lay all of his cards out at once.
"Mr Charles, I'm not sure I know what you're talking about." He said, let the man tell *him.*
"Oh Rufus, don't play coy with me, it's all over the news, Ada, and Dietmann, they're dead! Tell me it wasn't you! Tell me!" He demanded, Rufus could almost hear the tears banging against the inside of Isaac Charles' ducts, like they were locked inside, with a rapidly rising water level, begging to be released. He didn't say anything.
"Do you have any idea of what you've done Rufus? Do you know how much money you're costing me? Not

to mention time! Ada and I, we had a good thing going!" Whether the questions were rhetorical or not he couldn't tell, so he opted to remain tight-lipped once again. Isaac Charles was notorious for looking after his finances, and his propensity for cutting down anybody that messed with his ability to make money with the utmost of spite was well documented in the open air of public. The reality of it, behind closed doors, was much worse. Rufus knew this from first-hand experience, because *he* was the man that Isaac Charles usually sent to take his pound of flesh. Sometimes literally. How did he know that Ada was dead? The news wouldn't have had her name, only the situation, and how the hell did he know that Rufus was anywhere near it? It was almost like the man could read his thoughts, could see the visible of evidence of the cogs whirring in his face.

"You were *there* Rufus, you and four others, you were described in very vivid detail. She had herself followed. You went behind my back and climbed right into bed with the enemy! You've broken my heart!" Isaac Charles bellowed, now in his mind's eye Rufus could see him flouncing down onto a chaise longue, collapsing in a velour clad heap, the back of his forearm to his head. He didn't know what to say. What *could* he say? He might as well do what the kid Dietmann did and bite the bullet.

"Mr Charles, it wasn't me, it wasn't any of us. The bloke shot her and then he did himself. Seriously." He stated, calmly, and truthfully. A dramatic sigh almost pierced his ear drum.

"Oh, don't treat me like I'm an imbecile, do you think I'm an imbecile? Is that what you think Rufus?"

"No, of course not."

"Do you know what you've done?"

"But I haven't-"

"You've cost me millions Rufus, you and your petty squabbles, everything is ruined and you have cost me bloody millions!"
"Mr Charles-"
"You and your little friends have made a very powerful enemy today, a *very* powerful enemy!"
The line went dead, leaving Rufus in exasperated silence, perturbed by the fact that once his focus arrived back in the room he was staring directly at the huge painted cock of a bloke from *The Raft of The Medusa.* He didn't know what to think. Isaac Charles as an enemy would be recalcitrant and aggressive. He knew this because the man had told him once, when they had had a meeting regarding yet another of Isaac Charles' grudges. Rufus didn't even know what recalcitrant meant, but it sounded serious. The crux of the situation was that the damage was done, and it seemed to answer a very valuable question. He rubbed his face thoughtfully, his fingers rolling over the smooth, almost plastic-like feel of the scar on his cheek, like a fleshy pathway running down the middle of the rough artificial grass of his stubbled face-garden. He turned on his heels and explored the hallway looking for the others, finding them in a large study room filled bizarrely with skulls. Tom sat at the desk, flicking through papers, Cristiano at a computer, thumping a variety of password attempts, seemingly to no avail. Jess stood by the window, watching the ocean beyond it. Rufus cleared his throat to attract their attention, with success, and then tried to figure out how to tell them, he went with;
"I think I know who's in cahoots with your girl Ada."
He said with the palm of his hand feeling the texture of the hair on the back of his head, it felt greasy, it

needed washing. Tom's face looked at him expectantly, eagerly, and then impatiently.
"Don't tell me you're waiting til half past to tell us." He said, only half joking. Rufus smiled and shook his head knowingly, he *did* deserve that one. As he was about to open his mouth he was interrupted by Hurricane Liezel, whirling into the room.
"Who the fuck is Isaac Charles?!"

Chapter 20 - February

<u>Only A Fool Would Attempt To Control It</u>

The explosion rippled through the evening air of London. In Brentford a woman named Wendy thought it had started thundering, and sent her son to the garden to go and fetch the washing in. The opposite side of Kensington, in Peckham, it was assumed that somebody had been shot, and the expectation was that the sirens would start sounding in the distance, long before the blue lights would appear. Neither of those was true.

The ground rumbled, shaking barely dedicated crumbs of cement from buildings, had it been October then it would have performed the entire leaf-from-tree job of autumn in one go. The sound wave echoed across the sky, away from its epicentre. It gave way to a chorus of car alarms, singing to each other across the city as if they were dogs, communicating, and the screeching screams of hundreds of people, scattering in several directions. Some, the braver or more curious of them, ran toward the source of the explosion, cheering at the most recent piece of several pieces of excitement in their lives that were at somebody else expense, causing mayhem on Kensington Road. The more timid souls created a stampede through the narrow road away from it, taking with them police officers, cameramen, and Alex Green, intrepid field reporter and news breaker. The police cordon was now as useful as discarded ticker tape, once loved by a child of somewhere like New York, waving it around as a giant float of Spongebob Squarepants rolled by in some celebratory parade, now abandoned and awaiting the vigilant eye of a criminal serving community service, armed with litter picking grabber and a bin bag.

As chaos ensued all around him, Chief Inspector Philip Benson cowered in the stairwell that descended toward a basement flat. He knew that only a fool would attempt to control it, but these recent developments had given him an idea, and he only had a short time to act upon it. His nervous fingers danced over the keys of his phone, searching out the contact information that he needed. He pressed the phone to his ear, and awaited a response.
"Get the ARV in here now, we're moving in."

A Gigantic Dark Grey Turd

Another foot struck his head, another ringing in his ears, another flash of stars behind his eyelids. He'd curled up into as tight a ball as he could. His arms cradling the sides of his head but they couldn't protect all of it, the feet were relentless, wave after wave of stampeding shoes, all belonging to people that couldn't care less what they hit in their selfish personal sprint for safety. The metallic taste of blood in his mouth was beginning to make him feel sick, he hated it, and a sore sharp ache running across his face told him that his nose was broken. This was a very unexpected turn of events. One minute he was the centre of attention, the audience hanging onto his every word, it was the greatest, and defining moment of his career. At that point, when Wayne Cooper fed him the news, word for word, he was the king of the world. The hush afterwards, the furious look on the police chief's face, the other reporters hurriedly making their phone calls to check for confirmation of what he had said. It was a bold claim. It changed the entire game. *Will Thunder was not working alone.*

Nobody could have ever expected it. Then the explosion literally rocked their foundations, throwing the whole area into complete disarray. The last thing he saw was the forearm of a skinny guy with a goatee beard, his face didn't look too scared, but of course he was moving with the tide. It was probably that forearm that broke his nose. He felt like a jockey at the Grand National, taking an early lead but then fallen at the first fence, and been subjected to the clomping hooves of almost every horse on the field. Including his own. Eventually the stampede thundered off into the distance, the sound of the screaming and yelping subsided, and Alex Green rolled over on to his back. Every inch of him creaked in pain. In the sky above him smoke billowed, dragged along on a northerly wind from somewhere near Hyde Park like a gigantic dark grey turd, his eyes followed to as close to their source as they could, the grey became lightly tinged with orange, something was on fire. He wanted to move but his body was still just being thankful for being left alone, it wouldn't cooperate. What the *hell* had happened? The reality of the fact was that on top of the events here, London was currently being subjected to a terrorist attack too. Had they seen their opportunity, whilst the eyes of the world were on him? Who could say? Danny, the cameraman, came into his line of vision, looking down upon his colleague with concern on his face, dropping closer as he got to his knees.

"You alright mate? That was crazy." He said, before blowing through pursed lips, his cheeks being pumped up to their limit. Alex nodded as best he could with his bruised and bloody head against the concrete floor.

"Yeah." He croaked through the pain, already he knew that his lips were on their way, and would balloon before long. Another face joined Danny's above him, the Chief Inspector, looking decidedly less sympathetic than that of his friend.

"You stupid, stupid prick." He said, shaking his head, before turning his attention to Danny.

"Get him out of my sight, an ambulance is on its way."

Eyes Forward Cheech And Chong

From the relative safety of the backseat of the car he watched the flames dancing through the trees. He fancied that he could almost feel the heat from here, like when it was bonfire night in his childhood, and rather than pay for entry into the rugby club grounds, his mum used to stand with him by the mesh gates, and watch the fire from there, that toastie heat warming him to the core, home-made hotdog in hand, waiting for the fireworks display to begin. In the present day the fireworks had already begun. From his vantage point he saw the rubbernecking jackals moving together to view the display. They had dropped Liezel for something newer, more exciting, more dangerous. *He* would never do that. If he weren't here being held by these people, whoever they were, then he would be. They would all scatter to see their new spectacle, and he would remain, as loyal as ever.

The two blokes in the front of the car had not said much since the bomb went off, just did the same as him and watched the flames. Jake wanted to ask them something, but the one called Rufus had already told him that he had if he stepped out of line then he wouldn't let the weed thief stop him from shooting Jake between the eyes. He believed him too, there was a deranged look in his eyes when he had said it, and that scar on his face, you didn't get one of those unless you associated with shady characters. The weed thief, whose name he hadn't managed to catch yet, was playing the good cop in the situation. "Sorry kid, but you're coming with us." He had said at the time, having just saved his life from the mad man Rufus, and picked him up from the ground by the crook of his elbow, and handed him his bag. The weed thief's face was so much different from his partner's, he looked annoyed more than angry.

When Jake had had a chance to study it there was a strange playfulness in his eyes, like he wasn't a bad guy, but, well, Jake didn't know. Maybe it was just the drugs that clouded his own judgment. They had marched him through the trees, taking care to stay in the shadows, muttering to one another as they stayed behind him. At one point he felt inclined to turn to ask them where they were taking him but the weed thief had called out in a hushed tone.

"Eyes forward Cheech and Chong, behave yourself and you'll be reyt."

They hadn't walked too far before they were approaching a car, whose brand he didn't recognise, he didn't know much about automobiles in all fairness. When lads at college had raved about low profile tyres or twin exhausts he always joked about his trainers being all the tires he needed, or his arse being his exhaust pipe. He liked to think he was quite funny when wanted to be. He liked to think.

Rufus opened the door for him, and the other one told him to get in, sit still, and be quiet, and he duly complied. The pair of them had had a brief discussion before the Rufus one pulled out a mobile phone, turned his body away from Jake, but kept his eyes on the other bloke. Jake was sure he saw the other bloke nod, it was only subtle, and it could have been all in his head in the dark, but he was *sure* he had seen him

nod, right before the Rufus one did something on his phone, and then all hell broke loose. The evening sky over the tree lined horizon had exploded into a bright orange light, exactly in the same way as the bonfire from his childhood, and in the foreground of his view he watched his own face reflected in the same shade. His focus had shifted sharply to see the two men turn round, and climb into the car. Rufus in the passenger seat and his friend in the driving seat. Between them they didn't say a word. That was twenty minutes ago and Jake was beginning to wonder exactly what was happening. He felt tempted to ask them the question but every time his brain worked up any kind of courage his mouth refused to cooperate, so he simply sighed, and turned his head to watch the flames.
"Here we go." The driver, the weed thief, muttered to the one called Rufus, attracting the attention of the prisoner in the back. A figure was approaching the car, moving with a combination of haste and stealth. The blokes up front seemed to have been expecting it, and broke into welcomes when the figure climbed into the back beside Jake.
"Alright?" The driver asked, but the newcomer seemed not to want to return the gesture, they simply pulled the balaclava from their face, shook a pony tail loose, and looked at Jake directly in the eyes. *Those eyes.* It was like his world had shrunk to the size of a pea, not a marrowfat pea, not even a garden pea, but the kind of dried pea often found in a maraca. In it there were just him and her. A bubble from which the whole world had disappeared. The two in the front were gone, a blinding light circled her and only her. He couldn't stop himself, he had to speak, and he had to say something.

"Liezel?" He whispered, barely audible even to himself. Liezel looked him up and down, and spoke to the blokes up front.
"Who the fuck is this guy?"

Chapter 21 - January

Charlie Big Bollocks

"Oh fuck." Said Tom. Jess showed a slight glimmer of familiarity with the mention of the name, Cristiano remained entirely nonplussed, and Rufus turned to her with a resigned expression of a man who knew that they were doomed.

"So? Who is he?" Liezel asked again, *and more to the point, how is it that he has sent Ada photographs of me at work?* She thought to herself, but she wanted to know if he was a name they recognised. Certainly, to some of them, it was. Ada's phone had been locked, and Liezel did not want to risk it becoming block it by entering three incorrect PINs, so she had hooked the device up to her laptop, and raided the entire drive, taken copies of the call list, texts sent, and files received. His name had appeared on almost everything that Ada had been involved with. The first exchanges she had found were financial transactions, large sums of money between the pair. Liezel considered that maybe the guy was some sort of broker, maybe Ada was investing in property or some such, but the idea didn't seem to make sense. The deeper she delved into the device, she found exchanges of emails between the pair, discussing Liezel, and the tasks that she had been given. They talked of how much interest she had piqued, how many speculators there were. It didn't make sense. What were they talking about? Then she stumbled across the received documents, and the world seemed to crash around her ears, she could literally *feel* the colour draining from her face, like a rapidly emptying egg timer. Her stomach performed the kinds of somersaults that a family of circus athletes would struggle to pull off, even with years of training. The files. Every single file that Ada had placed before her. From the start, when they sent her on the first job, to research the guy in Arizona, showed her the images of his deviance, the child abuser, the one that had put her where she was today. It had come from Isaac Charles. The history of each and every one of them. The evidence, *he* had put it together, *he* was the one who put all of these people her way. But why? What did anybody stand to gain from sending her on these ridiculous assignments? She scrolled through her entire back catalogue of murder, saw the faces of her victims staring back at her, some were their police mug shots, some were photographs lifted straight from social networking sites, taken at arm's length with a wannabe cool pose. The memories of them all flooded back with each photo she had opened. Then it got worse, the next batch of pictures were of *her*. Somebody had been following her, gathering evidence of what she had done. There were hidden camera images from the homes of these people, the man Gary for example, there were pictures showing Liezel delivering boot after boot to his face, in vivid detail. With each photo there was a time, not in the time-of-day sense either, it appeared to be a stopwatch, a timer. The one of her wiping the blood from her foot onto the side of his armchair, that was taken at twelve minutes and thirty six seconds. The one where she finally put a bullet in his head, fifteen minutes and seven seconds. It didn't make sense. The room around her twisted out of all recognition, she *knew* that something wasn't right when it was happening, but couldn't put her finger on it.

With all of the files before her in separate windows she looked for some sort of correlation between

them, but nothing seemed to match, it was just a mess of information. Money going in and out of bank accounts, the files of the men she had killed, timed photographs of her killing the same men. And of course the Will Thunder file. She needed to focus, put some perspective on it all. Why would they time the pictures? Who were these speculators of which this man Isaac Charles spoke? How did the bank transactions tie in with it all? She needed answers, and it looked like she had the clues for the rest of them as to whether there was somebody else involved, so she had rushed down to them in here. She knew from the responses of Tom and Rufus that she probably wouldn't like the answer to her question, but she needed to know.
"Well?" She asked, one last time. Rufus seemed to want to respond first.
"This is what I was gonna tell you," He looked to Tom, and then the rest of them, before continuing, "He knows we were involved in Ada's death, I don't know how but he does. He said we've cost him millions, and that we've fucked everything that him and her had going on. He's the one who put me on to Ada in the first place, when she wanted someone to, you know? I've known him years. Everybody knows who he is, he's a fucking celebrity, a Charlie Big Bollocks. He creates superstars out of dickhead nobodies, puts them on telly, in the magazines, makes a lot of money off it too, and then he cuts 'em loose. It's like he can read the public like they were a book for kids, gives 'em what they want then moves on to the next big thing. But that's just a front. You couldn't even begin to know how much evidence of shit I've done that he's holding. He's a nasty fucker." He finished with a shake of his head, reflecting on the nasty part. Tom stepped forward.

"He used to work with Hoxton, like, me and Beefy, half the people we-" He turned to Jess, and stopped himself saying the word, "Most of the people Hoxton sent us for were 'cause of fucking Isaac Charles, it were like they were on a dual mission to wipe half the population of the world out, and they sent me and him to do it." He gestured toward Cristiano who nodded in agreement.

"Yes, a great many people we killed." The Spaniard confirmed, before Tom shook his head at him not to continue.

Still Liezel alone couldn't make sense of his involvement, so she shared with the others what she'd found out, describing it all in great detail. Even as she said it all again she hoped that something would fall into place, a linking piece of the jigsaw to put it right in her head. When she'd finished the others sat in stunned silence, looking to one another for some sort of answer for her.

"It's a game." The voice of Jess, who had sat and listened intently to everything that had played out before her, heard all aspects of the situation, and chose now to be the time to speak. She'd captured the attention of the other four, and it appeared that they wanted her to go on.

"If you check the bank transfers, I bet they match up to when you did what you did. Speculators, times on the photographs. They've been playing a game. They've been betting on how long it took you to finish them off. And this Will Thunder thing, they were going to do the same again, but we sort of spoiled that. I hate to say it, but if we want to get him to leave us alone, you're still going to have to go through with it."

The Big Passive Letterbox

She's hit the nail on the head, I know it. It's the only answer that makes sense. When Ada's got a dwindling gang of loyal servants, she's pretty much fucked if she thinks she's gonna get any more of those games that Hoxton set up. But she was that kind of lass, she would just *have* to prove that she could still do it, whether it was with or without the others. We're still coming up short with how she was doing it, how they got people to gamble on it, but my guess is that we'll find out soon, I never met the guy but I know that Isaac Charles likes to talk, I remember seeing him on telly back in my old life, he just would not shut up. I mean, seriously, if his own voice were a person he'd wine it, dine it, and fuck the shit out of it. For sure, if his own voice was a person, I think Isaac Charles would defo let *it* be the postman and he'd bend over and play the big passive letterbox. He loves the sound of it *that* much.

Liezel's eyes go all narrow, and dart down to the floor, thinking though what Jess has said, properly intensely too, then she looks back up.

"I was going to do that anyway, I've seen what he's done, and he's going to pay for that, but there has to be a way of taking the sneaky bastard out too, because once I do it, he's only going to want more and more. I can't allow that to happen."

Fair play to her, 'cause she's taken it in her stride, I'd go mental, knowing that people have been using me like that, putting my life at risk to make money. It looks like Ada's done a bit of a number on her, I bet she's wishing she got the chance to put a bullet in her before Dietmann. Rufus starts shuffling about a bit, and he clearly wants to say something, but his face is twisting like he's struggling to figure out how to put it. I don't think anybody else has noticed it so I feel moved to speak up.

"What's up Johnny Half Past?" I ask, I do enjoy calling people Johnny Something, like, it can define either their whole personality, or just a funny aspect of it. Beefy would be Johnny Muscles, Jess would be Johnny Pregnant Face, I don't know Liezel well enough just yet to warrant giving her a Johnny name, but for sure, I'll come up with something before all this is done with. It feels like we're getting to the end of it in some way or another, I mean, there can't be anymore after Isaac Charles, surely. If there is they can go fuck themselves, I'll meet them face to face and tell 'em as much too. I'll offer to pay for 'em a cock extension so they can literally go fuck themselves.

"He were pretty mad when he phoned me, what makes you think he'll even accept the offer? What if he pleads ignorance and we rile him up even more?" Rufus finally asks, and he's got something of a point, but how can we rile him up even more? He's already pretty much said we're at the top of his shit list.

"What have we got to lose?" Jess steps in, reading my mind. Rufus considers this, and shrugs.

"Suppose so. So how are we gonna play it?" He looks to all of us, and this is the tough bit. We got lucky with the Ada plan, 'cause it was a shit plan in all fairness, and fucking Rufus, with his predilection towards doing everything at strange times, almost fucked it up for us. We can't afford to be that lackadaisical this time round. Liezel's gonna try to take out Will Thunder, *Will fucking Thunder*. This is actually mad as owt. She's told us what he's been up to but I'm slightly struggling to believe it, I've not seen much of him this last two or three years, but he always seemed like butter wouldn't melt. Him and Johnny Lightning were so clean cut. You could barely imagine them having sex lives, let alone possessing cocks, they were like a pair of family-friendly eunuchs.

"Well, you're the one who seems to know the guy, so I'm afraid you're gonna have to be the one who speaks with him Rufus, find out what he wants from us, tell him what we're prepared to do. I need you to basically get on your hands and knees and beg him to let us do this to make amends. Once he agrees, we have to work out exactly how we're going to play it." Liezel says, leaning against the frame of the doorway, hands behind her arse, cushioning it, she's cool as a cucumber this one, good to have on board. Rufus is nodding but you can tell he didn't want to hear that. I'm racking my brains to think of a way to do it, I don't think he'd be daft enough to fall for the same shit trick that Ada did, he's not gonna want to meet us. He doesn't strike me as the kind of bloke who'd ever get his hands dirty in the grand scheme, he'll always be the bloke behind the bloke who gets his hands dirty. For a man who loves publicity so much he does a very good job of staying in the shadows. Then it hits me like a train. Publicity.

"I don't know, but why don't we play the shithead at his own game?" I pipe up, and it draws curious slash confused looks from the others, and I explain what I'm talking about. Rufus seems dubious, Beefy's not said much at all, just been trying to catch Liezel's eye. Jess and Liezel are nodding, their idea factories working overtime.

"Okay, I like it, Jess, can you find out everything you can about Will Thunder and Isaac Charles? Just go online, if these people are as famous as you say they are there's bound to be something out there that will help, I don't care how small it might be, get everything you can. I need to get back onto my laptop

and work this stuff out. Boys, stay here and carry on." And she disappears from the room again leaving us with our thumbs up our arses. I turn to the others with a shrug and a grin.
"Well that's us told then eh?"

An Entire River Of Bad Blood

Google throws up almost three million hits. The first of which is the Wikipedia link, and I suppose it's as good a place as any to start. The larger than life face of Isaac Charles smiles out at me, and it makes my skin crawl. I can see the predatory instinct in his eyes, and feel myself getting dirtier the longer I look at him. With a shudder I scroll down and scan through the information that Wikipedia is giving me. I never really knew much about him. I've heard *of* him, and he always struck me as a slimeball. It tells me where and when he was born, and it surprises me to see he's well into his sixties, but he only looks about forty, I don't doubt for a second that he's had work done. It goes into his career which I scan over, looking for anything that we can exploit, the best I can come up on here with is his connection to the Terence Wilcox Corporation, how he worked closely with them, in a kind of *You scratch my back and I'll scratch yours* situation, at the time it was the norm, so no eyebrows were raised, and then when Terence Wilcox 'died' and became Philip Hoxton the relationship disappeared, and Isaac Charles' reputation for being a ruthless operator grew ever stronger. I click back on the browser and the next link is the actual Isaac Charles Organisation's dot com, I doubt I'll find much there. As a master of spin, it will most certainly be pro-Isaac Charles propaganda, but there should be something to do with his current roster of clients. It doesn't take much exploring to find it, and there are the usual high-end names, Mike Rotch, Jack Knapton, Maxwell Brooks, among others. His regular client base plays like a who's who of top earning performers, and it's unnerving to know how powerful he actually is. Almost every story you could wish to hear about in the magazines, he has some part in. It makes me wonder what's actually real and what's not. I'd love to be a fly on the wall of a room when he's creating some alternative reality for one of his clients. The rest of the website is a showcase for his organisation, and not much else, so I click back again, and continue to scroll down the search engine's homepage. There are a variety of pieces about some charity work and what a great guy he is, and it strikes me that there's barely anything that makes him look anywhere near bad, but surely he can't control *everything* that's printed or said about him. There has to be *something*. It's all *Isaac Charles donated this* or *Isaac Charles saved the lives of that* and it just doesn't feel right. I get as far as the third page of links before I wipe the slate clean and rethink my approach. Into the search bar I type *Isaac Charles Will Thunder,* hoping that maybe there's a connection between them both, the number of hits that creates is well into the tens of millions. At the top there are images of them individually, a small thumbnail of Will Thunder in front of some sponsored boards with Johnny Lightning, my cursor hovers over it and it increases in size slightly, showing them to be at some sort of television awards ceremony. Next to that there's an image of Isaac Charles, that sleazy grin on his face again, his eyebrows waxed and shaped to within an inch of their lives, but his actual brow hangs over his eyes a little bit, leaving them in a perennial shadow, he honestly gives me the creeps. It's when I scroll down to actual links that I begin to get an idea of what's happening, beneath each link there are a couple of lines explaining why it's showed up on my search.

***Isaac Charles** in acrimonious split from **Will Thunder** and Johnny Lighting, as the entertainers have taken their business to Giles Baker...*

***Will Thunder** and Johnny Lightning: "We don't need **Isaac Charles** to succeed"...*

***Isaac Charles** tells **Thunder** & Lightning "You **will** regret this"...*

And it goes on, and on, and on. The penny slowly drops, they have history, and it looks like there's an entire river of bad blood flowing between them. It's starting to look less and less likely that the reason Will Thunder was picked for Liezel's attention was any kind of coincidence. If it wasn't for the mountain of evidence that is at Liezel's disposal I'd even think he was being set up. I set the screen to print and race through to the study.

Chapter 22 - February

A Disconcerting Silence

"ARMED POLICE GET DOWN! GET DOWN!" The Chief APO roared as the door was thrown from its hinges, giving way to a seemingly endless tentacle of men coated in body armour wielding automatic guns. An arm emerged from the tentacle to cast a smoke grenade into the room, as the last man crossed the threshold the tentacle evolved into a snake, none of the eyes within the snake could see much in there, but it was felt entirely necessary to remove visibility. Part of the snake broke away from the slithering body to clomp up the stairs and proceed to break down every door within the building. In the first room they discovered a computer, its standby light blinking away, as it had been left untouched for more than an hour. A small digital video camera sat on the corner of the desk, linked by AV cables to the back of the tower. On the floor splatters of blood had dried and crusted, and had they not had the gas masks on they would have smelled the strong ammonia stench from where the piss had soaked into the carpet and evaporated into the claustrophobic room. They moved on to the next room, the main boudoir, the bed was empty but had definitely been slept in, although the length of time since it had been slept in was not definitive. The policemen turned back upon themselves with a swift flick of the fingers from the head of the trio.

Downstairs the snake had dispersed and become a series of six foot smudges creeping through the smoke. There was a disconcerting silence about the place, a distinct lack of movement from anybody that was not law enforcement. Chief APO Neil Robinson

edged deeper into the smoke, this was not what he had been expecting. In the last available footage Esterhuizen was unmasked, congratulating the media for their good work, she seemed to welcome the release from the disguise. In the background Will Thunder still sat strapped to the chair, his face badly disfigured from the relentless beatings he had been subjected to. That wasn't that long ago. Now under the cover of the smoke the place seemed deserted, barren, empty, but Neil was not so naive that he would expect it to remain that way. They had smashed through the door quickly enough but she would have had time to gain some degree of cover. He stepped slowly through the room, at the front of his team, he always did this, never placed any of them at any further potential for harm than he would ever place himself. Even through the mist he could see that the walls were brightly decorated, covered in pictures that no doubt showed the entertainer in his element, but he would not allow himself to be side tracked by a celebrity's own self-importance. With each step he took he was pushing himself ever more toward uncertainty that the room was even occupied. His hand leapt up in a gesture for his team to halt as a muted whimper caught his attention. They each stood in tense silence, watching the back of his head expectantly. He scanned the edges of the chamber slowly, trying to locate the source of the whimper. As a silhouette twitched into his line of sight he tensed up, and raised his gun.
"Armed police, get your hands up." He instructed calmly, hearing his team each raise their guns as they found what he was aiming at. He took a step closer. "I said get your hands up." He stated again as his feet took another movement toward the silhouette, but still it continued to twitch, only this time the

whimper increased in volume, almost out of panic. Something clearly wasn't right here. Neil stepped once again. The smoke began to dissipate around the figure which was rapidly becoming human shaped, but it seemed to be almost floating as it twitched, ghost-like above the ground.

"What the fuck?" He heard one of the guys mutter to himself behind him. He was thinking the same thing himself as they edged ever closer to the figure. Its arms were wrenched up above its head, the feet hung heavy toward the floor, toes pointed directly to hell. As he approached the figure it became apparent that it was Will Thunder, hanging limp from the wall, his hands bound together and his mouth gagged. He gazed upon Neil and his team from his place upon the wall, and muttered something unintelligible from beneath the gag. Neil brought his own face closer to the hostage, who spoke again, shaking his head. He looked over his shoulder to the team, all held firm a few feet away, watching the situation play out. Will Thunder spoke that muffled phrase again, and his shoulders heaved beneath the strapped hands. He was laughing. The guy was *laughing.* Neil frowned underneath his gas mask, and turned once again to his squad before returning his attention to Thunder, who spoke once again through both the gag and the laughter. The chief APO reached out and pulled the gag from his mouth.

"Where is she?" He quietly asked the still laughing celebrity.

"Gone." He managed to say through the laughter and swelling around his face.

"Gone? Where?" Asked Neil, struggling to hold the concern from his voice. The celebrity shook, and then lowered his head.

"I don't know, she disappeared when the bomb went off, but she left that." The chief APO followed the guy's line of sight to the floor, and turned to collect what was there. It appeared to be a hefty bundle of paperwork strapped together within a manila document wallet. He wanted to open it, see what Esterhuizen was up to, but something scrawled on a yellow post-it note caught his attention. As one of the guys pulled Will Thunder from the wall and let him crumple into an exhausted heap on the floor the name on the yellow note leapt out at him. Philip Benson.

Albino Slug

The stoned fuzz had gone, this was more surreal than anything he had ever experienced in his life. For all the drugs he'd consumed in his life, like that time he'd lost a full day to the magic mushrooms that he and Kenny had gone searching for on a dawn raid of Fulton's Meadow, and spent untold hours with their backs to one another, just laughing their tits off. Or when he'd dropped four bombs of MDMA at Leeds Festival at once and floated around the huge dirty site with a feeling of pure wonderment coursing through his body, those surreal but fantastical times, were nothing compared to now. There were three faces looking at him in the darkness of the car but he was only concerned with one, hers. The weed thief had revealed his name to be Tom, and seemed endeared toward Jake since they both hailed from Yorkshire, Tom kept pushing him with questions as to whether particular nightclubs in Doncaster were still open, barely waiting for an answer before he went on about his own experiences within those establishments.

"Honestly pal, in Karisma I were hunched over the fattest line of coke you've never seen, it were like an albino slug that were busting for a big powdery shit, and I'm *that* close to hoovering it up my nostril," Tom said, holding his thumb and forefinger millimetres apart to illustrate the small distance he was discussing, "and this voice booms over the top of the cubicle, asks me what I think I'm doing. I look up, and there's this fuzzy headed bouncer frowning at me, but it's more like he's disappointed y'know? Like he doesn't want to kick me out but I've let him down. So I chance my arm, and I says to him 'Pal, I know you're gonna kick me out, but let me kill this bad boy before you do,' and y'know what? He looks at the slug I've got laid out and then back at me, and says 'Hurry up.'! He lets me finish it off, and walks me to the front door, all apologetic, like he's sorry for ruining me night!"

It wasn't long before Jake warmed to him, such was his enthusiasm, like he'd not met anybody from Yorkshire in a while, and had a lot of crap to release from his mind. In stark contrast Rufus in the passenger seat didn't say much as the car moved through the dark streets, in the side window he saw the reflection of the scar on his face illuminated periodically by the orange glow of the streetlights above them. Liezel remained quiet, aside from a token gesture of greeting when Tom had explained the situation, told her that they could use Jake, she remained in her own world, also staring out of the window, like Rufus. She was even more beautiful in person, her pale blemish-free face, he was truly astounded by her profile, by the skin that stretched around her small, but not tiny, skull, across her cheek and around her jaw. She caught him looking at her occasionally but paid him no mind, just turned back to the window and her own thoughts. He hadn't said anything other than the minor responses to Tom's banal questions, and given the danger he was in he felt no fear. He was in the back of a car with Liezel, that was all that mattered, and he would do anything in his power to help her, however that might be.

The car pulled up across from a hospital, the name of which meant nothing to Jake, he'd only really ever heard of Jimmy's, and he wasn't too confident that that was even *in* London. The car lit up ever so slightly with the pure white glow from the building opposite, Liezel pulled a mobile phone from her pocket and thrashed out a number. The other person spoke and she listened, and the other two sat quietly for a few brief moments as Jake performed a cursory glance between them. Tom and Rufus looked ahead, with seemingly no intentions of talking any more. His eyes turned to meet those of Liezel, who'd finished up on the phone and looked ready to speak, she was actually going to *speak,* to *him.* Jake's heart thumped in anticipation.

"So here's the deal. You seem okay Jake." Between the thumps his heart was released from its socket and rushed up into his throat like an English pisshead on holiday in Magaluf in a caged bungee rocket. He almost fainted. She thought he seemed okay. It was a start. Liezel pulled a cardboard wallet from the rucksack she had brought to the car, and handed it to him.

"You walk into that hospital and you ask for Chief Inspector Philip Benson. He's in there with Will Thunder. You won't speak with anybody except Philip Benson. When you speak with him you will tell him that you were pushed into a car by masked assailants, you could not recognise them from anybody else. You will tell him that you were driven here blindfolded, and then, as you hand him this file, I want you to give him this message, *Will Thunder is innocent.*"

I'm A Dead Man

The nightmare isn't over. It's far from over. Why won't they believe me? What have I ever done to anybody that I deserve this? I've done nothing. I'm in the hospital and the policeman, Chief Inspector Benson he calls himself, he's pushing these photos under my nose and sitting there in silence with a disgusted look on his face. What I'm seeing is me, getting my cock sucked by a teenage girl. That never happened. I told that bitch it had never happened but my words went over her head, they fell on deaf ears, whatever the hell you want to call it, she wasn't bloody listening. I can see the look in his eyes, this is proof that it happened, there's no point in me saying anything, I'd be wasting my breath. She might as well have killed me. I don't know why she put me through all of that just to let me go. Nothing makes any bloody sense. So I'm saying nothing, just looking at what I've already seen. The public hate me, my career is over, my life is over, I'm a dead man. How can I ever possibly walk the streets again? If I even get the chance to walk the streets again, that is. Because he's pushing another picture under my nose, the one where I'm supposed to be doing cocaine from the back of the prostitute. I know you won't believe me, but I have never done drugs in my life, I won't touch them, they scare me. I like to be in control of my facilities, I barely even touch alcohol. I feel so sick right now. The policeman is talking but I can't focus on what he's saying. I'm trying, I'm really trying but I feel so bloody sick. This slow motion flip book story of what I'm supposed to have done throws the next page into my line of vision, and it's me strangling the same girl. *Strangling* her. Yeah, it was as big a surprise to me the first time I saw it. I don't know what I'm going to do. They have me over a barrel, a very big, painful barrel and I can't help thinking that *I'm the victim here.* I'm the one who was held hostage, beaten black and bloody blue, abused, spat at, sentenced to death by the people who used to love me. I'm the one with broken bones and a broken spirit in the hospital. He's still speaking, I try harder to focus on what he's saying, but I'm still struggling, my thoughts are far louder than his words could ever be. The next thing he shoves in my face is a series of photos of me with people I've never met. I don't know how he has these pictures. I don't know how *she* had these pictures. Somebody enters the room, another policeman I think, but I can't be sure, and he leaves through the double swing door with them. The hospital room is quite big, the ceiling seems miles away from my face, but it probably isn't, another three beds fill it, but there aren't any people in any of them, I have the place to myself. To me, and the bleeping heart monitor which reminds me I'm still breathing, is if I could bloody forget. I try to count the bleeps, to distract my tired mind from my plight. I count one, two, three, and by the time I hit four a wave of nausea rolls over me as I remember things that she said, the things that the public had said about me, and I want to throw up.

Will Thunder Is Innocent

The youth standing before him looked riddled with disease. His greasy black hair, in dire need of a wash, hung shaggy over his eyes and thick brows. Tufts of

just as dark hair sprouted from his cheeks, like the kid had never learned to shave, but still made valiant efforts every now and then, swiping indiscriminately at his face in the dark. His hangdog expression gave the impression that he hadn't slept in months. Philip thought to himself that even after a nine hour stint in bed, and a shower, the kid would still look like he belonged to nobody. It was only the fact that he had dropped Will Thunder's name into conversation with the officer at the front door that he had managed to get this far, and gained an audience with the senior officer himself. Philip looked him up and down pointedly, and sighed.
"What could you possibly know about Will Thunder kid?" He asked, not expecting anything other than a weary mumble from him. He shifted uncomfortably on his feet, looking down at the document he held in his hand.
"Will Thunder's innocent." He said, as if he were in conversation with his shoes, and Philip wasn't even in the room. He spoke in a northern accent, maybe Yorkshire or Nottingham way out, so Benson wasn't sure he'd heard right.
"Say what?"
"Will Thunder is innocent." He repeated, he had definitely heard right. He stepped closer to the policeman who instinctively reached for his phone, as if he might ever need any back up against this scruffy urchin. The kid held out the document.
"They kidnapped me, drove me here and made me come look for you. They told me to tell you he were innocent. I dunno what's happening. They told me to give you this." He held the document face up toward Benson, and upon the face was a yellow post-it note, placed identically to the one that Liezel had left at Will Thunder's house, and once again, on the note, his

own name was scribbled. Without taking his eyes from him Benson tentatively retrieved the file from the extended fingers of the youth with one hand, and pulled the phone from his pocket with the other.
"Don't go anywhere." He instructed the kid, and briefly turned his back to make the call.
"Sir?" His underling answered, sounding almost surprised at the call.
"Kevin, leave him there, get back out here now, I need you to take this lad down to the yard, I'll explain shortly." He instructed curtly, ending the call as he swung round to face the kid, or at least where the kid was supposed to be.
"Fuck." He muttered. Predictably, the scruffy little wanker had done a runner.

A Fridge Full Of Fonzies

"You think he'll do it right?" Rufus asks to nobody in particular, so my guess is that he'll accept an answer from anybody, his attention looks to be taken by a tramp rummaging through a bin in a steaming alleyway. He doesn't look that old either, defo been dealt a shit hand that lad. Poor cunt. You've got to have hit bottom to have that as your only option haven't you? He seems to hit pay-dirt though, as he pulls some paper from the bin, and slides whatever tasty treat was in there into his appreciative chops from above, it seems stringy from this distance so I'd say the smart money was on kebab meat. Minging. Nobody's answered Rufus.
"I mean, we meet the guy a couple of hours ago, drag him at gun point, and send him in to ask *directly* for a copper, what if he starts shooting his mouth off?" This time he turns to me, like he expects me to answer, honestly, it feels like we've turned into

Laurel and fucking Hardy, bickering all the time. I can't wait to get all this done with so I can get back to Jess, get her back under this wing of mine. Yeah Beefy's looking after her, but he's not me. I'm the one should be protecting the gorgeous git that she is.
"So what if he does? The bobbies already know Liezel, all he'll say is there were two blokes called Tom and Rufus. He won't anyway, he's been looking at Liezel like she's made of gold. He's defo coming back for a bit of *Sarth Ifrikin* action!" I say, holding back on my natural urge to stick a *bom chicka wom wom* in there as I nod into the rear view mirror toward Liezel who smiles and shakes her head, cool as a fridge full of Fonzies that lass.
"Too young!" She calls from the back, "Stinks worse than a skunk too."
"Shoulda smelled him earlier, skunk was *exactly* what he smelled like." I laugh, but it's gone over her head, guess you had to be there.
So far everything's going just right. Jess, she's so fucking smart it's unreal. Everything she said to do has gone perfectly. Nobody's died, everybody got involved, and I'm not just talking about our new little gang, I'm talking about *everybody,* the whole of the country has picked up on the story, Jess properly did a number on Facebook, and the thing went fucking *viral.* Her *Hang Will Thunder* group grew faster than bacteria on yesterday's pizza, honestly, you could refresh it on your phone and it had got another few hundred likes, comments, pictures, everything. One guy had even put a picture of himself holding up a handwritten sign saying 'If this gets half a million likes Liezel says she will chop off Will Thunder's bollocks'! Some people man, for sure, they like to think of themselves as free thinkers but that mob mentality says they'll do or say owt if enough people

are doing and saying the same thing. I had to laugh at one guy calling himself *Danny Lovesdapussy Brown* who said 'send da dutty paedo wanker back to where he cums from', back to where he *cums* from, straight back inside himself into his own balls? Or Manchester? Either way, Danny Brown who loves da pussy played straight into our hands, the imbecile. So while Jess is playing cyber bully to an innocent man for the purposes of bringing down a guilty man, all the time Beefy is keeping an eye on her. Liezel's doing the hard work of course, you know all about that. Me and Johnny Half-Past are working away behind the scenes, feeding that daft sod Wayne Cooper information. That was a masterstroke in my not-so-humble opinion, by Jess, forget the police, go straight to the media. There's so many channels, so many outlets, that they'll break the law to get one over on the competition, to get that exclusive. Any normal person would have gone to the police with that information, when they're breaking their necks to find out who this nutter is that's got Will Thunder held hostage, but a newsmonger wouldn't ever do that, nope, for sure, a newsmonger would withhold it for their own sneaky benefit.

So yeah, they played right into our hands, the media did like, as predicted, and so far, so have the coppers. They were always gonna try to use the bomb distraction to mount an assault on Liezel, but then we were always gonna use it as a distraction to get her out of there. We took full advantage of Rufus' ineptitude when it comes to actually killing anybody, you know when the bomb went off? Well, yeah we used his skills in setting bombs, but as we promised Jess that there weren't gonna be any more deaths, so he just took a couple of trees out in Hyde Park, coated them in fuel, made sure they were gonna go up quicker than, if you'll excuse the paraphrasing of Alex Turner of The Arctic Monkeys, a shell suit on bonfire night. Caused some right havoc.

Now, this young Doncaster lad Jake, he's performed the final task in the huge jigsaw, and I wasn't lying when I said he'd been looking at Liezel like she were made of gold, maybe that wasn't strong enough an analogy, I think maybe he were looking at her like she were a pair of golden tits with nipples that were smoking the biggest spliffs you've ever seen, yeah, that's more like it. He'll be back for sure, he's not gonna want to miss out on potential fireworks in the sack with our *Sarth Ifrikan* friend, even if he knows that she wouldn't touch him with a stolen fanny. As if on cue, the scruffpot appears in the distance, head down, power-walking away from the hospital.

"Here is he look, knew he wouldn't let us down." I say, Rufus starts craning his neck past my big head, huffing a sigh of relief that I feel against, and then *in,* my ear, and it gives me an uncomfortable tickle that makes my neck spasm, much like the one I get when I'm having a piss.

"Thank fuck for that." He says, and there's no denying there's pure relief in his voice, soft lad must have been shitting himself. He's a strange one this Rufus, sometimes he reckons he's hard as fuck, then others he lets himself down by bricking it when he should just keep the faith. I shake my head out of sheer disappointment, I don't need to say anything, he knows he's done wrong.

Young Jake climbs into the back of the car, looking spooked as fuck, but he's done well bless him.

"All sorted kid?" I ask, trying to put him at some sort of ease, but before he can answer he opens his door again and leans out, throwing his rocks up all down the side of the car, and I have to laugh at that. For sure, I was like that once. As he slams the door closed, gasping for air through the sick in his throat I look beyond him and catch sight of a couple of fellas rushing out of the hospital doors, one of them's got a copper's uniform on, looking all over the place for our little hero in the back seat.

"Well done Cheech and Chong, get your head down." I tell him, properly chuffed that I backed the right pony.

After that, well, we get the hell out of dodge and head off to wait for the fireworks to start; Isaac Charles won't know what's fucking hit him.

Chapter 23 - January

A Pool Of Future Victims

"Well this *is* a turn up for the books Rufus, pray tell, why should I believe that you'll keep your end of the bargain? You've already broken my heart once, I don't know if I could take a second betrayal! I love you Rufus but believe me, I will *not* hesitate to ensure that your remains, and those of your treacherous cohorts are boiled in acid!" Isaac Charles sang into his ear, the guy never truly *spoke,* he just seemed to sing every word that came from his mouth, it belied exactly how dangerous the flaming bitch of a queen was.

"Mr Charles, we want to put this right, that's all. It's not just that though, Liezel's seen what Will Thunder's capable of, and she *wants* to end him, and if it means putting things right in the process then that's exactly what she'll do." Said Rufus, attempting to sound as sorry as he could. The others watched on hopefully, as they sat on a gradually mounting pile of evidence that Isaac Charles was in the process of setting Will Thunder up. Jess had come to them with a start, proof that there was most definitely a grudge between them. From that catalyst, and the information they had at hand, they were able to build a very decent picture of both the story of the fallout, and how Isaac Charles and Ada had been running their games together.

Based on emails between them, and the IP addresses that Liezel had spent time looking into at great length, it seemed that they had been welcoming 'anonymous' entrants to place bets on the exact time that Liezel lost her rag and killed her target. The first one was definitely not intended, she really was supposed to research and track her prey, and their behavioural patterns, assess their suitability for the time-honoured game of murderous hide and seek that had worked so well in the past. The game that everybody involved in the organisation had previously won, thus earning their stripes, and the respect of their peers. But she had bucked against her superiors, created an extra threat to their security, and rather than punish her directly they simply changed the game without telling her. Isaac Charles would always be the one to come to Ada with targets, and between them they would approach potential gamblers to participate in the game, to put their money forward and bet upon the precise moment when Liezel would stop a person from breathing. Those that failed to play the game, pun entirely intended, were then dropped into a pool of future victims by Isaac Charles, who would then have evidence of their depravity forged, and they would become the next target in the increasing number of games they were playing. This was how he worked, if you weren't with him, you were against him, and if you were against him then he would punish you. Unless, of course, he had a use for you, as he did with Liezel. She was apparently a disposable yet no less useful piece of meat that would continue to be called upon until the time which one of her intended victims got the better of her, or worse still escaped and had her apprehended by that country's authorities. Isaac Charles had even said as much in an email to Ada, the exact words were '*when the ungrateful harridan finally succumbs to her own stupidity we can always replace her.*'

    The lack of security around their communications was astounding, and now their own self-perceived immunity from danger between them,

the arrogance of power, had started to become their downfall. Ada's corpse could attest to that much. Eventually Isaac Charles sighed loudly, and emitted a high pitched purr which evolved into what could quite easily be mistaken for gibberish which evolved further still into actual words.
"Against my better judgement I am going to give you a chance Rufus, but only because it's you. You can tell your friends that they're lucky to know such a man as you, because a man such as myself is a *very* powerful enemy to have. I shall expect to be kept in the proverbial loop at all junctures. You can have just one chance to make amends Rufus, *one chance!* Please, I implore you, for your own sake, do not mess this up!"

Two-Headed Super Being

So he's setting Will Thunder up, he's making strangers place bets on how long it's going to take for Liezel to kill him, all because they fell out with one another. Call me naive but how can he be so cold about another person's life? Somebody he once claimed to have cared for? Is money really *that* important? I almost feel sorry for him. *Almost.*
The story is that Isaac Charles basically made the careers of Will Thunder and Johnny Lightning, he put them together, like in the same way a talent show producer might take a handful of talentless children and turn them into an auto tuned super group. They were apparently on a road to nowhere separately, and Isaac Charles convinced them that they would do a lot better together, that the world was crying out for a new generation of comedy duo. He was proved right, and they became an almost instant hit, overnight millionaires, and loved universally for their family friendly brand of humour. Isaac Charles had

taken these two lumps of personality-free clay, and created a wildly popular televisual super-being. But that was the thing, the two-headed super-being became aware of its own power, and together they conspired to remove Isaac Charles from their professional lives. Isaac Charles was widely believed to have blamed Will Thunder for putting seeds of mutiny into Johnny Lightning's head, pushed him to take the leap together, and they took their business, their very lucrative business, to Giles Baker, a professional competitor. The fallout was well publicised, apparently, having spent so much time out of the country it passed Tom and me by, otherwise we might have figured all of this out sooner, especially with Isaac Charles involved.

So I'm putting it to them that we ought to play him at his own game, push him so far into the public eye that he can't get out of it, too many people have died so far because of that man, I want our only ammunition to be evidence. I want to ruin his life the way that he has ruined so many others, if we don't have him locked away for the rest of his life he will never get a chance to reflect on the things he's done. Call me an idiot, maybe he does deserve to die, maybe he'll still be able to get at us from beyond the jail cell, but I don't think *everything* needs to be resolved with death. I will *not* bring my child into a world where violence and death are the only answers that anybody can think of.

As I'm speaking I can see that Rufus and Liezel are dubious, unsure of its chances of working out, but what else is there? We can hand the evidence straight to the police and risk it being swept under the carpet by corruption. We then run the risk of finding ourselves at the end of the barrel of a gun, *again,* or we can follow through with the plan that Isaac

Charles wanted, let him build up his gambling ring, let him *think* that we're doing exactly as he wanted, and when we have the world's attention, we leave only one name to blame on their lips. When I'm finished Tom is bristling with pride, so much so that he's looking round the others for a reaction with a smug face, that face where his chin juts out just ever so slightly and his eyes go kind of dozy.

"What do you think?" I ask, really not sure of how it sounded as I said it, maybe it's impossible. Tom's nodding and smiling, his eyes twinkle in my direction and even if the others don't like it, I feel on top of the world with the look of pride he's got just now.

"I like it, for sure, totally play the cunt at his own game." He says, "That'd blow his fucking mind!"

Now Cristiano's head is moving to the affirmative too, but he's still looking slightly confused.

"But how will you put the man in the eyes of the public as you say?" He asks, which I suppose is a fair question.

"Will Thunder." I respond, not meaning it to come out as mysterious as it does. Liezel's head raises to me. I feel moved to continue.

"I mean, Liezel, when you thought he was guilty you were going to punish him to get to Isaac Charles, now he's *not* guilty, we might still have to go down that path, only this time we make sure *everybody* knows you're doing it, turn it into news. Tom said it earlier. Use publicity. The same as Isaac Charles.. We need to get the whole world watching what you're doing, get the public onside, make them hate Will Thunder." I almost can't believe I'm saying this myself, Tom's looking impressed, and the rest are hanging on my words, wondering where I'm taking this, "Honestly, that part will be easy, Tom knows what our media is like, they all love a villain, especially when

paedophiles are concerned, they'll turn everybody against him. We can work the details out on how we increase public knowledge but that should be the basis. Eventually, we need to reveal that Will Thunder is innocent-"
"But what about me? We're going to do that while I'm *in* there?" Liezel interrupts me, but it's a valid question.
"No, we'll get you out, honestly, we'll figure the details out, I'm just talking here." I say, but I've slightly lost my train of thought now, and Tom picks up on it, determined to help me out.
"We're revealing that Will Thunder is innocent baby." He smiles, and I look to him gratefully.
"Yeah, that's when we hit him, the whole world suddenly hates themselves for wanting an innocent man dead, and more importantly, they hate the man that made them hate themselves, Isaac Charles will have *nowhere* to hide, he'll be stuck between a rock and a hard place. Between police that want to question him, and the public that want to kill him, he'll be finished."

Chapter 24 - February

The Illusive Mr Robert Knocker

As he sat at his desk Wayne Cooper tore the tamper proof seal from the padded manila envelope with as much eagerness as a child at Christmas fingering the edge of a wrapped square box that they just *know* is that iPhone that they'd demanded of their underpaid and overworked parents. It had been hand delivered to him by a northern tramp who would have been laughed out of the building if he hadn't introduced himself with the words 'Mr Robert Knocker sent me. Will Thunder is innocent.'. Wayne had wanted to ask him if he were the illusive Mr Robert Knocker himself but the slouching, baggy way that the kid presented himself was very much the opposite of the talkative, confident and witty voice of his mysterious informative aide. This kid was far from talkative, just dropped the envelope into Wayne's hands and left. He seemed antsy and nervous, his bloodshot eyes refusing to meet Wayne's. How the hell the lad had managed to get himself in with whoever it was that had been feeding him information he couldn't even begin to imagine. He wasn't about to start speculating though, he had much bigger fish to fry, in the form of the actual evidence that said Will Thunder indeed *was* innocent.

Mr Robert Knocker had already fed him plenty of information, enough to keep the other channels a million miles behind *Politickle My Funny Bone* in the exclusive stakes, like the identity of Liezel Esterhuizen, and then more recently the fact that Will Thunder had not been working alone, which he made the controversial call to release before it hit Philip Benson's radar. Partly because the law man had been so fucking shady about his own information, but primarily because this was *his* fucking story, and the stranger had entrusted *him* with the information to do with it as he damn well pleased.

He pulled the papers from the envelope and laid them out on the table, the document must have been two inches thick at least, and were accompanied by what looked like a covering letter, headed with the words *'Read Me First'*, so he did.

Mr Wayne Cooper,

The stinky kid who delivered this package is a friend of mine, if for whatever reason you feel the need to detain him, then do not, you've got a bit more on your plate than a fidgety tramp.
The package you have received is an exact duplicate of one that Chief Inspector Philip Benson has received, so do not worry your head about sharing this information with him, he knows what you know, and he also knows that you know. You are the only two people to hold this information. The reason you have received it too, is that the police cannot be trusted to reveal this information and could easily be brushed under the carpet, and we cannot accept that. Will Thunder is innocent, to our knowledge he has never fingered any children, he has never received blow jobs from young fans, he has never killed any hookers, we're not even sure he's even had sex before. We told you he wasn't working alone, that wasn't strictly true, he wasn't working at all, we just needed to keep you on board. The evidence you hold in your hand incriminates Isaac Charles, yep, THE Isaac Charles, as the man who tried to set Will Thunder up, he is the man who has attempted to coerce Liezel into murdering the poor funny man, but has come unstuck because of his own

greed. Unfortunately for Isaac Charles, the papers you have hold vital evidence that he has ordered the deaths of dozens of people, he has ruined the lives of dozens more, and has been involved with organised crime for over two decades. He has politicians, the police, celebrities, and news editors, to name a few, in his pocket. We know we can trust you, Wayne Cooper, because you were so gormlessly excited when presented with snippets of information, you presented it to the world with all the prejudice we might expect from a seasoned news vulture.

Don't be scared to bring this news to the public Wayne, you're about to save a lot of lives. You, and only you, are responsible for them. If you sweep this under the carpet as the police might, you're signing the death warrants of those people. Their blood will be on your hands. Remember that Wayne Cooper.

Mr Robert Knocker.

Wayne Cooper shook his head, this couldn't possibly be real. Isaac Charles was involved in organised crime? Surely not. His hands pushed the cover letter to the back of the pile and he began to pore over the so called evidence that he had been entrusted with. The copies of emails could be forged easily, if Isaac Charles had forged evidence of Will Thunder's depravity then surely these people could do the same. The photographs were just as professional and credible than those he had seen on the live feeds and the website created by Liezel Esterhuizen. He just couldn't believe that Isaac Charles was as all-powerful as the letter suggested. He had made his way round to some paperwork to suggest that the PR man had paid a hit man to murder a French politician, before the phone in his office rang, shitting

him up somewhat. He was tempted to leave it to investigate the 'evidence' some more before he thought better of it and picked up the receiver.
"Wayne Cooper." He greeted.
"Ahhh, Mr Cooper, darling, a friend of mine has brought to my attention the fact that you hold some rather scurrilous documents which make very naughty accusations against me and my reputation, Isaac Charles here, ought I remind you that I have some very powerful lawyers, and we will take your company to the cleaners should any of those accusations make it to air?" That familiar camp voice echoed down the line and shook Wayne Cooper to his core. His breathing thinned to almost nothing, and he felt his arsehole physically twitch. The receiver dropped from his clutch and he scrambled through the paperwork for the cover letter. His eyes scanned over the sentence again... *He knows what you know, and he also knows that you know. You are the only two people to hold this information... He has politicians, the police, celebrities, and news editors , to name a few, in his pocket...* Benson. Surely not? It didn't matter. Wayne Cooper hung the telephone up on Isaac Charles and grabbed the papers, before rushing from the room. The bright artificial light burned through his skull as he passed desk upon desk of low level serfs, each working within their own bubbles. He heard the voice of Sophie the intern quietly and conspiratorially ask him if he wanted to go for a drink after work but it didn't sink into his brain, it deflected the insinuation that he might get laid like Batfink's wings like sheets of steel would deflect bullets. He was far too preoccupied. The show went live in less than an hour, and he had a strong feeling that Benson would be undertaking Isaac Charles' business as soon

as humanly possible, if he was going to get time to do this, it was going to be extremely tight.

You've Ruined Me Life You Fat Bitch

"Ladies and gentleman, my name's Barney Cowper, I'll be your warm up guy for the show tonight! It's promising to be a good one! What about that Will Thunder eh? Four days strapped to a chair, beaten black and blue, now that bastard knows what it feels like eh? You ask me he deserves everything he gets, but I'm not here to wax lyrical, I'll leave that to the professionals in a bit. No, I'm here to tell you all jokes! Who likes a good joke?" The crowd around her cheered and clapped, a woman in front of her who seemed to be going slightly bald around the crown, and with atrocious pale white cornflakes coming away from the scalp around the roots of her hair, leant in to her companion and told him that she liked jokes, with not even a hint of irony. Claire hadn't enjoyed jokes for a while. It was like her laugh had been stolen, and locked away in a cave fifty miles below the sea, somewhere it could never be retrieved, in a million years. Although she didn't enjoy jokes this middle of the road comedian, at a halfway point in his career, too successful for open mic nights at a back street comedy club, not successful enough to be invited to appear on one of the multitude of television panel shows, was providing enough of a side-track for the time being. "I were talking to me mate the other day, and he says to me, he says 'I were in the shop the other day and the girl behind the counter had the biggest knockers I've ever seen, proper massive they were, and instead of asking for a bag of taties, potatoes like, instead of asking for a bag of taties I asked for a bag of titties! It were a proper Freudian slip like' and I got to thinking that that's almost exactly what happened to me the other day, I were sitting eating breakfast with the wife at the table, and instead of asking her to pass me the milk, I says 'You've ruined me life you fat bitch'!" The balding crusty scalped joke-fan in front of her almost passed out from hyper-ventilation at the apparent hilarity of his joke, bruising the arm of her companion in the process as she repeatedly punched it in order to get over how funny she found the joke. Claire got it, it just wasn't funny. Behind Barney Cowper there was Gareth Bennington-Lane sitting in pride of place at the centre of the panels, several backstage mosquitos buzzing around him, applying licks of make-up, filling his brain with lines, and advice. But then the crowd of mosquitos dispersed as a man who appeared to be the head honcho parted them like a Moses parting a human Red Sea, his arms waving, pointing firmly at a load of papers in his hands. He looked very flustered, and Claire might have paid him more attention had she not seen *him. He* was there, in all his fat, sleazy, ignorant, racist, liberty taking fucking glory. As he sat there he leered down the top of some poor unsuspecting young employee of the show, undressing her with his eyes, exchanging a brief conspiratorial glance with whoever that was, messing with his microphone. *Dirty old men,* Claire thought as she shivered to her core. Her life ended the day he raped her. His life would end today.

Fuck The Lawyers

Gareth Bennington-Lane listened to his producer in open-mouthed shock. Things just got more and more bizarre around here. When he'd started on *Politickle*

My Funny Bone the show had simply been a weekly light-hearted dig at the week's events, a cross between *Question Time* with its occasional politicians invited to say their piece and show the world that they really were human after all, and a showcase for up and coming comedians to show just how cutting edge their comedy could be. Now, however, in the wake of this Will Thunder debacle, it had pushed the limits on exclusive reporting, gone out every day of the week, and broken viewing figure records for a Channel Four programme. This latest revelation threatened to blow Gareth Bennington-Lane's mind. Was Wayne Cooper really going to go out with this?
"What have the lawyers said?" He asked of his producer.
"Fuck the lawyers, if we don't run it now it'll never go out." Wayne replied, clearly in a place where his heart was ruling what his head might, on another day, have stopped him from doing. Isaac Charles represented one of the people sitting across from him. For all of Mike Rotch's faults, Gareth Bennington-Lane considered him an alright bloke, he didn't know that accusing the man who represented him of being a serial murderer would be a good way of concreting a good professional relationship.
"If this isn't true Wayne, they'll string you from the nearest lamp post." He warned, but he knew that look in the other guy's eyes. Whatever they had lined up in the wake of Will Thunder's release from captivity was being shelved, the news had moved on already, they were definitely going with it.
"I know, but if it is, then I won't be the man who didn't run it." Cooper said, and then explained how he wanted this to go.

You're Pretty Much Fucked

"Philip, you need to stop that fool from doing what he's going to do, this could ruin me!" The shrill whine emanated from the loudspeaker of the phone which sat upon the knee of the Chief Inspector as his car powered through the streets of London toward the modest television studio from which the programme was filmed.

"Isaac, I'll do what I can, but you're going to have to accept that you're pretty much fucked." He said, his eyes firmly on the road.

"If I'm *fucked*, as you so crassly put it Philip, then believe me, I'm taking everybody down with me, *everybody*, don't think that I won't. It's in your best interests to ensure that this goes no further!" The predictability of the threat irritated Benson. He was clean, or at least as clean as any policeman was, anything that Isaac Charles thought he had on him was small chips compared to the shit storm the PR man faced. Benson wasn't going over there to stop the revelation for Isaac Charles' benefit anyway, he was going there with the intention of putting a stop to Wayne Cooper's one man mission to sour any relationship that the media might ever have with the Met, and to find out how the hell he was getting all of this information. Of course it was the same person, or people, it would seem, that had sent the scruffy urchin into the hospital looking for Benson, hopefully Cooper would have a bit more information.

"Philip? Philip? Are you still there?" He'd forgotten that Isaac Charles was still on the phone.

"Isaac, I told you, I'll do my best." He reiterated. He was fucked if he was going to let the PR man dictate to a Chief Inspector. As influential and powerful as he was, he needed to understand that he wasn't above the law. Chief Inspector Philip Benson had not risen to his current position through bending to corruption. Isaac Charles began another rant but Benson was in no mood to hear him start the same record so he hung up the phone and continued in his drive to the studio.

<u>Are We Gonna Enjoy The Show Today</u>?

Wayne Cooper stood beside the studio floor, his knuckle had become a permanent fixture between his increasingly clenching teeth, so much so that he had begun to draw blood but barely noticed. The warm up comedian was wrapping his bit up.
"Okay, I've been Barry Cowper, you're all bloody magic, are we gonna enjoy the show today?" He asked loudly, to which the audience responded with enthusiastic cheers to the affirmative.
"I said, are we gonna enjoy the show today?!" He repeated in the time-proven manner which almost always yielded the same results, a louder, even more enthusiastic response.
"Lovely stuff, lovely stuff. Okay, ladies and gentlemen, I want you all to put your hands together for your charming host, Mr Gareth Bennington-Lane!" He roared and welcomed the nervous presenter to the floor and the show went live.
Bennington-Lane skipped onto the stage and took his place between the guests. With a nervous fidget he had not displayed in any of the previous editions, he spoke directly to the camera.
"Hi, and welcome to Politickle My Funny Bone, tonight's edition of Politickle My Funny Bone, um, welcome, today's guests are the ubiquitous Mike Rotch, and left wing politician Daisy Beckford."

Wayne Cooper wasn't convinced that the public schoolboy bastard would be able to pull this off, it wasn't shaping up to be the Earth shattering exclusive that it promised to be. He was stuttering over his words, his eyes rarely making any kind of contact with the lens. He should be seeing this as his crowning glory, not shitting himself from the lawyers, and the effeminate wrath Isaac fucking Charles. Cooper felt an overwhelming urge to storm on stage and do the job himself, because Bennington-Lane was in huge danger of fucking it up.

"Well, the Will Thunder situation has reached its next stage, did you see it? It was carnage. Bombs, and stampedes. It was as if we'd all be transported to Baghdad in nineteen ninety one! The police stormed the building only to find out that Liezel Esterhuizen had disappeared, leaving Will Thunder to face the music. Everybody else is still calling for his head, but guess what?" He paused, and looked to Cooper, who nodded to him, *do it!* The presenter stalled, as if the words wanted to come, like a baby after its mother's waters had broken, but was just too damn big to get out of her vagina, but just stuck in his throat. Cooper willed him on, *say it!*

"But guess what?" He repeated, his gaze looking up to the audience, the fearful look became one of confusion. Wayne Cooper followed his line of sight, to a young woman leaping two steps at a time down the gangway that separated the audience into two. It seemed that they were the only two people that had seen her, because the security guy, Malc, stood still with a gormless look on his face, watching Gareth Bennington-Lane, waiting for him to finish the revelation. The girl was dark eyed and skeletal, her brown hair flowed behind her and acted as testament to how fast she was actually approaching the stage.

Various members of the crew had begun to notice a strange air around them as her figure finally made it onto the screen, and inexplicably masked the entire frame of Mike Rotch's rotund body. The camera picked up that her right arm swiftly rose above her head before disappearing to the space between her and the tubby comedian, the more eagle eyed viewers would have also spotted that the arm was attached to a hand which wielded a twelve inch knife, but she moved so fast that the only one fully aware of its presence was Mike Rotch, as she plunged the knife into his neck, and twisted with every ounce of strength that her body could summon. The blade ripped apart his sterohyoid muscle and interior jugular vein, sliced through the front of his oesophagus and into the back of it. The twisting tugged and wrapped them tight around the blade, and as Malc the security man finally pulled his finger out and leapt into action amidst confusion and screaming from all around him, pulling the girl kicking and wailing from atop Mike Rotch, she ensured that she continued to hold tightly onto the knife, and ripped his throat from his body. The fountain of blood spattered and coated the aghast face of Gareth Bennington-Lane, and soaked the dull, mumsy green dress of the silent, stunned Daisy Beckford.

Wayne Cooper didn't move, he simply stood watching the carnage play out before him. He couldn't speak. Couldn't move. Couldn't even begin to make sense of what had just happened. He wanted his eyes to blink but they were struggling to pay any attention to anything he wanted, he needed to shut out the horrific sight of Mike Rotch's twitching body slowly slumping to the floor, and as any resistance by his heels to halt the descent was wiped out by the dark

wet pool of blood that surrounded his seat and he eventually disappeared behind the long panelled desk.
The studio descended into terrified chaos around him as the familiar form of Chief Inspector Philip Benson appeared beside him.
"Do you maybe want to cut your cameras off?" He asked, and at that point Wayne Cooper was ashamed to acknowledge that that hadn't even occurred him.

<u>Breaking News Just In</u>

"Breaking news just in, the controversial comedian Mike Rotch, real name Barry Pratt, has been brutally murdered in the last hour. Rotch, thirty eight, was appearing live on the topical panel television program Politickle My Funny Bone, when a woman from the audience broke onto the stage and stabbed him in the throat, fatally wounding him in the process. Reports are in but unconfirmed that his killer was Claire Swift, the woman that he had recently been accused, but cleared, of raping. The most horrific aspect of his murder was that it was committed live on television, and the producers have come under immediate fire for allowing the act to be aired at all. Wayne Cooper, the producer at the centre of the storm has stepped down with immediate effect, issuing the following statement"
"It is with great regret that I have decided to resign from my post as producer of Politickle My Funny Bone, although the fault was not entirely my own, I understand that I must take responsibility for my own inaction surrounding the tragic events which have happened and hope that this gesture will go some way to making amends for allowing Barry Pratt's death to be broadcast. My thoughts and

condolences are with the family of Barry at this sad time, let us hope that justice is served swiftly and to the full extent of the law."

"More on that story as we get it. In other news the explosion that rocked Hyde Park has been branded a *dangerous prank* by Scotland Yard, who were said to be following up various leads, specifically around the source of the highly complex C4 explosives that were the apparent cause, but have been quick not to attach the blame to any terrorist cells. A senior member of the Met has said that the perpetrators were lucky that there were no fatalities."

"Also in the last hour several people have been taken in for questioning in relation to the Will Thunder kidnap case, including his comedy partner Johnny Lightning, real name John Thorne, and the duo's former publicist Isaac Charles. Chief Inspector Philip Benson has said that the investigation was in its preliminary stages, but that he had substantial evidence to suggest 'serious foul play' surrounding the case, and had mentioned that he would be in discussions with police forces across Europe in the coming days. Mr Benson refused to discuss the disappearance of Liezel Esterhuizen, the woman who had been publicly holding Will Thunder, real name William Walters, hostage, stating that the investigation had had several critical developments and that Liezel Esterhuizen was only one of a number of people that he needed to speak with."

"Strange that, it does make you wonder what it could all be about doesn't it? I'm sure we'll find out soon enough."

"Sport now, and in the FA Cup fifth round replay at the Emirates Arsene Wenger's Arsenal were stunned by a single goal from struggling Championship side Barnsley who booked their place in the quarter finals against Arsenal's north London rivals Tottenham Hotspur..."

Chapter 25 - February

Another Damned Inconvenience

"This is not happening Miles, tell me it's not happening!" Isaac Charles wailed from behind his desk, his forehead in one hand, and the handset in the other. The lilac coloured satin shirt that he had been wearing for three days had begun to crust slightly from the excessive sweating caused by nervous expectation that his world could come crumbling down at any moment. The under-arm patches had started out as a darker shade of lilac, they could perhaps even be described as purple, but the longer that time passed, they had begun to swing to the other end of the spectrum, more an off-white with a hint of pink. This was most unlike the usual behavioural patterns of one Isaac Charles, the man usually liked to change his clothing at least twice a day, to ensure that they remained as fresh as the moment they were placed on his body. Although he rarely wore the same outfit twice, he did own two copies of the every outfit for exactly that kind of situation. His mouth tasted like crap, utter crap, as he hadn't even found himself in a position where he could brush his teeth for fear of throwing up the Seroxats that had comprised the closest things to a meal he had consumed since the fools that worked for Scotland Yard had come knocking on his door. His lawyers had worked night and day to ensure that everything was in order and had managed to secure bail yesterday, allowing him to at least get home and close any open wounds that might come back to him and infect his chances of getting away with the whole sordid affair. The thing was, that Rufus and his damned cronies had somehow found access to his emails to Ada, God rest her soul, and had shared everything that had passed between them with the police, and the media, with great relish.

The only shining light of hope of the whole situation was that the crazed lunatic had attacked and murdered Barry when the troublesome Wayne Cooper had intended to spread the bad news to the world. Of course there was the inconvenience that the professional relationship with character of Mike Rotch had been a very lucrative one of late, *yet another damned inconvenience,* but Isaac Charles would much prefer the death of the irritating fool over his own downfall, so it was what it was. The police could be contained to a degree, they had chinks in their armour, but had his own naughtiness been unleashed upon the world, well, that would be the end of him.

His lawyer sighed heavily at the other end of the phone, it was a sigh that said more than any of the multitude of words that might spill from his mouth, but Isaac Charles did *not* pay him to deliver bad news by way of sigh.

"I do *not* pay you to sigh Miles, I pay you, and I pay you handsomely, *very* handsomely, to work! Tell me something good!" He bellowed.

"Mr Charles, I've tried to find a loophole in the law, there's nothing, they have your balls in a vice-" He was interrupted by the PR man.

"Miles! How crude!"

"Okay, I'm sorry sir, the evidence they have is water tight, they have you ordering the deaths of several people, they have you organising illegal gambling operations, and they have you bribing officials-"

"And can these officials-" Isaac Charles stopped abruptly, almost uncharacteristically.

"Mr Charles?" The curious voice of the lawyer said, Isaac Charles didn't know but Miles was almost wishing that he had dropped dead at the other end of the phone. In actuality he wasn't far wrong, but the PR man spoke.
"Miles, I'll call you back." And hung up the telephone. There had been a small circle of hard pressure placed upon the centre of the back of his skull, and he had a very good idea of what might be causing that pressure.
"Please, whoever you are, don't kill me." He whispered as his hands slowly raised to the air, he did not wish to make any sudden movements or loud noises that might make a nervous trigger finger squeeze by accident.
"Not sure that's gonna be possible." That voice, no, surely not *that* voice. Out of pure horror Isaac Charles' mouth dropped open, and commenced emitting a pained squeak, barely audible to begin with, but gradually louder and louder as the shock worked its way into his system. He didn't want to turn around and make it real, but a heavy hand pulled him round upon the chair. *That* voice was joined by *that* face, and reality smashed head first into Isaac Charles like a wrecking ball. A single tear balled up above the bottom lid of his right eye, and undertook a lonely journey down his obsessively shaven and moisturised face before hanging like Tom Cruise on a rock face from his chin and dropping down to his lap. He and his intruder faced each other in silence, with the barrel of a gun between them. Isaac Charles thought sadly to himself that if he believed he could be wronged any more than he already had then he was dead wrong.
"Rufus? Why?" He asked sadly, for all of his over-the-telephone posturing and wailing, Isaac Charles

actually felt his heart break today, but there was no change in Rufus' eyes as he briefly looked to his watch, and shrugged.
"Why not?"

Sortabix?

As the bullet rips into his face, at sixteen minutes past twelve by the way, and explodes the back of his head across the room behind him I feel a release of pressure from my chest. It's like nothing I've ever felt before. I know what Isaac Charles is capable of, I know that he has no loyalty to anything or anybody unless it has a monetary value to it, I know that if I had allowed him to live I would be on the long list of people he would drag down to try to save his own skin. He's better off dead. I can't spend too much time thinking about this, the police will be back around soon enough, and I don't intend to be here when they show up.

The drawers of the heavy duty filing cabinet are open, unsurprisingly, he thought he was untouchable, above anything, so fucking arrogant. I finger the lips of the files in there and find what I'm looking for, my name emblazoned across the top, before I pull it from the drawer and stick it under my arm. Before rigor mortis sets in I prise open the fingers of his left hand, and put the gun in there. I had thought about making it a botched robbery but it's just as clichéd as a pretend suicide so it's six of one and half a dozen of the other, and anyway, I might as well do a mixture of both.

From Isaac Charles' pockets I extract the key and step lightly up to the walk-in wardrobe in the master bedroom. It's an eye-hurting array of purples and greens, like he was a walking Bruiser Bar, the chewy ten pence apple and blackcurrant flavoured sweet, loved them when I was a kid. Once my eyesight has recovered from the initial shock I make my way to the safe at the back and insert the key. The door swings open and I grab at the cash that's in there, stuffing it on top of the file I took from the drawers, into the small bag I've brought with me before I lock up the safe and put the key back into Isaac Charles' pocket, whistling a happy tune as I exit the property. I told you I'd get paid from these shit heads!

I climb into the car and breathe a sigh of relief as I pull out, and look at the file. I'm free of everything that that cunt held over me. Everything I've done wrong in life is in here, and now it's in my hands. I don't know how much I've managed to get away with in terms of cash but that's not important, it was the principle of the matter, even if I'd managed to snatch a fiver I'd be happy.

"Sortabix?" Tom asks, I don't even know what *sortabix* is, he talks some shit that kid, honestly, some absolute bollocks, but I'm feeling good, so I play the game.

"Sortabix." I confirm, and he shifts the car into first, pulls us out of the driveway and onto the road.

I don't know what I'm gonna do with myself now, I could go and find Charley, sit her down and try to explain why I did and said what I did, I *could* do that, but I probably won't, she doesn't need that. I know Tom and Jess are planning for a quiet one now, there's nobody chasing them anymore, so why not? Under assumed names I think, but they don't know what, I know what I'd pick, John Fogerty. For sure, as Tom might say. Liezel and Cristiano, I dunno, they'll figure it out I reckon, they've taken the weird little stoner Jake under their wing, I'm sure they'll all be

just fine, I know *he* will, as long as he's got Liezel around him. To be fair, I'm not too fussed, I've spent too much time watching other people's backs, it's gonna be good to get back to Rufus time.
"You didn't miss did you?" Tom asks without looking at me, but I can see that mischievous look in his eyes, he's winding me up.
"Fuck off." I chuckle, he's not a bad guy Tom, I know he'll look after Jess and the young one, it's all he knows, and that's not a bad attribute, I wish I could be more like that sometimes.
"You never told me how you got the scar." He says, settling down again, a level of comfort attained between us now, I know he's been itching to ask since we met.
"It's a long story, I'll tell you another day." I reply, and I probably will.

Epilogue

"Mr Brown?" Her head sticks out of the door, I almost forgot that it was my name, like, the name I'm using now, but she catches my eye and I'm up like a shot, my face obviously asking all sorts of questions. The girl smiles at me, I know she's done this smile a million times before and she'll be doing it a million more in the future, that smile that says *ah bless.* Usually I'd feel patronised as fuck but that's not gonna be me today, for sure, my stomach is in mouth, and I'm right there in front of her, eyes wide and expectant, *just tell me!* The grin slowly extends into the start of her saying something, and eventually she blurts it out.

"Congratulations, she's a beautiful baby girl."

You fucking beauty! You absolute fucking beauty! A weird prickling feeling hits me and I can feel my eyes welling up, I'm about to start wailing here!

"Do you want to come and see them?" She asks, do I want to come and see them? Do I want to fucking see them? Lead the way Missy, let me feast my peepers on my girls!

In the room I see Jess first, she looks beaten up, bless her, but she's still gorgeous, how does she do it? And she's smiling at me, and then back at this pink little ball of skin in her arms.

"Hi daddy," She says, "Meet Natalie Florence, your daughter."

Jess holds my little girl up toward me and I take her in my arms, and she's tiny. I mean, so *tiny,* so *fragile.* It's at this exact moment that I realise that all this time I've been waiting to grow up. Expecting it to happen overnight, whilst I slept. It doesn't happen. It's now. Now I see this tiny little life that's depending on me forever, *now* is the point that I feel myself grow up. I can't say it happens for everybody, there are some shit dads out there, but I will *never* be one of those blokes. I can already see into the future, my two girls taking the piss out of me. Going to town with Daddy's credit cards to spoil themselves now and then. And I'll be honest with you, I welcome it. These two girls can skint me every day of the week, because you know what? This is what it's all about. Drugs? Maybe now and then, but *never* when this little angel is around. The world isn't perfect, it never has been. Scumbags will always be scumbags. Corruption will always be around. Yeah, the world isn't perfect, but for sure, *for surely sure,* in this little rural hospital somewhere in Wales where me and Jess have settled, with the love of my life on one side, and my daughter in my arms, mine is.

For exclusive material, short stories and ranting diatribes from Tom, why not drop him an email at
Mrrobertknocker@live.co.uk

Afterword and Acknowledgements

It won't be long before you see something like the story of this book happening, I promise you. We're *that* close to it. Social networking runs our lives. It *ruins* our lives. It's the first thing we check when we wake up, and it's the last thing we check before we go to sleep. I'm the same. I watch the lives of everybody I've ever known play out on a little blue box on my phone, it entertains and inspires me. So to everybody on my *Friends List,* thank you for not thinking before you type.

Also big thanks to my wife Rebecca for putting up with me constantly disappearing to do a little edit, or indulge in a little self-marketing, you are an absolute star. You know you are.

Thanks to Joe for telling me the *Freudian Slip* joke, to Keith Nixon, Laura Chambers, KTC, and of course my mum, for previewing it for me. But most of all thanks to you, for thinking that a story that I had to tell you was worth hearing. Big love.

> If you enjoyed this then go and have a look at
> Paul Carter is a Dead Man

Bad Moon Rising: Written by John C. Fogerty 1969.
Performed by Creedence Clearwater Revival.
Fortunate Son: Written by John C. Fogerty 1969.
Performed by Creedence Clearwater Revival.

Printed in Germany
by Amazon Distribution
GmbH, Leipzig